"You're a good [man,] Gabe Tennert."

Ciara met his gaze directly so he'd know how sincere her words were. "But that doesn't mean you owe us anything. If you ever want to back off—"

She'd have sworn a hint of color touched his cheeks above the close-cropped beard. "I'll tell you." He nodded and started down the steps.

Before Ciara reached the kitchen, she heard the ripping sound of the first porch board being pulled up.

She wondered what Gabe would have done if she'd gone up on tiptoe and kissed his cheek. And whether his beard would be stiff and scratchy or more silky under her lips.

And, oh God, what would have happened if he'd turned his head at that precise moment, and her kiss fell on his lips instead?

She hadn't felt this kind of honeyed warmth low in her belly in longer than she could remember.

It was foolish beyond words to let herself develop some kind of crush on her reclusive next-door neighbor, who would probably be appalled if he knew.

Dear Reader,

A friend of mine who was a school counselor said once, "There's a leper in every classroom." I knew immediately what she meant. There is always at least one child who is shunned, teased, even bullied. He may be overweight. She might come to school wearing dirty clothes and smelling because of her home situation. He could be hyperactive, she could be an easy victim because she cries instead of returning taunt for taunt. A girl may physically mature much earlier than the others, while boys are at risk if they mature too slowly. Any behavior that is even slightly "off" serves like a red cape to a bull. It's a painful phenomenon that says much about human nature. Fortunately, many of the children who go along with the taunting grow into good people.

Many of the victims mature and learn to fit in—or find the niche in life where they can belong. As a fiercely protective mother myself, I've wondered what I would have done if one of my daughters had been that victim. Confronted with her helplessness to change the school dynamics, my heroine in *More Than Neighbors* decides to move far away from their previous school district, and to homeschool. She believes she can shield her son from all of life's slings and arrows—which, of course, is impossible. Her new next-door neighbor is at the top of the list of people most unlikely to get involved in any way.

Fortunately, they're both facing some big surprises! And, hey, who doesn't love the gruff, quiet man suppressing a world of pain who is still incapable of being unkind? Trust me, Gabe's a keeper!

Hope you enjoy getting to know this set of neighbors!

Janice Kay Johnson

USA TODAY Bestselling Author

JANICE KAY JOHNSON

More Than Neighbors

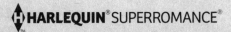
HARLEQUIN® SUPERROMANCE®

Recycling programs for this product may not exist in your area.

ISBN-13: 978-0-373-60892-8

More Than Neighbors

Copyright © 2015 by Janice Kay Johnson

This edition published by arrangement with Harlequin Books S.A.

For questions and comments about the quality of this book, please contact us at CustomerService@Harlequin.com.

Printed in U.S.A.

www.Harlequin.com

An author of more than eighty books for children and adults, *USA TODAY* bestselling author **Janice Kay Johnson** is especially well-known for her Harlequin Superromance novels about love and family—about the way generations connect and the power our earliest experiences have on us throughout life. Her 2007 novel *Snowbound* won a RITA® Award from Romance Writers of America for Best Contemporary Series Romance. A former librarian, Janice raised two daughters in a small rural town north of Seattle, Washington. She loves to read and is an active volunteer and board member for Purrfect Pals, a no-kill cat shelter. Visit her online at janicekayjohnson.com.

Books by Janice Kay Johnson

HARLEQUIN SUPERROMANCE

The Baby Agenda
Bone Deep
Finding Her Dad
All That Remains
Making Her Way Home
No Matter What
A Hometown Boy
Anything for Her
Where It May Lead
From This Day On
One Frosty Night

The Mysteries of Angel Butte

Bringing Maddie Home
Everywhere She Goes
All a Man Is
Cop by Her Side
This Good Man

A Brother's Word

Between Love and Duty
From Father to Son
The Call of Bravery

SIGNATURE SELECT SAGA

Dead Wrong

Visit the Author Profile page at Harlequin.com for more titles

CHAPTER ONE

A FLASH OF movement over at the old Walker place caught Gabriel Tennert's eye the moment he hopped out of the box truck he'd just backed up to the open doorway to his barn workshop.

He owned thirty acres himself, and the neighboring place was of similar size. The Walker house and land had been posted for sale a good three, four years now, with no taker. An occasional looker, that's all. Gabe hadn't minded Ephraim Walker as a neighbor, given that they'd spoken only when Gabe went over to check on the old man. Not being sociable, Gabe had been happy once Ephraim was gone to have the house sitting empty.

But, now that he was looking, he couldn't miss the candy-apple-red van parked in front. Even squinting, though, he didn't see a soul to go with the vehicle. Whoever had arrived in it must have gone in the house.

Lookers, he reassured himself. Or a new real-estate agent, checking out the property. One or the other came along now and again. Far as he knew, nobody ever made an offer. This small town north of Spokane, Washington, didn't have much to draw newcomers. Once viable, farms like his and Ephraim Walker's were good these days mainly for running a few head of cattle or keeping some horses, like he did. The hour drive to Spokane was fine for delivering finished cabinetry, but would be pushing it for a daily commute, and there weren't many jobs in an almost entirely rural county. Winters were harsh in this northeast corner of the state, the landscape pretty but not spectacular enough to attract much in the way of tourism. The town of Goodwater had been deceptively named; the creek that curved around the town and along the back of his property was pretty enough, but dwindled to barely a rivulet by late summer.

Whoever those folks over at the Walker place were would go away like all the others had once they saw how run-down the old farmhouse was, he told himself.

Sure were here early in the morning, though.

Dismissing the unpleasant possibility of acquiring actual neighbors, Gabe went about loading the cabinets he would be installing in a handsome old house in Hillyard, once a town in its own right but now a neighborhood in Spokane. Gabe did a lot of work for homeowners in Hillyard and Corbin Park, both neighborhoods designated as historic. More in Corbin Park, although he'd seen an upswing in Hillyard, which was having a revival after years of deterioration. Because of the designation, homeowners of the handsome Victorian-era houses in both areas had to comply with some restrictions when they remodeled. Ready-made cabinetry wasn't acceptable. His specialty was solid wood cabinetry built to 19th century quality. He could do a more modern look, but rarely chose to.

Once he was loaded and on his way, his day went smoothly. The remodeling contractor was on hand with a couple of his men to help with unloading and installation. Gabe had measured, cut and built to accommodate floors and walls subtly and not so subtly out of plumb, no surprise in an old lady that had passed her one hundred and thirtieth birthday. He approved the dark gray granite countertops. Although not historically proper, they would look fine with the richly stained cherry cabinets.

After gently running his hand along the satin surface of a tall pantry door, he left, feeling his usual mix of satisfaction and something like grief at letting go of his work. He'd started with raw wood, measurements, some ideas from the homeowner and his own conception, and then he'd put one hell of a lot of hours into those particular cabinets. Unless the house was featured in a magazine, he'd likely never see them again. He thought he was entitled to some goodbye pangs.

He stopped for a burger and fries in Mead before driving the rest of the way home. He was nodding along to Darius Rucker playing on a country station, his headlights picking out the narrow two-lane road ahead, when he came even with the Walker place and through the darkness saw something that shouldn't be there. Lights.

His foot lifted from the gas, even tapped lightly on the brake. What the hell…?

But he knew. Somebody had moved in. New owners or renters, didn't matter, not if their presence meant vehicles coming and going all hours, the possibility of loud music, kids yelling, dogs chasing his quarter horses. Goddamn it, his doorbell ringing with a friendly new neighbor standing on his not-so-welcome mat.

He shook his head, accelerated again and turned into his own long driveway a minute later. He had to get out to open the broad doors of the outbuilding he'd converted to a garage for the box truck, a horse trailer and his pickup. Soft nickers carried on the warm spring air, in case he'd forgotten he had hungry animals waiting for their oats. The welcome was enough to have him smiling as he unloaded his tools and hung them in their places in his workshop, then measured servings of a molasses-and-grain mix into two buckets that he carried to the open lean-to, where the mangers and water trough were.

His gelding and mare might have been looking forward to their evening treat, but they took the time to say hello with nudges and whuffles before plunging their noses into the buckets and crunching with enthusiasm. The air was redolent with hay, horse and manure. In another month, the lilacs around the house would come in bloom, adding their sweetness. After telling his horses what fine animals they were, Gabe leaned back against the fence and enjoyed the quiet of the night. He pondered the reality of new neighbors, but thought the absence of any racket coming from next door was a good sign. The evening was early enough; a herd of kids would surely be making some noise, wouldn't they? Or teenagers would have cranked up their music. Maybe a young couple had rented the place and would move on when the solitude got to them. Hell, maybe Ephraim's son and his wife, who had to be in their sixties if not seventies, had decided to sell their house in Seattle and move into Dad's.

He felt his mouth curve at the unlikely thought. Ephraim's son, whose name Gabe couldn't recall, had spent years trying to persuade his father to move to assisted living on the west side of the mountains and cursed him for a stubborn old fool for refusing.

It did cross Gabe's mind as he let himself into his house to wonder when he'd gotten so set in his own ways. He was closing in on forty, sure, but late thirties wasn't middle-aged, was it? Yet here he'd become as staid in his habits as old Ephraim himself. He didn't let the thought linger, though, because he knew to the day when it had happened. When in a searing minute he'd been left alone and known he'd never try to replace what he'd lost.

If the new people tried to intrude... Well, he'd have no trouble setting them straight. He knew what signals to give to hold people at a comfortable distance. He could be pleasant and still be read just fine.

He took a beer from the refrigerator and decided he wouldn't waste any worry on problems that probably wouldn't arise. Maybe he'd trailer Hoodoo up toward Calispell for a good ride come morning. He often took a few hours off work after finishing a major job.

Sleep came easily.

"MOM, I'M BORED."

Ciara had been standing on tiptoes to set the empty case that had held her sewing machine on the shelf in the closet. Nudging it as far back as it would go, she sighed and turned to face her son, who was gazing at her expectantly. Lately she'd been disconcerted every time she looked at him. She swore he'd shot up three inches this year, and was now, at twelve years old and not far from his thirteenth birthday, lanky and several inches taller than she was.

"How can you be bored?" she asked. "You can't possibly have put your own stuff away yet."

He grimaced. "No, but that's boring."

She leveled a look at him. "You know how irritated you get when something isn't where it belongs."

"But nothing belongs anywhere yet," he complained. "I don't know where things should go."

Hiding her exasperation, she escorted him to the bedroom he'd chosen and discovered that he'd barely begun to unpack. Apparently, it had been obvious to him that clothes did belong in dresser drawers, because most of what had been in his suitcase had made it that far. Otherwise, he'd opened boxes but not taken anything out. She should have realized he'd be paralyzed by so many decisions. He liked things to stay the same.

"We brought all your furniture," she pointed out. The moving truck had arrived midmorning, as promised, and the movers had unloaded with astonishing haste. Furniture had all gone into the rooms she'd designated, but not necessarily in exactly the ideal spot. Maybe that was the problem for Mark. "Do you like where the bed is?"

He was strong enough to move his own furniture around, but dithered so much over where each piece went, an hour passed before he seemed to be satisfied. Then, of course, he was hungry.

Well, okay, she was, too. And really, what was

the hurry? They could take their time unpacking. This move was their new start, and she wanted it to be a happy one.

As she dumped a can of soup into a saucepan on the stove, Mark gazed wistfully out the window toward the neighboring pasture. "I want to pet that horse. She's real pretty."

"What's the rule?" Ciara pulled cold cuts out of the refrigerator. How did he know the horse was a she? Was it obvious even from a distance?

"I can't go near the horse until the owner says it's okay," he repeated by rote. "But he can't say it's okay until we go talk to him."

"Even then, I don't want you to go into the pasture," she said with a spurt of alarm. "You'll have to wait until the horse comes to the fence."

"Mo-om. Most horses are friendly."

"They bite. They kick."

He rolled his eyes, which she probably deserved. The truth was, she didn't know anything about horses. The closest she'd come was to pat the neck of whatever pony Mark had been able to ride at the zoo or fair when he was much smaller. He was the one obsessed with animals in general and horses in particular. He read about them; he drew them; he talked about them. And now, a real, live specimen grazed in the pasture a bare stone's throw away from his own house.

She eyed him suspiciously as she put together

sandwiches, stirred the soup and poured it into bowls. Usually he was good at following the rules, as long as she made them specific enough. But the temptation this time…

"Sit down and eat," she said.

He did as she asked, but paused between bites to inform her that horses liked carrots. "And sugar cubes. We could buy some, couldn't we?"

She didn't know if grocery stores stocked sugar cubes. They had never made an appearance on her list before.

Somehow or other, she'd have to work horses into the lesson plan. How, she couldn't imagine. As had become her habit, she put off worrying about it to another day. Truthfully, she was apprehensive about the whole homeschooling deal. She'd graduated from high school what seemed like an awfully long time ago. Mark was particularly advanced in math, a subject she'd been weak in. Given his insistence on precision, that went with his personality.

She'd bought ready-made materials to meet state requirements for a seventh grader, though, so how hard could it be? And once the internet was hooked up, limitless resources would become available.

I can do this.

Her mantra usually calmed her. She *had* to do this, for Mark's sake. The whole move was about Mark, reducing the stress that had had him coming home from school in tears half the time. She was still enraged when she thought about her last meeting with the middle-school principal, who had made it plain he thought Mark, the victim, was to blame for being bullied. If he'd respond differently to the little creeps who were taunting and beating him, they'd leave him alone, the principal had explained despite her mounting outrage.

She had risen to her feet and glared at him. "My son is kind, smart and gentle. And you're saying *he's* the one who should change? The boys who trip him, steal his lunch, rip up his schoolwork and beat him up, they're just boys being boys?"

He'd stuttered and fumbled, but clearly the answer was yes. That was what he thought.

She had marched out, her mind made up in that instant. Not only would she homeschool, but she and Mark would move, too. Start over, where he wouldn't already be pigeonholed. As it happened, she had been considering quitting her front counter job at a medical clinic and focusing full-time on a hobby that had somehow been transforming into a business.

Now was good.

It wouldn't hurt to put more distance between Mark and his father, too. Mark's constant disappointment at the excuses and cancellations could be moderated by the fact that regular weekends with his dad were clearly no longer possible, and obviously Jeff *couldn't* come to sports games or any special happenings. Better than for Mark to be hammered by the knowledge that his dad didn't want to see him.

She'd intended to give Mark a few days off before they started with the schoolwork—at the very least, she had to get her sewing room/studio unpacked before she could return to work. Orders for her custom pillows wouldn't magically be filled unless she applied herself.

Reading and applying himself to worksheets and projects would keep Mark occupied so she could go back to work, though.

"We need to grocery shop," she said. "We can stop at the neighbor's going or coming, introduce ourselves and ask about the horse. Okay?"

"Yes!" her son said with satisfaction.

Once they had finished eating, she insisted he unpack at least one of his collections before they went anywhere.

If it hadn't been for that blasted horse wandering so close to the property line, she'd have expected Mark to go for his rocks and minerals. He liked all the sciences, but especially biology and geology, including paleontology. He'd been excited about doing some fossil hunting in Eastern Washington. After a session on the internet, he'd informed her that trilobites could be found in Pend Oreille County a little to the north, fossil plants in Spokane County and graptolites—whatever those were—

right here in Stevens County. Something else that could be worked into his science curriculum in the form of field trips. Ciara had been trying very hard not to let him guess how unenthusiastic she was about prowling dry, rocky ground or fresh road cuts in the hot sun. As excited as *he* was, he probably wouldn't notice if she whined nonstop, though, or if they encountered a rattlesnake. Caught up in one of his interests, Mark tended to be oblivious to anything and everyone else.

Oh, God—*were* there rattlesnakes locally?

A number of Mark's teachers had hinted that his intense focus was somehow abnormal, that he needed to learn to "moderate" his enthusiasms, to respond appropriately to his classmates rather than shutting them out or being astonished that they weren't as captivated as he was by whatever currently interested him.

Gee, had it ever occurred to those teachers that his behavior meant he was exceptionally bright? And that those interests should be encouraged, not *dis*couraged? Apparently not.

Her blood pressure rose just thinking about it. She found herself not folding fabrics as carefully as she should before piling them onto shelves.

New start. Who cared what those teachers had implied?

Once she felt calmer, she took a break to see how Mark was coming along, and found that he had chosen, big surprise, to get his animal figurines and books displayed rather than the rocks and minerals and his few precious fossils. The figurines had to be anatomically correct to join his collection, of course. He could and did pick any one up and talk endlessly about it. Only a few days ago, while he was carefully wrapping each before setting it in a box, he'd lectured her about what made an emu different from an ostrich.

Answer: emus were native to Australia, ostriches to Africa, the coloring was different, an ostrich was larger and faster. In fact, it was the world's fastest two-legged animal, clocking in at forty miles an hour while emus trailed at only thirty miles an hour. And, he had added earnestly, just as he had the last time she heard the same lecture, ostriches only have two toes on each foot, while emus have three.

"Ostriches are the only members of the ratite family with two toes, Mom," he had informed her, as if this was a fact that should make her shake her head in wonderment.

And yes, she already knew that kiwis, rheas and cassowaries also belonged to the family.

Ciara knew, God help her, a whole lot she wished she could forget.

And so what if he was fascinated by two-toed birds instead of who the current NBA leading scorer was? She couldn't believe the mothers of most twelve-year-old boys shared their sons' enthusiasms, whatever they were.

"Groceries," she announced, after admiring the ranks of creatures displayed by species and family on the shelves of a tall bookcase.

"Yeah! But we can stop next door first, right?"

Ciara ruffled his hair. "Right."

Which meant that, ten minutes later, she turned into the driveway just past the next mailbox on their rural road. Weirdly, it was paved, a black-top smoother than the road. Hers, two dusty strips separated by a hillock of sturdy wild grasses, was more typical, from what she'd seen. This made for a nice change, though, and didn't raise a plume of dust behind her Dodge Caravan.

She braked beside the farmhouse, which was in considerably better shape than the one she had just bought. Personally, Ciara thought it could be improved by a more imaginative use of color. Once she got around to having their house painted, it wouldn't be white, that was for sure.

"We should ring the doorbell," Mark said.

"It doesn't look like anyone ever uses the front door," Ciara said doubtfully.

"I'll go ring it anyway." Without waiting for an answer, he loped across the neatly mowed lawn and bounded onto the porch. A minute later, he came back. "No one is here."

There weren't any visible vehicles, it was true.

The doors on both barns as well as a couple of out-buildings were closed.

"We'll try again on our way home from town," she suggested. "Maybe they're at work."

"Do you think they have kids?"

She glanced at him, trying to decide whether he sounded wary or hopeful. Given how much trouble he had making friends, she'd expect wary. She hadn't said to him, *Let's move somewhere so isolated, you won't have to interact with other kids your age at all*, but that had been her goal. At least, until she could introduce him to others in a controlled way.

"No idea," she said. "Mr. Garson didn't say." Mr. Garson was the Realtor she'd dealt with. She wished now she'd asked more about the nearest neighbors, but it was a little late. "Come on, let's go do our shopping."

Goodwater had a dusty charm and an old-fashioned Main Street with the type of independent businesses that had vanished from larger towns, including hardware, appliance and clothing stores, a pharmacy, a sporting-goods store with a large banner in the window promising Uniforms for All Local Teams and a special on soccer shoes. Ciara stole a look at Mark, who was gazing with interest at the sidewalks, stores and cafés. Would he like to play soccer? She couldn't imagine. His feet had grown even faster than the rest of him. He literally tripped over them. Maybe something this fall…

The grocery store turned out to be adequate. More expensive than Ciara was used to, but that wasn't unexpected. It might be smart to plan a trip every few weeks to stock up at a Costco or Sam's Club or suchlike in Spokane. She could make an outing of it for both of them.

In the frozen-food aisle, a plump woman about Ciara's age stopped her cart to smile at them. "You must be visitors. We don't get many strangers here."

"I just bought a house. I'm Ciara Malloy, and this is my son, Mark."

"Hello, do you have a horse?" Mark asked.

The woman laughed. "No, but half the people hereabouts do. I'm Audrey Stevens. I live right in town. My husband is an attorney, if you come to need one."

Ciara smiled. "Not yet, fortunately."

"Do you have a dog?" Mark asked.

"Yes, a small one. Since our yard isn't very big," she explained, probably in response to his expression. Mark thought dogs ought to be large. He couldn't understand why anyone had bred a perfectly good animal to be purse-size.

Since he tended to be literal, Ciara was pleasantly surprised that he'd held off reminding her that she'd promised they would get a dog as soon as they moved. After all, in his mind, the move had probably been complete the minute they drove up to the house last night.

"Which house did you buy?" the friendly woman asked, reclaiming her attention.

"It's on acreage. We dealt with the former owner's son. Um…something Walker. I think the owner was Ephraim Walker. The name stuck in my head."

"So would Ephraim, if you'd known him. He was the original cranky old man. One of my husband's best clients. Ephraim liked to sue people."

Ciara chuckled at that, trying to imagine excuses to file a lawsuit. "He must have been popular."

"Oh, he wasn't so bad when he was younger," Audrey said tolerantly. "Who wouldn't get cranky if they lived into their nineties? I'll bet the place needs work."

"Yes. Can you recommend any local contractors?"

Audrey could. Seeing Mark's restlessness, Ciara accepted Audrey's phone number so that she could call later, when she had paper and a pen in hand. Maybe she could find someone to mow the pastures a couple of times a year, too. Or would anyone be interested in renting the pasture? Of course, it would be hard to keep Mark away from any four-footed creature who lived on their own property.

Pleased by the idea of making a friend, Ciara moved on, buying generously. As skinny as he was, her son had an enormous appetite.

They were no sooner in the car than Mark reminded her that they had to stop at the neighbor's again. Wonderful.

They pulled into the black-topped driveway to find a pickup truck and horse trailer parked in front of the second barn.

Mark leaned forward. "Mom, look! There's another horse!"

Ciara couldn't have missed the fact that a man was backing a horse down the ramp. The one in the pasture was just plain brown; this one was a bright shade that was almost copper, with a lighter-colored mane and tail, two white ankles and, she saw as she got out, a white star on its nose.

"A chestnut," Mark declared, having leaped out of the car faster than she could move. "And I'll bet it's a quarter horse. The other one is."

Trust Mark to know the subtle difference between breeds, even though he'd probably never seen a quarter horse in real life.

"Mark," she said sharply. "Wait."

The horse's hooves clomped on the pavement when he reached it. He shook his head, sending his mane flying, danced in place and trumpeted out a cry that made Ciara jump and brought an answering call from the pasture.

"Mo-om!" her son begged, all but dancing in place himself.

The man holding the rope barely glanced at

them before turning his back and leading the horse around the side of the barn.

"Really friendly," she mumbled.

"What?" Mark said.

"Nothing."

"Can we go watch him turn his horse out to pasture?"

"No, we'll wait here like the polite people we are."

"But Mom—" he begged, expression anguished.

"No."

It had to be five minutes before the man reappeared. He hadn't bothered hurrying, that was for sure. He'd probably hoped they would go away if he took his time.

She felt a stir of something uncomfortable at the sight of him walking toward them, although she wasn't sure why. He wasn't incredibly handsome or anything like that. Nobody would look at him twice if he was standing next to her ex-husband, Ciara started to think. But as this man came closer, she changed her mind. If nothing else, he was... imposing.

Like the already-pastured horse, his hair was brown. Not sun-streaked, not dark, just brown. So was the close-cropped beard that made his face even more expressionless than it already was.

He was large, likely six foot two or even taller, and solidly built. Either he spent a lot of time in a gym, or he did something physical for a living. His stride was long and yet somehow collected, as if he controlled his every movement in a way most people couldn't.

He was only a few feet away when he said, "May I help you?" in a deep, quiet voice that was civil while also sounding remote.

"That was a quarter horse, right?" Mark said eagerly. "I've read all about them in books. Why do you have quarter horses when you don't have a ranch? They're best for herding cattle, you know."

To his credit, the man barely blinked. "I do know. In fact, both mine are trained for cutting."

"Is that what you were doing today? Why don't you keep some cows here to practice on?"

Was that a smile glinting in eyes that Ciara decided were gray? "The next-door neighbor—" he nodded to the north "—runs a herd and lets me, er, practice on his." He held up a hand to stop her son's next barrage of questions. "And today I went on a trail ride."

"Oh. What I wanted to know is—"

Ciara cut him off. "That's enough, Mark." She met the neighbor's eyes. "We stopped by to introduce ourselves. We bought the place next door."

"I saw lights last night." He didn't sound thrilled.

"We arrived late yesterday. The moving truck came and went this morning."

"I see."

"My name is Ciara Malloy, and this is my son, Mark. He really likes horses and is hoping you won't mind if he pets yours if and when they come to our fence line."

She sensed more than heard a sigh. "That's fine."

"Do they bite?" she had to ask.

"Only if they think your fingers are carrots."

Mark lit up. "Do they like carrots? I wanted Mom to buy sugar cubes 'cuz horses like them, but she didn't. Maybe they'll come to the fence if I give them something to eat."

"An occasional treat is fine," the man said. "And I do mean occasional. Sugar isn't healthy in large quantities for horses. A carrot or two a day won't hurt anything."

"Cool!" Mark exclaimed.

"Do you know how to give a horse a treat so he doesn't mistake your fingers for food?"

"I can just hold it out like that, can't I?" Mark demonstrated.

Another near-soundless sigh. "No, you have to remember that horses can't see your hand when you hold something out. If you have a minute—" he glanced at Ciara with his eyebrows raised "—I'll give you a demonstration."

"You mean I can pet them now?" Mark bounced like an excited puppy. "Mom, did you hear?"

"I heard. Yes, that's fine."

"Give me a minute." The man disappeared into

the barn briefly, reappearing with a fistful of carrots. Maybe he was nicer than he appeared; he'd obviously guessed that feeding one measly carrot wasn't going to cut it for her son.

She trailed man and boy around the corner of the barn, seeing the fence ahead and a kind of lean-to with a big enameled bathtub filled with water and a wooden manger beside it. The horses currently stood side by side, both grinding hay in their mouths.

Mark raced forward. One of the horses swung away in apparent alarm, and the other threw up his head.

"Gently," the neighbor said. "You have to be quiet and calm or you'll scare them. Keep your voice down. Make your movements slow."

"Oh. I can do that." Mark tripped, fell forward and had to grab the fence to keep from going down. Both horses shied and ended up twenty feet away.

Their owner cast a look at Ciara in which she read understandable desperation. If he wasn't used to kids—

"Gently," he repeated.

"I'm sorry." Mark quivered with passionate intensity. "They'll still come to me, won't they? So I can feed them?"

"Greed will overcome them," the man said drily. He whistled and held up the carrots. As speedily as they'd departed, the horses returned.

Ciara stayed a few feet back, watching as Mark learned how to hold out a treat on the palm of his hand, where horses liked to be stroked and how and what they didn't like. He laughed when their soft lips tickled his hand as they whisked pieces of carrot off it, and laughed again when one blew out a breath with slimy orange bits of carrot that got on his face. He asked what their names were and nodded solemnly at the answer: Hoodoo and Aurora. Both apparently had long, unintelligible names under which they were registered with the Quarter Horse Association, but they didn't know them. The man had come up with Hoodoo; Aurora was used to that name when he'd bought her. He corrected Mark when he described Hoodoo as a chestnut; for some reason, that coloration was called sorrel when it came to quarter horses.

"Hoodoo is prettier than Aurora." After a sidelong glance, Mark placed one foot on the bottom rail and his elbows on the top rail in exact imitation of the neighbor. "Do you think she minds?"

"I doubt horses think in terms of *pretty*. And Hoodoo is actually her son. I did have her bred the once."

"Will you again? That would be amazing." Her son swiveled enough to look over his shoulder. "Wouldn't it be amazing, Mom?"

"I'm sure it would. Now, say thank you, Mark. We need to get those groceries home."

"Do we have to?" His shoulders slumped when he saw her face. "Okay. Now they know me, I'll bet they'll come when they see me with a carrot."

She mouthed the words "thank you" at Mark.

"Thank you, mister," he said obediently. "You didn't tell us what your name is, did you?"

"Didn't I? That was rude. I'm Gabe Tennert."

"It's a pleasure to meet you," Ciara said, holding out a hand.

He looked at it for longer than was polite before gently engulfing it in his much larger hand. The rough texture of his calluses sent a tingle through her and, she suspected, warmed her cheeks.

"Thank you for stopping by," he said, leaving her in no doubt whatsoever that he wasn't at all glad for their visit.

"We're going to get a dog," Mark told him as they walked back to the van. "Mom said we could as soon as we moved."

"If you do, please make sure it's one that won't chase horses or cattle." There was no flexibility whatsoever in that deep voice now.

That was reasonable, Ciara supposed.

Mark got in, and she circled to her side.

"Do you have other children?" Gabe Tennert asked.

She paused. Somehow, she didn't think he was hoping she'd say yes. "No, only Mark."

He nodded brusquely. "Good day."

Before she had so much as gotten the key in the ignition, he had hopped into his pickup truck and began maneuvering to back the trailer into an empty slot inside one of the barns. He didn't even glance their way as she turned in a circle and started down the driveway.

Ciara surprised herself by wondering whether he had a wife.

CHAPTER TWO

ALWAYS AN EARLY RISER, Gabe was outside forking hay into the manger when the school bus passed the next morning. Without thinking about it, he'd known it was coming; the brakes squealed at every stop, and the Ohlers a couple of properties past the old Walker place had two kids that rode the bus.

Now he turned, thoughtful, when the bus lumbered on past without stopping next door. Would have made sense, when Ms. Malloy and her boy were in town yesterday, for her to have registered him for school, wouldn't it? Today was Wednesday, though; maybe she meant to give him the rest of the week to settle in before he started.

April was a funny time of year to move, when it meant pulling a kid out of school and him having to start in a new one at the tail end of the year, Gabe reflected. Usually people with kids tried to move during the summer. Maybe this was following a divorce?

He shook his head as he unlocked the big double doors and let himself into his workshop. Why was he bothering to wonder about the new neighbors?

All he cared was that they stayed on their side of the property line.

He always had several projects going at various stages. Today he settled down immediately to measure and mark what would be the pins and tails of dovetail joints, these particular panels to be sides and backs of drawers. He almost never used any other kind of joint but dovetail for drawers, liking the solidity and elegant appearance. Although they could be cut with router and jig, he preferred to use traditional hand tools.

Securing a solid board of alder with a vise, he reached for a dovetail square and pencil. Despite the care required, long practice meant he was able to let his mind wander as he worked to mark where cuts would be made.

That boy—Mark—was an odd duck. The mother hadn't said how old he was, but he had to be almost a teenager. Middle school, at a guess. What had he been? Five foot nine or ten, Gabe thought. Clumsy, but a lot of boys were at that age. Gabe's mouth twitched. God knew he'd been a walking disaster for several years in there, when he was outgrowing pants and shirts so fast, his mother despaired. Sometimes he'd felt as if those gigantic feet had been transplanted onto his legs during the night. He had to stare at his feet when he was walking to make sure he was setting them down where they belonged. Unfortunately, that didn't work when he wanted to run or climb a ladder or even race up the bleachers in the gymnasium.

It wasn't the clumsiness that suggested the boy was a little off. And maybe Gabe was wrong—but he didn't think so. Mark's excitement was more like a younger kid's than a near-teenager's. The way his mother seemed to be coaching him, too, as if he were a kindergartener who hadn't yet learned to say please or thank you.

Grudgingly, Gabe conceded the kid had been nice enough, though. And he had known a surprising amount about horses and the breed of quarter horse in particular for someone who obviously had done his learning from books or on the computer rather than real-life exposure. Was the mother thinking of buying a horse for her son? Gabe hoped she wouldn't rush to do so without seeing that he get some lessons first. And making sure the enthusiasm wouldn't wear out three months down the line.

He continued to work methodically, out of habit marking the "waste" sections—the parts he'd be cutting out and discarding—with Xs, then, finally, reached for a dovetail saw as his thoughts reverted to yesterday's two visitors.

The mom had an unusual name. Ciara. Irish? Probably. She was exceptionally pretty, he had to admit. Eyes so blue, a man more susceptible than he might liken them to the sky just before twilight or the vivid gleam of sapphire. Hair darker and not quite as bright as Hoodoo's sleek sorrel coat. Envisioning it, he thought, *bubinga*. Bubinga was an exotic hardwood he liked and used on occasion. Harvested in West Africa, it was a reddish-brown with fine, dark lines that created interesting patterns, as if the coloration was made up of distinct strands. Yeah, that was it, he thought, pleased with the comparison.

She had the complexion of a redhead even if her hair wasn't quite the classic red or auburn. Creamy pale, with a scattering of freckles on her nose and cheeks. A pretty mouth—not too thin, not too plump. She was a couple inches shorter than her son, five foot six or so, at a guess, and willowy. Long legs and long fingers, too. Gabe wasn't sure why he'd noticed that, but he had, when she laid her hand briefly on her son's shoulder in a sort of gentle caution. Seeing her do that had sent an odd little shiver through him, as though—

He frowned, discovering that his own hands had gone still, and he was staring into space, his attention no longer split. Ciara Malloy had filled his head, and he didn't like it.

—as though she'd been touching *him*. The sensation had been eerily real. Her hand could have been resting on him. He'd liked her touch.

Too long without a woman, he thought irritably, while knowing he wasn't going to do anything about it. He missed sex—damn, but he missed it. The idea of bar pickups and one-night stands held no appeal, though, and his couple attempts since Ginny's death at having an ongoing lover hadn't ended so well. Maybe in the big city there were women who only wanted a casual lover, but here in Goodwater, anyone he hooked up with started envisioning diamond rings and moving in. Since he couldn't imagine wanting that again, well, he'd decided he could survive living celibate, as long as he avoided temptation.

Which meant it would be safest all around if he had as little to do with these new neighbors as possible.

Comfortable with his conclusion, Gabe reached for the saw. No reason the pretty mom and boy would be interested in *him*. They'd make friends soon enough, and he'd be nothing but the reclusive man next door, whose horses they happened to see out their kitchen window.

There might be a whisper of sadness when he thought of himself that way, knowing he'd end up like Ephraim Walker, a man who, toward the end, had had to depend on the distant kindness of people who didn't even much like him. And Ephraim, at least he'd had a son.

But Gabe knew himself well enough to be sure he didn't want to risk again the kind of devastation he'd barely survived once. He let the brief sadness go and concentrated on something that did give him pleasure—the texture and smell of fine woods, the miracles his hard work and skill wrought from plain-looking beginnings.

He was like the most ordinary of boards, he decided, solid, reliable, but nothing astonishing likely to spring out at the touch of stain or linseed oil, and that was fine by him.

CIARA REACHED THE end of a seam and grabbed her small scissors to snip the threads. Without the whir of the machine going, the silence of the house struck her.

If Mark had finished the reading she'd assigned him, he was capable of concentrating by the hour on drawing or looking up something that interested him on the internet. Still…it was awfully quiet.

"Mark?"

No answer, which meant he wasn't in his room. She left the pillow cover she was working on sitting in a small heap on her worktable and went to check Mark's bedroom anyway. Empty. So neat, it belonged in a model home, but that was just Mark. One argument she'd never have to have with him was over cleaning his room.

She headed downstairs, calling his name but receiving no response. The social-studies book lay closed on the kitchen table, neatly aligned with the square corners of the table. The worksheet beside it appeared to be filled out. She flipped it over to be sure he really had finished. Yep. Ciara felt a twinge of worry that it had been way too easy for him. And boring. If she found some reading on local Indian tribes, or early white settlement in Eastern Washington, maybe that would be more gripping than standard stuff about the executive branch of the federal government. But he did have to learn the basic stuff, she reminded herself, and she had to be sure he'd pass end-of-the-grade-level tests, which meant sticking to the standard curriculum, didn't it?

A worry for later. All she had to do right now was get him through the last couple months of the year. Then she could plan better for eighth grade.

There was no reason to be concerned because he'd gone outside. It was a nice day, and he was mostly sensible. She could guess just fine where he was. Those damn horses fascinated him, despite the fact that they were refusing to come to the fence no matter how he waved carrots at them or tried to whistle like their owner did.

But when she stepped out onto the porch, she saw them peacefully grazing down the slope toward their own barn, and no sign whatsoever of her son.

"Mark?" she called again.

She gave brief thought to returning to work. What kind of trouble could he get in? Even if he'd

wandered as far as the road—and why would he?—
no more than a vehicle or two an hour went by.
More likely he'd wanted to explore the back section
of their land, including the creek, which should be
safe enough. Yesterday she'd looked up the distri-
bution of rattlesnakes in Eastern Washington and
been relieved to find they were rare to nonexistent
in this upper corner of the state.

Ciara went back into the kitchen, grabbed a soda
from the refrigerator and popped it open. Maybe
she'd walk toward the creek herself, just to be sure.
She'd feel better to definitely know that he hadn't
left their property.

"HI. ARE YOU BUSY?"

Gabe straightened from the bin of boards he'd
been sorting through and saw Mark Malloy standing at the entrance to his timber store. This corner
of the barn, walled off from the rest but for a wide
doorway, held his supply of solid boards, veneers
and smaller pieces of exotic woods. This space
had a ceiling, unlike the rest of the barn with its
high rafters and loft that hung over what had been
stalls. A dehumidifier protected his stock of wood.

"This barn is my workshop," he said. "Yes, I'm
working."

"You don't look like you're working."

"I'm choosing some pieces of maple for a particular job." He didn't know why he was explaining, but did.

"Oh." The boy came to his side and gazed into the bin. Right away, he asked why Gabe didn't just grab a bunch of boards.

Gabe found himself explaining his criteria for this and other jobs, again without entirely understanding himself. He didn't want to hurt the kid's feelings, he told himself, but wasn't sure that was exactly it.

Mark helped him carry half a dozen boards to his Felder saw.

"Your mom know where you are?"

"She was working."

Lucky Mom.

"But she wouldn't mind. She said I couldn't go into the pasture, but she didn't say I couldn't visit you," Mark confided with a winning smile.

"Shouldn't you be in school?" Gabe asked, leaning one hip against a workbench. Or had school already let out? It occurred to him belatedly that Ciara might have driven her son today.

"I'm homeschooling." The kid's tone was odd, maybe stilted. "I went to school back where we used to live—you know, near Seattle—but Mom got mad at the school so she said *she* could be my teacher."

Gabe knew he shouldn't raise questions; all that

would do was encourage the boy. But he was curious enough to risk it. "What grade are you in?"

"Seventh."

"I see." No, he didn't. Did the mom want to give Mark an education steeped in religion? Or did she just not think it was fair for him to have to start at a new school so late in the year? "If you're not going to school, you'll have to find a way to make friends around here," he commented. "It's probably too late to sign up for Little League."

Mark grimaced horribly. "I'm not very good at baseball."

"Basketball? You're tall for your age, aren't you?"

"I guess, but I'm not very good at that, either. I hated PE."

"You'll grow into your feet," Gabe said, nodding at them.

"How do you grow *into* feet?" Mark laughed nervously. "That sounds weird."

"It's a saying." Gabe did some more explaining, this time about how bodies grow in fits and starts, and not always in a well-coordinated fashion. His own feet had reached their final size—a twelve— long before he'd attained his current height.

"Is that why baby horses—I mean, foals—look so different?"

"That's right. They have to have long enough legs to reach their mother's teats to nurse and to keep up with her when she runs. In the wild, they wouldn't survive if they couldn't run as fast as the herd. But it takes time for the rest of their bodies to mature so they're in proportion."

"Oh." The boy shuffled his feet and hung his head. "I don't think Hoodoo and Aurora like me. They won't even take a carrot from me."

Gabe knew why; he'd seen the kid a couple of times at the fence, jumping up and down and waving his arms and yelling to get the horses' attention. God knows what kind of strange creature they thought he was, but it was unlikely to be a flattering conclusion on their parts.

"Did you remember what I said about staying quiet and moving slowly?"

His expression became mulish. "But if I just stand there, they ignore me!"

Smart horses. Gabe wished he could ignore the kid, too.

CIARA WENT OUT the kitchen door and made her way toward the creek that ran at the back of the property. In front, the land was all pasture, but sloping down behind the house was the beginning of a kind of open, dry woods that continued as far as she could see. The trees were evergreen, but there was no understory like there'd be in Western Washington, with ferns and salal and salmonberries, all encouraged by the generous rainfall.

Instead there was thin grass and otherwise bare ground that she imagined would be really dusty once summer came.

Were there fish in the creek? She speculated about whether Mark would enjoy fishing. After a moment she made a face. She couldn't picture him being willing to knock a wriggling trout he'd caught on the head to kill it. Or doing something as gruesome as cutting off the head. And Lord knows *she* didn't want to do that part.

She ought to let him wander in peace. That was part of the beauty of owning a good-size piece of land, wasn't it? If there was a raging river back here, that would be different, but he couldn't drown in the creek, not unless he slipped, cracked his head on a rock and ended up unconscious and facedown in the water.

Her steps quickened. He did trip an awful lot. Still— Mostly, she just wanted him to let her know when he went outside and when he came back in the house. Plus, she didn't know the dangers here. This was so different from any place she'd ever lived.

The day felt pleasantly like spring, blue sky arching overhead. Trees she thought might be cottonwoods clustered along the creek. Even so, it didn't take her long to determine that Mark wasn't here, either.

She cupped her hands and yelled, "Mark!"

There wasn't any answer this time, either. Mild concern morphed into the beginnings of apprehension. She was running by the time she reached the house again. After bounding up the steps, she called his name one more time, but the same quiet met her. Damn it, where could he be?

Had somebody come by that she hadn't heard? Would Mark have gone with anyone without having told her?

She grabbed her purse and car keys then raced back out. She'd go from neighbor's to neighbor's, driving slowly in between. She wouldn't panic yet. A boy Mark's age had no reason to feel a need to check in constantly with his mother. He wasn't inconsiderate, exactly, but the idea of her worrying wouldn't cross his mind.

Gabe Tennert's first, she decided. Mark had been intrigued by him. Neither of them had yet met the people on the other side or the ones across the road. Although there were obviously some kids at the house a little ways down. Maybe—

She drove down her long driveway faster than she should have, dust pluming behind, turned right on the two-lane road then right without even signaling into Mr. Tennert's driveway. As cool as he'd been, she was trying not to think of him as Gabe. That was too…friendly.

And friendly was the last emotion she'd feel if

she found out he'd been letting Mark hang out without insisting her son call home first.

Gabe knew mad when he saw it, and there it was, vibrating in front of him, in the person of Ciara Malloy.

Mark didn't seem to have noticed. "Mom! Look at all these cool tools Mr. Tennert has. And he's like me. See? He has a place for everything, and he says he never quits work without putting every single tool away and cleaning up every scrap of wood and even sawdust." He sounded pleased and awed. He hadn't been as impressed by the huge band resaw or the pillar drill, grinder and sanding machines as he'd been by Gabe's regimented ranks of clamps and the rolling chest with multiple drawers that held his tools, each placed as precisely in a slot designed just for it as a surgeon's tools might be in the operating room.

"You disobeyed my direct order," his mother said from between tight lips. She shot a fiery look at Gabe.

"I didn't!" her son cried. "You said I couldn't go in the pasture, and I didn't."

She stared at him. "If you didn't cut through the pasture—"

"I went down the driveway and along the road. Didn't you see my bike? Though it would be a lot faster if I could go through the pasture, Mom.

Then I wouldn't have to ride my bike on the road. The horses wouldn't hurt me." Momentary chagrin crossed his face. "They won't even come near me."

She planted her hands on her hips. "Okay, new rule. You need to tell me if you are going to leave our property. *Always*. No exceptions."

"But Mom! You say I can't interrupt you when you're working. That's already a rule."

"Then you wait until I take a break."

"But Mom—!" Even he seemed finally to notice she was steaming. "Are you mad?"

"I was scared when I couldn't find you." She transferred her gaze to Gabe. "Didn't it occur to you I'd be worried?"

"I did ask if you knew where he was," Gabe said mildly. "He said…" He frowned, unable to remember exactly what Mark *had* said. "I'm right next door," he added.

"He knows better than to bother you, especially in the middle of a working day."

"I'm not bothering Mr. Tennert," Mark assured her. "Am I?" Eyes as blue as his mother's met Gabe's. The beseeching expression was his downfall. Damn it, the kid *was* a bother. Gabe would really like it if Ciara forbade him visiting. But looking into those eyes, he couldn't bring himself to be that blunt. It would feel like kicking a puppy.

"Ah…a little break didn't hurt anything. I'd have kicked him out pretty soon."

"I wish you'd show me how to use your tools," the boy said wistfully.

Gabe cringed at the idea of those uncoordinated limbs anywhere near a whirring saw blade. Hand tools, though...

"Whatever he says, you cannot pop over here whenever you feel like it and bother Mr. Tennert," Ciara said. Her sigh was almost surreptitious. Did she have as hard a time crushing the kid's hopes as he did? Gabe wondered.

"Make it Gabe," he suggested, glancing at the boy. "Both of you."

They beamed at him. "Oh," the mother said. "My name's Ciara. Did I tell you that?" She spelled it for his benefit, and he nodded. Spelling never had been his strong suit.

"I could give Mark a few lessons in using hand tools," Gabe suggested, even as he thought, *What the hell?* "Unless you're hiring someone to come in and do a sweeping remodel of your house, maybe he could take on a project or two. Learn how to strip and sand windowsills and moldings, say. The doorknob on the front door could use to be replaced."

Her expression changed slowly to one of suspicion. "How do you know?"

"When Ephraim got old, he needed somebody to check up on him." He shrugged. "Make sure he hadn't fallen, that he'd gotten out of bed, looked like he'd been eating. I drove him to some doctor appointments, too."

"Oh." She looked almost disappointed, but her face had softened, too. "That was nice of you."

"I'd known him a lot of years," he said simply, although that wasn't all there was to it. Ephraim had expressed gruff sympathy after Ginny and Abby were killed, then went back to treating Gabe the way he always had. He didn't stare at Gabe every time he saw him with pity or avid curiosity, which made seeing him tolerable at a time when Gabe was avoiding everyone else.

"If you mean it," she said slowly.

Mean what? Then he remembered. Oh, hell. He'd offered to teach her son to swing a hammer and apply a scraper and use sandpaper and maybe a handsaw. He considered himself a decent man; he didn't hurt people's feelings on purpose, and was rarely rude. Mostly, he limited the amount of time he had to spend with them, which allowed him to be polite when he was forced into company.

Well, this time he'd give a lesson or two then make excuses. Maybe start closing the barn doors when he was working instead of leaving them standing wide open. Or tell Ciara that he didn't want to be bothered. *She* could be the bad guy so he didn't have to be.

"A little time with Mark won't kill me," he said,

and couldn't help wondering at the expression of astonishment she wiped quickly from her face.

"Why don't you give us your phone number, so Mark can call and find out a good time instead of just showing up?" she suggested.

He had some business cards in a drawer and took one out. He handed it to Mark, who stood closer. "You won't lose that?"

"It's really your phone number?" The kid inspected the card then turned it over as if he expected it to squirt water at him or produce a toy gun with a flag that said, *Bang*. What was with these two?

"It's really my phone number." He glanced at the boy's pretty mother. "You might want to post it when you get home, in case you have an emergency."

She thanked him. He escorted them out, reminding himself he was being neighborly, that's all. Not so different than with old Ephraim. A single woman and a twelve-year-old boy might have a crisis they didn't know how to deal with. He got the feeling they were coming from a very different environment than a county with barely over forty thousand residents. Most Seattle suburbs probably had that many people. Here, those forty thousand people were spread over one hell of a lot of empty land. Seemed to him Colville, the biggest city in the county, didn't even have a population of five thousand. Goodwater claimed a grand total of 1,373 people, which put it in the largest few cities in Stevens County. That didn't include the home-owners outside the city limits, of course, but still, living here wouldn't be anything like what these two knew. Gabe had to wonder why in hell they'd made a move so drastic. Had Ciara even seen the house before she bought it?

Gabe watched them leave, hoping he hadn't bit-ten off more than he was willing to chew. As he walked back into his workshop, he frowned, try-ing to figure out why he'd made an exception to his usual No Trespassing philosophy.

Maybe it was because the boy seemed so… needy. Yeah, that was it. And yes, he was odd, no question, but seemed unaware of it. At least, he'd shown no sign of being aware until Gabe had ex-pressed his willingness to give him some time. Then he'd seemed perplexed, as if he wasn't used to anyone welcoming him.

Gabe gusted out a sigh. Yeah, that had to be it. His offer had nothing to do with the boy's mother. In fact, he stood by his belief that he'd be better off *not* seeing her any more than he could help.

IT DIDN'T TAKE Gabe twenty-four hours to regret his offer.

That happened when, late morning, his mo-bile phone rang. Unfamiliar number, but local. He always tried to answer in case he was going to pick up a new contractor or client.

"Can I come over now?" an eager voice asked. "This is Mark," he tacked on belatedly. "You know. I live next door."

Gabe almost groaned. But…hell. He was at a logical stopping point. "Sure," he said. "But this is a working day for me, so you can't stay long."

"Okay!"

"Make sure you tell—" Realizing he was talking to dead air, Gabe gave up.

Because he was paying attention today, he heard the soft sound of bicycle tires on the asphalt not five minutes later. The kid popped into the barn. Nothing unusual about his attire for a boy his age: jeans, a plain T-shirt and, in his case, red canvas Converse shoes. His sandy hair was spiky and disheveled.

"I want to learn to make something," he announced.

Not what Gabe had had in mind, but he reluctantly conceded that it wasn't a bad idea. It would give the boy a sense of achievement. The high point of Gabe's day in high school had been shop class, where he'd been introduced to woodcrafting. Mark wouldn't get anything like that as long as his mother insisted on homeschooling.

"We can aim for that," he agreed.

"But what can I make?" The boy gazed trustingly at him.

"A box." That had been his first project in shop class, and thanks to a good instructor and his own perfectionist nature, it had ended up beautifully constructed. He kept it in his bedroom and was still proud of it.

Mark brightened. "You mean a wood box? I like boxes. I could keep stuff in it."

"That's the idea. But we won't start on it today. You need to practice on scrap wood first."

He was a little surprised to discover how quickly Mark took to measuring and how much pleasure he took in the tools Gabe showed him. Most kids that age would want to be slap-dash. When Gabe gave him a challenge, Mark measured and remeasured, his concentration intense.

He knew rulers and tape measures, of course, but was fascinated by the LDM—laser distance measuring—something Gabe rarely used but owned. His favorite was the angle gauge, which looked like two straight-edge rulers hinged together at one end, and was designed to measure the angle between adjacent surfaces. The kid understood the concepts right away, too, and Gabe began to suspect he might be good at math, as Gabe had been himself.

He let Mark do a little sawing by hand, but

they hadn't gotten far when Mark asked if he was hungry.

"Because I am. Do you have anything to eat here?"

Apparently, he was inviting himself to lunch. Gabe hesitated, not wanting to set a precedent, but decided feeding the kid a sandwich wouldn't hurt anything. He'd send him home afterward.

"Yes, but let's clean up first."

That wasn't a concept this boy had any trouble with, either, as it turned out. He remembered where each of the tools had been kept, and wiped them clean with a rag and put them away as carefully as Gabe would have. Apparently, yesterday's admiration for Gabe's meticulous storage had been genuine. He used a small hand broom to clean up his minimal amount of sawdust and then looked at Gabe expectantly.

His phone rang while the two of them were putting together sandwiches.

"Gabe? This is Ciara. I'm just checking to be sure Mark is still with you."

"Yes, we're having lunch right now. I'll send him home as soon as he's eaten."

"You didn't have to feed him."

"I won't make it a habit," he said, thinking that he liked her voice, which had a lilt to it. It made him think of the creek out back, when the water rippled over rocks.

"All right." Suddenly, she sounded awkward. "Um, just let me know if—"

"If?" he prompted after she fell silent.

"If he's bugging you."

He didn't say, "Pretty sure that'll happen soon. Any minute, in fact." He had a bad feeling his patience today had created a monster. He settled for "I'll do that" and ended the call, thoughtful.

Parents said that kind of thing all the time. He was sure his own mother had. But Ciara sounded more…resigned than he'd expected. Because she knew her son was a little unusual?

Mark chattered unaffectedly all through the meal. He wanted to know when he could start his box.

"After you learn some basic skills."

"Can I ride one of the horses?"

"Maybe."

"When?"

"Someday."

"Can I today?"

"No. I have to work."

Thanks to his mother, he did seem to understand that adults had to apply themselves to their jobs. But when Gabe asked what his mother did for a living, he was vague.

"She used to work at a doctor's office. You know. She made appointments and stuff."

"What about now?" Gabe didn't even know why he was curious, but he was.

"She sews." His forehead crinkled. "Sometimes people send her something and she uses it to sew, like, I don't know, a pillow or something. It's boring," he concluded.

Gabe laughed, raised his eyebrows at the boy's empty plate and said, "Time for you to go home now."

"You don't have cookies or anything?"

"Afraid not." Desserts for Gabe were store-bought, and therefore rarely worth the bother. Sometimes he thought nostalgically about his mother's home-baked cookies, but not often.

"Can I come again tomorrow?" Mark asked eagerly.

Precedents, Gabe reminded himself. "Depends how involved I get. Check with me tomorrow."

"You mean, I have to call *every* time?"

"Unless we've made arrangements in advance."

"Like, today you say I can come tomorrow."

"Right. But I'm not saying that today."

"Oh." His shoulders sagged a little, but he let Gabe steer him toward the door without further protest.

Nonetheless, it seemed like forever before Mark

finally got on his bike and pedaled back down the driveway.

Gabe shook his head and made his way to the barn.

His generosity today was going to bite him in the ass. He knew it. As he set up to get back to working, he practiced nice ways of saying no.

CHAPTER THREE

"CAN'T YOU TAKE a break *yet*?" Ciara's son asked from where he stood in the doorway.

Oh, why not? She reached the end of the seam, lifted her foot from the sewing machine pedal and turned with a smile. "What's up?"

"Gabe says I can't come today."

His despondency was all too familiar, as was the starburst of frustration and hurt for him that filled her chest. He had come home so excited yesterday, so…proud, as if he'd done something right. And now—

She wanted, quite fiercely, to detest Gabe Tennert, but in fairness couldn't. He'd been nice. That didn't mean he was obligated to become her son's best buddy.

"I'm sorry, honey," she said gently. "He's a busy man."

Mark's expression brightened. "But he says I can come tomorrow. That I don't have to call or anything. He said ten-thirty. We made an appointment." He savored the concept. "Maybe he'll let me have lunch with him again."

"Really?" Ciara hoped he hadn't noticed how amazed she sounded.

"Yeah. So what I was wondering is… You promised we could get a dog. So can we go today? Please, Mom?"

Oh, Lord. She was never going to get anything done.

"Why don't we wait for the weekend?" she suggested in an automatic delaying tactic.

He looked at her as if she had a screw loose. "But tomorrow is Saturday, and that *is* weekend. And I'm already going to Gabe's." He paused in apparent pleasure at the idea and then continued. "And they might not be open on Sunday."

She supposed that was a distinct possibility. Ciara had done some research on animal shelters and rescue groups after she'd bought this house, and decided the Spokane Humane Society would offer the largest selection of dogs and puppies to choose from. Plus, she and Mark could be pretty sure they'd be saving an animal from euthanasia, although she didn't plan to mention that to Mark if it hadn't already occurred to him.

"I can check online—"

"But why not *today*?"

She leveled a look at him. Her tolerance for whining was low. The hope in his eyes was her undoing, though.

"Oh, what the heck." She smiled. "Today it is."

"Yeah, Mom!" He jumped, spun in what might have been intended to be a sort of breakdance, crashed into the door frame and almost fell down. "Ouch!"

Laughing, Ciara swept him into a quick hug, about all he'd tolerate in the way of physical affection, and said, "Let me change shirts, at least. We'll have lunch while we're out."

"And we have to get dog food and stuff, too."

"Right." She reflected on that. "Before we pick out a dog. We don't want one to have to sit in the car, all by himself, while we're shopping."

It had turned out that the one balmy day was pure trickery; late April in Stevens County was *cold*, not springlike at all. A new puppy would be more likely to freeze than overheat if left for any length of time in a car. There were other dire possibilities, though. She wouldn't be thrilled if their new dog ripped up the upholstery of the van. Howling nonstop wouldn't be great, either.

"Lots of stores you can take your dog in, you know," he informed her, trailing her to her bedroom.

She could just imagine. Odds were he'd choose a puppy. One that didn't know how to walk on a leash yet. Oh, and would piddle anywhere and everywhere. Part of her really wanted to insist they bring home an adult dog, but she'd already made up her mind to let Mark make the decision, within reason. He was a kid; kids were entitled to experience the fun of owning a puppy.

"Let's shop first anyway," she said.

CIARA SNEAKED ANOTHER look in her rearview mirror, which revealed the same astounding sight as the last peek had, ten seconds before.

She and Mark were going home with not one dog, but two. And it was her fault.

At least both were adults, she consoled herself, snapping her gaze back to the unwinding road ahead. Theoretically potty trained.

Horse trained, now that was another story.

Watson's information suggested he was a Labrador retriever-hound mix. Read: mutt. He was short-haired, chocolate-brown, with a white chin, chest and three white paws. The history—or maybe it was a wild guess—said he was two and a half years old. In theory, past the chewing-everything-up stage. He clearly had plenty of youthful energy, though. The moment Mark was allowed inside the kennel with Watson, he'd leaped up high enough to cover Mark's face with his tongue. Mark had erupted in giggles.

"He's supposed to be great with cats and definitely is with other dogs," the attendant told her encouragingly. "A little obedience training wouldn't be a bad thing, but he really wants to please. I suspect if he's told what's not acceptable firmly enough, he'll learn quickly. Our volunteers who walk the dogs have been pleased with his attitude."

"What about horses?" Ciara had asked, remembering the steel in Gabe Tennert's voice saying, *Please make sure it's one that won't chase horses or cattle.* No flexibility there. She wasn't sure he'd understand the concept of a learning curve.

The attendant gazed at the same information Ciara could see. "I'm afraid we have no idea," she admitted.

Ciara had retreated to let Mark get better acquainted with Watson, and shortly found herself back in front of a kennel where an elderly dog named Daisy lay with her chin resting on her front paws, her eyes, slightly clouded with cataracts, fixed on each visitor who stopped. Upon seeing Ciara back for a second time, she thumped her tail a couple of times but didn't bother getting up. Ciara wasn't sure whether that was because she'd lost hope, or because her obvious arthritis and excessive weight made heaving herself up more effort than she went to without a clear reward.

The attendant had trailed her. "Daisy is such a sweetie. But given her age…"

She didn't have to finish the sentence. Daisy was a shepherd mix. At eleven-plus years, she wouldn't appeal to many potential adopters.

Ciara found her gaze fixed on the card that said, *Good with cats and dogs.*

No, she told herself. The dog was for Mark, not her. He needed a pet that could keep up with him, that was fun.

Daisy's tail thumped a couple more times, and she hoisted herself to her feet. Her gait was rather stiff when she came forward to allow herself to be patted.

"She'd do well on glucosamine," the other woman said. "Her owner was elderly, and I suspect she didn't have much chance for exercise."

This is too big a commitment to make out of pity, Ciara told herself, with what she hoped was resolution.

"I want Watson," Mark said, right behind her.

The attendant started. "Oh! Did you latch the kennel door?"

"Yes, but he didn't like it when I left."

A mournful howl rose, which started a sympathetic barrage of barks and howls from other shelter dogs. Daisy's ears twitched, but she only wagged her tail a couple more times.

"Crap," Ciara mumbled.

"Mom! You won't let *me* say that."

And that's when the attendant suggested craftily, "You know, dogs are pack animals. They love having a dog companion as well as a human family. If you'd consider taking two, I'm sure we can waive Daisy's adoption fee, given that she's a senior and her chances—" She took a quick look at Mark and changed her mind about what she was saying. "Given her age."

And so it was that Mark was buckled into the middle of the backseat and had not one, but *two* dogs draped over him. Watson had bounded into the car. It had taken two of them to lift Daisy so high.

A little late, it occurred to Ciara that they'd bought a reasonable amount of food for *one* dog. For two, they should have bought more. Plus, Daisy should probably be on a diet formulated specifically for seniors, and Ciara could already envision the hassle of getting each dog to eat his or her own food instead of the other's.

She sighed.

Daisy's tail thumped against the door. Or maybe it was Watson's. Or both.

Mark laughed, and Ciara's mouth curved into a reluctant smile.

Hey, on the good-news front: one of the two dogs crowded on the backseat wouldn't be interested in tearing around the pasture chasing horses.

GOD DAMN IT.

The sharp sound of a whinny had brought Gabe out onto his back porch Saturday morning before he'd had more than a couple swallows of his coffee.

Both horses bolted across the pasture, manes

and tails flying, and right behind them came a brown bullet.

A dog.

An expletive came out of his mouth even as he took off at a run for the pasture.

He didn't bother with the gate, instead planting a hand on the top rail and vaulting over. Hoodoo and Aurora spun past him, the dog in close pursuit. He whistled sharply, and the dog actually hesitated then stopped. The animal's whole body swung with its tail. A long, pink tongue lolled out.

"Come," Gabe snapped, and to his mild surprise the dog obeyed. Gabe was able to wrap his fingers around what appeared to be a brand-new collar, from which two shiny, silver-colored tags dangled. One was the expected rabies tag; the other, bone-shaped, gave the dog's name as Watson and his owner's name as Mark Malloy. The phone number was now familiar to Gabe.

Not letting go of the collar, Gabe walked the dog out of the pasture, in the side door of his garage and popped him into the cab of his pickup. Hoping like hell the damn animal wasn't still young enough to want to chew whatever was in front of him—say, the seat upholstery—Gabe hurried back to the house to grab his wallet and keys.

When he returned to the pickup, Watson barked happily, slopped a big kiss on his face before he could evade it and thrust his nose out the window when Gabe lowered it a few inches to entertain him during the short drive.

His jaw ached from clenching his teeth by the time he pulled up in front of the neighboring house. Ciara burst out the front door before he could get out.

"Oh, no!" she said. "Watson went to your house?"

Despite his severe aggravation, he couldn't help noticing how gracefully she moved, and how much he liked her long, slim body in tight jeans and form-fitting T-shirt.

Do not *get distracted,* he ordered himself.

"What was the one thing I said?" It came out as a roar. "Don't get a dog that'll chase livestock!"

"Oh, no," she said again, more softly.

Watson, still in the cab, barked at her.

She tore her gaze from the dog and fastened it on Gabe. "The thing is the shelter doesn't know how most of the dogs do with horses or cows. When I asked, they gave me blank looks. Probably Watson has never seen a horse before. I…I'm sure he can learn."

She kept talking. There was something about a potential obedience class, and a learning curve— he tried to imagine how that would work—and she concluded by saying maybe she could pay to have wire mesh fencing added to his board fence along their property line.

He shook his head. "That's a mighty long property line. Unless you're made of money…"

The alarm that widened her eyes was answer enough.

They both fell silent for a moment, looking at each other. Her expression was oddly defenseless. Maybe because it was so early in the morning. At least she was dressed, but the hair he'd so far seen captured in a braid hung loose and was tousled enough, he had to wonder if she'd brushed it yet. Sunlight caught fire in the curls.

"I didn't think," she admitted at last. "I let them out when I first got up—"

"Them?"

He swung around, expecting to see another dog tearing through his pasture. The Hound of the Baskervilles.

"You won't have to worry about Daisy." She turned, too. "I wonder where she is."

A second dog toddled around the corner of the house. Her legs were stiff, and the effect with her too-well-rounded body was more of a waddle than a walk. As she got closer, Gabe saw the milky film in her eyes that went with her graying muzzle.

He crouched and held out his hand. "Here, girl."

Her tail swung a few times, and she came right to him, accepting his scratches and soft words.

Finally, he straightened. "Her, I'm okay with."

Ciara's face became mutinous. "You're not telling me we have to take Watson back. That would kill Mark!"

Gabe groaned and let his head fall back. This was every bit as bad as he'd imagined. No, there weren't little kids next door running around screaming, but the one kid who was here didn't disappear daily to school, either. Instead, he wanted to be *friends*. He wanted *lessons*. He'd be calling every damn day if Gabe didn't shut him down. And now a cheerful young dog with no manners at all had been added to the mix.

He lowered his head to see Ciara watching him anxiously.

"If he attacks one of the horses or Henry Beem's cattle, you have to either find him a home where there's no livestock around, or you'll need to have him put down. Do you understand?"

Her chin trembled a little bit. "I understand."

The foundations of his anger began to crumble. *Damn it,* he thought again. *This* felt like kicking a puppy, too, even though she was now glaring at him.

"All right," he said abruptly, wheeled and opened his door.

The dog exploded out, jumping and barking in delight because he was free, and now there were *two* people to love him. No, the front door was opening. Mark came out on the porch, and now there were three. Jubilant, Watson leaped up the steps to greet his boy then sprang back down and headed for Gabe.

"Sit!" he snapped.

The dog looked astonished, but his butt did momentarily touch the ground. Didn't last long—next minute he was jumping on Gabe, trying to kiss his face again.

"Sit," he repeated, this time laying his hand on the dog's head to quell his quivering desire to spring back up.

"He knows how to sit." Mark grinned in delight. "See, Mom? He's already trained."

"Do you have a leash?" Gabe asked grimly.

He looked puzzled. "Yeah."

"Go get it."

While her son was gone, Ciara said, "I'm so sorry. I did ask."

"You ever think of checking in town? Somebody around here probably has puppies that have been raised around animals."

"No-o." She drew the word out. "I researched shelters. We got Watson and Daisy at the Spokane Humane Society. I meant to get only one. You know, for Mark. But I was afraid nobody would take Daisy, and I thought maybe she'd have a calming influence on Watson."

Daisy had planted herself at Ciara's feet, appearing completely content.

"They already have those names?"

"Yes. I asked if they'd been named at the shelter, but those are the names they came with, so I thought…"

Gabe nodded. "It's something familiar. They should be able to keep them."

Her smile brought something to life inside him he'd never wanted to feel again. "That's what I thought, too."

Gabe tore his gaze away, concentrating on the dog squirming in front of him. He released him from the sitting position but whistled sharply every time he got too far away. When Mark returned with a short red leash, Gabe had him fasten it to the collar. "Now go get some carrots, if you have any."

"Mom bought lots!" Mark raced back into the house, almost falling halfway up the porch steps.

Gabe winced in sympathy despite his irritation. *I am still irritated,* he assured himself, although his emotions had already become way more complicated than that, as seemed to happen every time he got close to these new neighbors. Either of them.

Once the boy returned with carrots in hand, Gabe led a parade to the pasture fence. Even Daisy roused herself to toddle along behind.

Gabe was far from sure the horses could be persuaded to come, but eventually they got near enough to be sure one of those humans was Gabe, and that there were carrots in the offing. Every time Watson barked, Hoodoo and Aurora neighed and shied away, but Gabe had Mark put his hand around the dog's muzzle while reminding him sternly to "Sit," and eventually he was able to persuade the two horses to come to the fence for their treat.

There was a lot of backing and shying, but finally Watson touched his nose to each of theirs, and Gabe made sure they all stood there long enough for the animals to develop some level of comfort with each other. He knew damn well it wouldn't last, but it was a start. He just hoped the dog was high-spirited rather than having a killer streak. He didn't think Mark would take it well if the dog he'd picked out to be his had to be put down.

"Use the leash a lot these first days," he instructed him. "If your mom is okay with it, you can walk him in the pasture, as long as he's *always* on the leash."

After a moment, she nodded. Reluctantly, he thought, but she must have been able to see the sense in his suggestion, and had surely become convinced his quarter horses were too scared of her son to want to trample him to death.

"Why don't you pet them?" he suggested, having noticed she was hanging back like she had last time.

He stayed where he was to gentle the horses, which might have been a mistake. She stepped close enough to allow a citrus scent to rise to his nose. Probably shampoo. He studied her fingers as she tentatively stroked one sleek neck and then the other, giving a surprised squeak when Aurora lipped her fingers.

"Her mouth is so soft!" Ciara exclaimed.

He couldn't help thinking her lips looked soft, too. So did her skin. It was exceptionally fine-pored, more like a young child's than an adult's. In self-defense, he began to scratch Hoodoo's poll. He couldn't remember the last time he'd been so tempted to touch a woman. Hell, if he laid a hand on her, she'd probably jump six inches and shy away just like one of the horses did to an unwelcome surprise, he thought ruefully.

But the face she turned up to him was alight with pleasure. "They're so friendly! They're just like dogs."

For that moment, all the guardedness he'd seen in her was gone. Those eyes, huge and bright, shone with delight. And the way her mouth curved...

He'd have sworn he heard a cracking sound, the first ominous fissure in the Grand Coulee Dam, holding back the weight of enough water to wreak havoc through the whole Columbia River basin. Nobody else seemed to hear the sound, originating in his chest, where he'd built walls he would have sworn were rock solid.

Panic spiked, and he took a step back.

Irritable, that was his defense.

"Just so you remember, horses weigh two thousand pounds," he reminded her and her son.

She shot a worried look at the boy before fixing her gaze on Gabe again. "Do they ever, well, step on you?"

"Yeah, I've had horses step on a foot. Sometimes they don't even notice. That's why it's a good idea to wear boots around them." He glanced at Mark. "You have any?"

"Uh-uh. Maybe I should get some, Mom."

"Is leather really good enough?" she asked Gabe. "Or do you get steel-toed or what?"

Amusement eased his panic. "You ever seen a cowboy boot coated in steel?"

"Is that what I should get him? Cowboy boots?"

"Yeah, probably," he said in resignation. Sure as hell, he'd be putting the kid up in the saddle before he knew it. Might have to do it on a lead line, if Mark didn't turn out to have any more ability to center his weight when sitting than he did on his feet. Quarter horses had been bred to turn on a dime, whether their rider went with them or not.

"Well, okay." Ciara gave him another sunny smile that had him backing up yet another step. "Thank you for…well…"

His eyebrows climbed. "Not shooting the dog?"

The boy grabbed his dog's collar. "You wouldn't!"

His mom's smile turned to a glare. "Don't say things like that!"

Gabe chose not to say anything.

Her eyes narrowed. "Do you *have* a gun?"

"A rifle. Yes, I do, ma'am." *Ma'am*—that was good. Distancing.

"You hunt?" Her voice spiked with disapproval.

"I was raised hunting," he said. "My family needed that meat on the table. But no, actually, I don't."

"Then why—?"

"Do I keep the Remington on hand?" He hesitated, not wanting to tell her it had been a gift from his dad, which at the time had meant something. In these parts, giving your son a fine rifle was a way to acknowledge he'd reached manhood. His father hadn't been very good with words, but sometimes he'd done something that had made Gabe glow with pride. Not often, which is maybe why those rare moments stuck with him. "Anyone with livestock has to worry about coyotes or wolves," he said instead. "If I heard someone breaking into my workshop, I'd reach for it, too."

She looked shocked, giving him an idea how she'd cast her ballots. His mouth twitched. If he was right, she'd be in a minority in this corner of the state. The thought made him wonder anew what she'd been thinking, a woman raising her child alone, buying a house so isolated, in a county where she and her son might both have trouble fitting in with what neighbors they did have.

He glanced from her outraged face to Mark's. The kid was kind of dorky-looking to go with his personality. Lips a little too big and loose, expression too open. Gabe's amusement faded. Sure as hell, Ciara Malloy had gone for isolated on purpose. He just hoped she hadn't made one hell of a mistake.

He dipped his head. "I need to be getting back." He met Mark's gaze. "You want a dog, teaching him what's acceptable and what isn't is your responsibility. You understand, son?"

The boy nodded. "Yes, sir."

"All right, then." Gabe walked back to his truck, not allowing himself any softening chitchat. Whatever that strange feeling he'd had when Ciara smiled, he had to have imagined it.

He was going to be pissed if he was back here in two hours because the damn dog was already in the pasture nipping at his horses' heels again.

"Sir? I mean, mister...I mean, Gabe?"

The driver's-side door was open; he didn't have a lot of choice but to glance back.

Neither woman nor boy had moved. The old dog had settled her butt and looked as if she'd be content never to move. The young dog, however, was getting antsy.

"Yes?"

"I can still come to your place this morning, right?"

Oh, hell. In his exasperation, he'd forgotten. He

wanted to say, *You've already wasted enough of my day,* but the apprehension coupled with hope that the boy couldn't hide stopped the words in Gabe's mouth.

"Yeah," he said gruffly. "I'll be expecting you."

He took one last look as he started the engine, bothered by the knowledge that he wanted to see warmth again on Ciara's face. That it would be easy for a man to get to crave the sight of that expression.

And there it was, just as he'd envisioned it, and the crack in his protective wall groaned a little as the damage done to it allowed further weakening.

He drove faster than he should have down their long, dusty driveway.

STARING IN DISMAY at the math problem Mark didn't understand, Ciara wished she'd escaped to her workroom immediately after breakfast instead of making the mistake of lingering to ask if he needed any help. She'd mostly been okay with the seventh-grade math in the original curriculum, but once she downloaded the kind of work he'd already been doing in his advanced class, she was lost.

What's more, this was the first major download she'd tried since discovering high-speed internet wasn't available. In moving to such a rural location, they'd apparently lost a decade or two. Dial-up was torturous.

"This is geometry, isn't it?" she said unhappily.

"Um...*yeah*."

"Sarcasm is not appreciated."

"Well, it's about angles."

"I can see that," she snapped. It showed a shape—God help her, she didn't even know what the shape was called—and wanted to know the sum of the angle measures in it. She'd taken geometry in high school and hated it. "You know, if you're going to work on this stuff, I'll have to review it in advance to be any help to you."

"But Mom, it's only eighth-grade math!" her son exclaimed.

Gee, and she hadn't already felt stupid enough.

"Do you know how many years it's been since I took this stuff?" she asked. "Things like percentages I use once in a while in real life. Geometry, never."

"Oh."

They both stared at the peculiar shape.

"Maybe Gabe knows the answer," he suggested.

Because you had to know angles to shoot a Remington rifle?

"'Cuz he has this cool gauge that measures angles!" Mark said with new enthusiasm. "So he must understand them, right?"

"You have my blessing to ask."

"Yeah!" He grabbed the worksheet and stuffed it

into the daypack that already sat on the table. "It's time for me to go anyway."

"You've got the cookies?"

"You saw me put them in the pack."

"Right." Of course she had.

Anxious mother that she was, she walked as far as the front porch and stayed there while he pedaled down the driveway, turned right on the road then up Gabe Tennert's nicely paved driveway. When he disappeared from sight behind the house, she figured he'd made it safely. Watson, nose pressed to the screen door, whined miserably. He'd wanted to go, and he didn't understand why he couldn't. Ciara shuddered at the thought of him in Gabe's workshop.

He almost escaped when she opened the door, but swift use of her foot allowed her to slide inside and latch the door. "Not a chance," she told him and went upstairs. He followed, of course, while Daisy lay at the bottom, watching sadly. She could barely handle the couple of steps from the back porch to the yard; a whole flight was out of her capability. Watson, on the other hand, would want to go in Ciara's workroom, where he could do as much damage as he would in Gabe's. The damage wouldn't be as expensive, but Ciara couldn't afford it.

She shut this door firmly in his face, too. He moaned but then subsided. As she plugged in her iron, she hoped her neighbor had a sweet tooth. Although she still found him alarming for reasons she hadn't altogether figured out, ones that didn't have anything to do with the fact that she also found him sexy, he'd so far been exceptionally nice to Mark. Oatmeal-raisin cookies were probably inadequate thanks, but she didn't know what her next option would be.

Did he cook, or was he the kind of single guy who lived on microwave meals? Maybe tonight she'd bake bread. Everyone liked homemade bread. And if he kept letting Mark go over, she could invite him to dinner one of these nights. That would be the nice thing to do, wouldn't it?

Steam puffed from her iron, and she gasped at the realization of how long she'd left it pressed on the delicate damask she was working on. Damn, had she burned it?

No, she saw in relief, but that was pure luck. She had to concentrate. Why on earth was she worrying about what a man she didn't even know liked to eat? Mark's sixth-grade teacher had been a man, and she'd never once considered sending him home-baked cookies.

Yes, but he'd been *paid* to teach her son. Nobody was paying the closemouthed, bearded guy next door to spend any time at all with Mark.

She winced, wondering what he'd think when Mark whipped out the geometry worksheet.

And then she wondered what Gabe Tennert would look like if he shaved off that beard.

CHAPTER FOUR

"IT'S A HEXAGON," Gabe said absently. "Six sides."

The boy's forehead crinkled. "I thought it was a polygon."

"It's that, too." Gabe explained that a polygon was a closed shape that usually had straight sides. "A triangle is a polygon."

"Tri." Mark's face brightened as if it were lit from within, like his mother's did. "Three."

"Right. Four sided is a…?"

"Quadrangle."

"Five sides makes it a pentagon."

"Cool," the boy decided. "So how do I figure out the sum of the angle measures in a hexagon?"

"Do you know what the measures of the angles of a triangle add up to?"

"A hundred and eighty degrees," he said triumphantly.

"Good." Gabe got out a ruler and pencil and showed him how to divide the shape up into triangles, then watched as Mark divided it into four triangles. He was able to multiply 4 times 180 in his head and come up with the right answer, which Gabe thought was pretty good.

"I don't remember getting to geometry until high school," he commented.

"My school did it in eighth grade. Except, if you were ahead, you did the eighth-grade stuff in seventh. Then if you were pretty good, you could skip Algebra 1 and take geometry as a freshman."

"Gotcha." Gabe nodded. "You okay with the next problem?"

They talked about a couple more, after which he put the worksheet away but pulled out a lidded plastic container. "Mom made cookies. She thought you'd like some."

Gabe's fingers were peeling the lid back before his brain gave the order. "What kind—" He inhaled. "Raisin oatmeal. My favorite."

"Really? I thought she should make chocolate chip. That's *my* favorite. But she says these are better for us."

"I like chocolate chip, too," Gabe admitted. "I wouldn't turn them down. But these are great." He took a bite and closed his eyes to better savor the burst of flavor. "Really great," he mumbled a minute later.

He gobbled two before he remembered he shouldn't waste the time eating when he was supposed to be—teaching, he guessed. He turned his mind back to his woodworking class and said, "I want you to do some measuring, and then you can experiment with the saw."

Having seen how clumsy Mark was, Gabe did a lot of talking about safety precautions but was still a little unnerved when they got to the stage of practicing first with a handsaw, then a jigsaw and finally a circular saw. Interestingly, he found that the boy was both careful and precise. His focus was as intense as Gabe's was when he worked. Gabe began to relax. They talked about the options for corner joints and decided that for Mark's first effort, they'd go for a rabbet joint, good-looking and relatively simple.

He did some marking, chose clamps for his scrap lumber and practiced cuts with various saws. They talked about woods, and Gabe explained what his next stage was for the three separate cabinetry jobs he had going. Mark eventually decided to use cherry for his box; he liked the rich color of a darker stain better than the look of light woods. Truthfully, Gabe did, too, although he especially liked being able to use contrast.

It felt companionable putting sandwiches together with the kid again, with the bonus today that they both ate a couple more cookies. Gabe carefully put the top back on the container. Ciara had sent a couple dozen. That would keep him in cookies for…well, that depended on how greedy he allowed himself to be, didn't it?

He evaded the boy's hints that he'd like to learn to ride, too—half the day was already shot—but he did allow Mark to feed a couple of carrots to the horses again before he sent him home.

Gabe pretended he was just giving himself a minute to decompress when he stood outside watching the boy pedal home, but he knew better. He felt some sense of responsibility. The road didn't have much of a shoulder. It wasn't ideal for bike riding.

He was disconcerted to find he was smiling when he walked back into his workshop.

"THAT DOESN'T SMELL very good."

Ciara turned to see that Mark had appeared in the kitchen.

"Shut the door," she said hastily—too late.

Watson burst into the kitchen, leaping to put his paws on her chest, his wet tongue catching her chin before she could take evasive maneuvers. She had to fend him off with an elbow. "Mark!"

Eventually, he propelled the reluctant dog out of the kitchen and latched the swinging door. Ciara hoped the young dog would learn enough manners soon so that they didn't have to exile him from any room where they were cooking or eating, but for now, she was grateful for the door. In their previous house, she wouldn't have had any way to keep

Watson from putting his paws on the dinner table and snatching food off Mark's plate.

Above the whine that penetrated the closed door, she said, "This is a new recipe. There's nothing in it you shouldn't like." She carried the casserole dish to the table and set it on a hot pad. "Try it."

"I don't like it when foods are all mixed together," he said disconsolately.

"You like raisin-oatmeal cookies. Flour, sugar, oatmeal, raisins and several other ingredients, all mixed together."

"That's different." He sighed loudly and plopped down in his place.

"You like spaghetti," she pointed out.

"It's not new!" he burst out.

Ciara only laughed. "Try this casserole. It may surprise you."

She poured them both milk, dished up the peas she'd chosen because they were a favorite of his and sat down herself. She watched as he used the serving spoon to transfer a minuscule amount of the cheesy hamburger bake onto his plate, but said nothing.

He stared down at his plate. "Dad said he'd call tonight. Do you think he already did and we didn't hear it?"

Familiar tension felt like wires strung through her body being pulled tight. "I think I'd have heard the phone, but you can check voice mail. *After* dinner," she added, reading his mind even before he started to jump to his feet.

"But Mom—"

She took a bite to give herself a minute. "It's only six-thirty. If he said this evening, it'll probably be later anyway."

Mark hunched his shoulders and stabbed at his peas. Several went skittering off his plate. "He'll forget. He always forgets."

He was right. Jeff did always forget. She wished he wouldn't make promises at all, however casual. He *knew* how literal Mark was. In his world view, if you said you were going to do something, you did it.

"Your dad is pretty busy these days," she said gently. New wife, new baby, promotion at work. Out with the old.

No, not fair—the new family and promotion at work had absolutely nothing to do with his disengagement from his first son. That happened as soon as he began to suspect Mark wasn't a chip off the old block. The son he had once described as a "retard" was *her* fault, he had declared. Jeff was unimpressed with the reality that Mark scored at 95 percent or above on most standardized tests given in school.

"You know what I mean," he'd growled.

Yes, she did. He meant Mark wasn't a swaggering, sports-crazy, rough-and-tough boy's boy. Instead, he was thoughtful, given to intense interests—none of which his father shared—and, at least so far, spectacularly *un*athletic. Ciara could not understand how any of that made Mark unlovable to a parent.

"How'd things go with Mr. Tennert today?" she asked in an attempt to divert him.

It worked. His face brightened. "He said to call him Gabe, you know."

"Right." She was trying to stick to Mr. Tennert, who sounded like a neighbor, versus Gabe, who was a sexy guy she found herself thinking about way more often than was healthy.

"It was good." He chattered on, explaining how today they'd worked on finding the missing angles in triangles and quadrilaterals.

At one point she leveled a look at his plate, and he took a tiny bite then a larger one before he continued his enthusiastic recitation about complementary, supplementary, vertical and adjacent angles. Ciara pinned an interested smile on her face and tuned him out.

"He remembers everything about geometry," Mark concluded with satisfaction. "That's good, because I think it's cool."

Panic briefly raised its head. What if Gabe Tennert lost interest in helping Mark with his math?

I can research anything, she reminded herself. *I am perfectly capable of staying ahead of a seventh grader.*

It was humiliating to know she wasn't buying her own pep talk.

Gabe had also had Mark sawing assorted pieces of scrap lumber. He'd done some miter cuts today, and Gabe had shown him how to mark intended cuts so as not to make a mistake.

"Mark them." Her son cackled. "Get it?"

She produced a chuckle.

This was Thursday. She hadn't encountered their neighbor since their Saturday morning confrontation over Watson chasing his horses. Having seen the bone-deep reluctance on his face, she'd honestly been surprised when he'd let Mark come down to his workshop later that same morning. She was even more surprised that he had scheduled appointments thereafter, meaning Mark had disappeared for up to two hours to the neighbor's both Tuesday and today.

She was trying to keep her distance, but had expressed her gratitude by sending a loaf of freshly baked bread with Mark on Tuesday and a Bundt cake today. Mark had reported an enthusiastic reception for both the cookies and the bread. She asked now about the cake.

"He said you don't have to send stuff every time."

"Oh." Ciara was disconcerted to feel let down. "Does he not like desserts?"

"He had, like, a *humongous* piece of cake while

he helped me with my math." Lines appeared between Mark's eyebrows. "So I don't know why he said that."

Her spirits rose. "He was probably being polite."

He stared at her. "Why is it polite to say he doesn't want your food if he really likes it?"

Ciara told herself it was just the age, or maybe being dense about the games people played in the name of civility was a boy thing. She explained why people said, "Oh, you didn't have to," when that wasn't really what they meant at all. Mark appeared to be listening earnestly, but his expression never cleared.

Her suspicion was confirmed when he said finally, "People are weird."

Well, yes, they were, but Mark nonetheless had to learn the art of telling polite lies. Right now, if he'd been required to take a standardized test on this particular art, Ciara was afraid he'd score somewhere in the first percentile. He always said what he was thinking.

It seemed like every time she took the phone after he'd spoken to his dad, the first words out of Jeff's mouth were, "For God's sake, do you know what he just said to me?"

Um…the truth?

It was surprising how often the truth came out sounding awfully rude.

"When are you going back to Gabe's?"

"Saturday. Tomorrow he's going to a house to make measurements for cabinets. I wanted to go with him, but Gabe says I can't 'cuz it's going to take him most of the day and he knows I have to do schoolwork."

"I don't suppose he often builds cabinets for houses in Goodwater," she said thoughtfully. She wondered if anyone in this small town could afford him.

"This house is at someplace called Medical Lake. Gabe says it's called that 'cuz people used to think the lake water cured them of all kinds of diseases."

In her initial search, she'd browsed houses online in Medical Lake. As in much of Eastern Washington, real-estate prices were staggeringly low compared to the Seattle area.

"There's sort of a castle in Medical Lake," she told him. "It was built by an English lord."

"Can we go see it?" Mark asked eagerly. "Maybe we could go with Gabe."

She shook her head. "In the first place, he hasn't invited us. Plus, I think I remember reading the castle has been turned into an apartment house, and there isn't much to see anymore."

"You mean, you can rent an apartment in a *castle*?"

Mark had enjoyed touring Craigdarroch Castle in Victoria, British Columbia, almost as much as he'd liked the natural-history displays in the Provincial Museum there. Craigdarroch, built in the late 1880s, was no more a real castle than the one in Medical Lake—which had probably been built in roughly the same decade, come to think of it.

"I wish he'd let me go with him," Mark said, sounding sad.

Ciara took a deep breath. "Maybe we should invite Gabe to dinner tomorrow night. Or Saturday, if he'll be back too late tomorrow."

"Can we?" He pushed back his chair and jumped to his feet. "Can I call him? Right now?"

She hoped this wasn't a huge mistake. She was torn between discouraging Mark from forming any deep attachment to a man who might lose interest in him any day—and, okay, keeping her own distance for personal reasons—and bribing said man to keep providing something Mark obviously needed desperately.

Something his father would never give him.

"I think this is one invitation that should come from me," she said firmly. "He needs to know it comes from me."

"Then will *you* call him right now?"

"After dinner. Sit," she ordered.

He sat. From then on, all he talked about was how cool it would be, having Gabe here. He bet

Gabe could show him how to make Watson sit. 'Cuz he knew *all* about animals. Had he told her...?

Oh, Lord. What if Gabe Tennert politely declined her invitation? Mark would be heartbroken.

The phone rang. Once more, Mark erupted from his seat.

"I bet that's Dad!"

He returned a moment later with her cell phone, his expression downcast. "It's that man who came out here about the floors."

She accepted the phone, saying brightly, "It's still early," even though she knew damn well Jeff wouldn't call.

What was she thinking, letting Mark get attached to a man whose only connection to them was a property line?

Even as she greeted the local contractor who was ready to offer a bid on refinishing floors, all she could think about was their next-door neighbor's slow, deep voice and a face not quite as expressionless as she suspected he wanted it to be.

CIARA DID LET him call his grandparents that evening, and took a turn talking to them herself. Dad said hello, there was a Mariner game on and gave the phone to Mom, who laughed.

"He started watching so he could sound intelligent when clients commented on games or players or whatever, and now he won't miss a game. Bridget, too."

"Bridget?" Ciara repeated. That, she'd have to see to believe.

"You know, if you gave your dad a chance, he could get Mark interested, too."

Ciara snorted.

Mom laughed again.

"What about you?"

"I still can't figure out why I'd want to waste hours watching grown men adjust their balls—and I'm not talking about the stitched leather kind— and stare intently at someone crouching behind the plate holding one finger or two fingers down between his thighs. Or, come to think of it, just below his balls."

Ciara laughed hard enough to get tears in her eyes. Only her mother. "Have you expressed this opinion to Dad and Bridget?"

"Yes. Bridget said there is only one ball, and what am I talking about. Your dad snorted wine out his nose."

"I miss you," Ciara said with complete sincerity.

"We miss you, too, honey. We're dying to see your place. Just let us know when you're settled enough to welcome visitors."

"I will," she promised, disturbed to find herself torn between an aching need to see her family, and a reluctance to let reality intrude on the new life she and Mark were creating.

FRIDAY, GABE WAS disconcerted by how much he anticipated having dinner with the Malloys, mother and son. He tried to convince himself it was only that he didn't get good, home-cooked meals very often. His own repertoire was basic and pretty limited. After the samples of her baking he'd devoured, he was willing to bet Ciara would feed him something mouthwatering.

Usually after a long day like this, he'd have stopped for a burger or even a pizza somewhere on the drive home. There weren't many places to eat out in Goodwater, and when he did occupy a booth in one of the two cafés, people insisted on pausing to talk.

Not like I won't have to make conversation tonight, he reminded himself, but was perplexed to realize he didn't so much mind the idea. He was used to Mark; that had to be it. And Ciara—well, she seemed like a comfortable enough woman, except for her looks, which stirred him into a state that wasn't comfortable at all.

It felt odd to turn into the driveway before his own. The horses wouldn't like their dinner being late, but they could live with it. He winced at the dust rising to coat his truck. He'd paved his own driveway to avoid jarring and potentially damaging a finished cabinet or piece of furniture, but he was particular enough about his vehicles, keeping them clean had been a bonus.

Before his pickup even rolled to a stop, the front door sprang open and Mark and Watson burst out. Gabe yanked on the emergency brake, turned off the engine and jumped out before the dog could leap up and scratch the paint on his truck.

"Down!" he ordered, and the surprised mutt aborted his delighted spring.

"No leash?" Gabe asked.

The boy's gallop down the steps had been only slightly slower but considerably less graceful than the dog's. "He's getting better. He comes right away when I call. See? Watson. Hey, boy, come here."

The dog kept big brown eyes trained on Gabe's face. His tail swung wildly.

"Watson!"

"It's okay," Gabe said. "He's excited because I'm new, that's all." He laid a hand on Mark's thin shoulder and gently squeezed. "You're right. He seems a little less excitable."

"Mom makes me take him out for runs all the time." His face scrunched. "She says I need the exercise, too."

Gabe laughed. "She's right."

"Mom made one of my favorite dinners. I told her I bet you'd like it, too."

"So what's this favorite dinner?"

Watson whirled around them as they walked toward the porch. Gabe noted how many boards on the steps were cracked. Might be an ideal example of good, practical carpentry Mark could help him with.

"Manicotti. Mom makes really great manicotti."

Gabe's stomach growled. Lunch seemed like a long time ago.

Daisy was waiting on the porch, her tail wagging. He stopped to give her a good scratch and speak softly to her, even though Watson and Mark were seething with impatience. They all entered the house together.

"Mom won't let Watson in the kitchen when she's cooking or when we eat," Mark confided. "Only tonight we're eating in the dining room— you know, because you're a guest—so I have to shut him in my bedroom. He might howl."

"I suppose you can't put Daisy in with him."

"Uh-uh. She can't climb the stairs."

"She looks good, though," Gabe observed. "I think she's walking a little better."

"Mom's giving her some pills the vet suggested. Do you know Dr. Roy?"

"He takes care of my horses. Rides in cutting-horse competitions, too."

"Really?"

Gabe nodded toward the staircase. "Why don't

you go on and take Watson up? I'll go say hello to your mom."

"Okay." The two raced up the stairs, sounding, as Gabe's mother would have said, like a herd of elephants.

He pushed through the swinging door into the kitchen then stopped, hit with sensory overload. The manicotti smelled amazing, and Ciara was bent over, removing garlic bread from the oven. The sight of her in tight jeans and a frilly lemon-yellow apron made his mouth water in a different way. She either heard the door or his stomach growling again, because she swung around quickly, her eyes startled.

"Oh! I heard your pickup, but I thought maybe Mark had dragged you upstairs to see his room."

Gabe ambled forward, hoping he looked un-threatening, although he wasn't sure why it mattered. It might be best if she did find him in-timidating. "No, he's currently dragging Watson upstairs to lock him in solitary confinement."

Ciara made a face. "I swear that dog's last fam-ily must have let him help himself to food right off their plates. I refuse to gobble down my meals, ready at every moment to defend my food."

Gabe found himself smiling at the picture. "Might be good for your reflexes."

"More likely it would cause indigestion." She

tilted her head. "Was he coming right back down? Dinner is ready to go on the table."

"I think so."

Feet thundered on the stairs.

"Can I carry anything?" Gabe asked.

She gave him the salad bowl and carried the glass baking pan filled with manicotti herself, using crocheted potholders, then went back for the garlic bread.

"This is our first meal in the dining room," she said, pulling out her chair.

As he took his own seat, Gabe looked around reflectively. As with the rest of the house, Ephraim had let the room get shabby. In retrospect, Gabe felt guilty that he hadn't done more to help. At the time, he'd thought his neighbor would be insulted at any implication he was letting his place get run-down.

The house was solidly built, older than his own, Gabe thought, but the wallpaper was peeling, the wood floors were scratched and had lost much of their finish, and the molding needed either to be refinished or painted.

Ciara handed him the spoon to serve himself first. "Do you know Vince Mays? Audrey Stevens recommended him." Her thoughts had obviously paralleled his, or else she'd been able to tell what he was thinking. "I may hire him to refinish the floors. Although now I'm trying to figure out how we can do it and keep living here."

"It would be tough," he said honestly. "Especially with the dogs."

She sighed. "I may put it off, but now I feel guilty since he came all the way out here."

"I was thinking the front porch steps need replacing. Mark could help me do the job. It'd be a good learning experience for him."

The boy's face lit with pleasure. "I can? You mean, saw the boards and nail them and everything?"

"I don't see why not." Gabe helped himself to some broccoli then passed it to Ciara. Their fingers brushed. He felt like he'd just touched a hot burner.

"I can't ask you—" she began.

"You didn't. I offered. Mark's old enough to be doing some of the basic work, once he learns how."

"Really?" She must have heard how doubtful she sounded, because she glanced at her son, but he was glowing and appeared not to have noticed. Gabe had come to realize that Mark didn't notice much about what other people were thinking or feeling. He was oblivious to the subtle cues that worked for most people. Discouraging him would have taken more cruelty than Gabe wanted to employ.

"Why not?" he said. "He's doing fine with what we've been working on."

He had a feeling she wouldn't have wanted him to see her surprise, but he did. He pondered it as they all started eating. Was the boy such a screw-up, then? Gabe wouldn't have guessed it. He seemed smart, and his concentration was impressive. Gabe liked that he was meticulous, too. He hated making mistakes as much as Gabe did.

The first bite of manicotti had him stifling a moan. This would be one of his favorite meals, too.

Ciara asked questions about Goodwater, mentioning folks she'd already met. He told her most people stocked up on groceries and other supplies with an occasional run to the city, the way she was talking about doing. She wanted to explore fabric stores in Spokane one of these days, too, which had Mark grimacing and the corners of Gabe's mouth twitching. At that age, hanging around a fabric store would have been his idea of a fate worse than death, too.

He eyed the manicotti, wondering if it was too soon to take a second helping. Or would she expect him to eat his broccoli first?

She saw the direction of his attention. "Please, have more."

He didn't hesitate, but tried to disguise his gluttony with some conversation. "Mark says you have your own business, but he was a little vague about what you do."

She gave her son a fond look. "That's because he doesn't see the appeal. I make custom pillows. Decorative ones," she added after seeing Gabe's blank expression. "I also sell one-of-a-kind pillows in a bunch of small home-decor-type stores, but my specialty is using a piece of fabric that holds sentimental value to someone as the centerpiece of a pillow." This time, she smiled at his bemusement. "Say you were the starting forward for your high school basketball team, and you've treasured that jersey all these years. Instead of it being stuck in the bottom of a drawer, I cut it apart and use it with some complementary fabrics to make a pillow that looks really cool on your family room sofa. It's right there, making you happy because you're reminded more often of your glory days, plus people notice and comment on it, and you can laugh and say, "Isn't it a kick?" But hey, now you get the chance to tell people about your stardom without having to figure out a way to work the conversation around to it."

Gabe considered the idea. "That's damn clever. Sports jerseys, huh?"

"That's only an example, although I've had people send me a bunch of those. But I've sewn lacy pillows out of wedding or prom dresses—the prom ones are fun for girls to take to college for their dorm room. I can make gorgeous pillows from tattered family quilts that might have been thrown away otherwise. An Olympic gymnast sent me her leotard. I sewed a whole set of pillows from a World War II uniform with the patches as accents.

I never know what I'll get, so I try to keep a varied selection of fabrics to go with anything and everything. Sometimes I have to head out to search for something that'll work, but…hmm, I have a certain style, and I like certain looks." She shrugged.

"How do customers find you?" he asked, deeply intrigued.

"Website. My business is called Pillow Talk."

"Sounds racy."

She grinned. "If that draws attention…"

"I'll have to take a look at it."

Her nose looked cute when she scrunched it up. "Except it has a whole lot of pictures showing examples, which means it would take you twenty minutes for it to load. It never even occurred to me there were places still without high-speed internet."

"Yeah, browsing the internet isn't something you do in a hurry in these parts. There's talk that high-speed is coming, though. The cable TV company is working on bringing it to us."

"That I could get excited about."

"Me, too," Mark interjected. He'd been getting restless, Gabe had seen out of the corner of his eye. Mom's business didn't interest him. "There's all these cool sites, but they take so long they're hardly worth it. And the library in town is so *small*."

Gabe raised his eyebrows. "Goodwater is a small town. We're lucky to have a library at all." He suspected he sounded defensive, but didn't care. "You can order anything that's in the system, you know, and interlibrary loan is faster than you'd think."

"I've already ordered a few books, and Mrs. Upton was really helpful," Ciara put in.

There was something in her voice, though, that made him wonder. Gloria Upton might be helpful, but she was also a busybody. Gabe didn't know of any other kids in the area who were being home-schooled. Gloria might have been scandalized by the very idea that this newcomer didn't think Goodwater schools were good enough for her son.

Come to think of it, did that have something to do with Ciara's decision to teach Mark at home? Had she wanted a rural lifestyle, but assumed her kid was too good for the small school in a back-water town like this? And this from a woman who obviously couldn't handle the math her son was supposed to be learning?

Would she tell him why she was homeschool-ing if he asked? Maybe—but probably not in front of Mark if her motivation was specific to him and not more general, as in having to do with her re-ligious beliefs.

He couldn't remember the last time he'd both-ered speculating much about anyone's life or rea-sons for doing anything. Better not to ask, he told himself. Keep this relationship casual. He was en-joying sharing his skills with Mark more than he'd expected. It took him back to that shop class and

Mr. Avery, who had meant a lot to him. Paying it forward, he thought; that was all he was doing. And he was getting some damn good food out of it, too.

"Apple pie, anyone?" Ciara asked.

Oh, damn. Bad enough that she was pretty and that he didn't dare let himself look too long into eyes that made him want to be a poet. Now she was assaulting his defenses in a whole new way.

CHAPTER FIVE

EVERY TIME THE renewed whine of the circular saw penetrated the closed doors and windows, Ciara's anxiety rose. Mark could lose a finger or a hand in less time than it took to blink. Should she really be trusting a man she didn't know that well? In the week since he'd first come to dinner, she had had him once more, but that was it. She still hadn't figured out why he was giving so much time to Mark, or how he could be so patient.

"I couldn't believe my eyes when I saw Gabe Tennert out there with your son," Audrey Stevens said. When she'd called earlier, Ciara had invited her to come by for a cup of coffee. She could use the distraction. Otherwise, she was afraid she'd be outside hovering.

Her several phone conversations with Audrey had wandered from the subject of reliable local plumbers, electricians and carpenters into personal interests. It had turned out that not only was Audrey a fount of local knowledge, she was a quilter like Ciara used to be, when she had time.

"He's been really nice to Mark," she said now,

pretending her ears weren't acutely tuned to the sounds outside. As long as there weren't any screams…

Surely they'd give up soon, as chilly as it was out there. She'd peered out earlier to see the thermometer reading only forty-two degrees Fahrenheit. They were now in the first week of May. When was spring around here? June? she thought indignantly. July? And neither Gabe nor Mark was bundled up the way she would have been, if she were doing outside work.

"Don't get me wrong, I've never seen him be anything but kind," the other woman assured her, in a tone that suggested she was giving the devil his due. "He rides in cutting-horse competitions. I don't know if you're aware of that."

"He's mentioned it."

The whine was replaced by silence then the steady thud of nails being driven. Thank God. Mark would live with a swollen thumb.

"Gabe has friends from that. But otherwise…" Audrey hesitated. "He stays to himself."

"I…had that impression," Ciara admitted. "Would you like a refill?"

"Thanks." Audrey grinned. "Your coffee is better than my coffee."

Rising, Ciara found the empty bag that had held the beans and held it up so the other woman could see the logo featuring a stylized bull. "Chimayo

Coffee Company. I don't suppose the local store carries it, but it's worth ordering online."

Audrey accepted a fresh cup, inhaling the rich, dark aroma. "I'm sold."

It had been a long time since Ciara had made a new friend, so she was warmed by this budding relationship. She knew Audrey was the driving force; between work and being a single mother, Ciara didn't have time to look for activities where she'd meet other women.

Men—well, she was off men. A disquieting whisper suggested, *Except for Gabe.*

Ridiculous. He was a godsend for Mark, assuming he didn't abruptly lose interest. That was all.

"He was married and had a daughter, you know," Audrey said abruptly.

"What?" *Had* a daughter? Alarm speared Ciara. What did that mean? He'd lost contact?

"I'm not just gossiping," this new friend said slowly, before making a face. "Oh, well, I guess it is gossip, but you should know."

"Know what?"

The steady beat of the hammer was like background music. Occasionally, she heard Mark's voice, but Gabe's was too deep and quiet to carry. Plus, she suspected he said only an occasional few words of direction or encouragement. He wasn't a big talker. The couple of times he'd come to dinner now, she could tell he'd been making an effort.

"His little girl was only five. She'd just started kindergarten." Audrey's brown eyes were fixed on the past. This wasn't just gossip; sadness had transformed her plump, usually happy face, reminding Ciara that, in a town this size, everyone knew everyone. "They'd gone to see *The Lion King* at the INB Performing Arts Center in Spokane. Abby was so excited. On their way home, a drunk driver ran a red light and rammed into the passenger side of Gabe's truck. Abby was killed immediately. His wife, Ginny, lived for a couple of days in a coma but never came out of it. He was a quiet man even before that, but since then…he's never been the same."

Ciara had listened with horror. Of course he'd never been the same! If Mark was killed, what would she have to live for? And his wife and child both? For the first time, she fully understood the desperate reluctance she'd seen on his face when Mark had been so insistent on being friendly. It was a miracle that Gabe had let down his guard as much as he had.

"That poor man," she murmured.

The next second, she also understood the odd flash of resignation she'd seen in his gray eyes when he saw Audrey getting out of her car. He must have guessed she'd fill Ciara in on his history, if she hadn't already. Ciara wondered how a man as private as he seemed to be endured the pity he must see on people's faces every time they saw him. And the knowledge that, in a community this small, everyone knew his tragic story and probably whispered about it when he appeared in the grocery store or post office. In his place, she'd have been tempted to move away.

She winced at what she'd just said. *That poor man.*

She would have to be very careful not to look at him any differently when he and Mark came in.

"Did you grow up around here?" she asked. "Have you known Gabe long?"

"Not that long. No, I'm actually from Moses Lake. I met my husband when we were both at WSU. He went to Gonzaga for law school, so we stayed in the area."

Ciara nodded. Gonzaga was in Spokane.

"He grew up in a small town and wanted his own practice. Of course he has to be in Colville a lot, since that's where the courthouse is, but, with an office here, he attracts clients from this part of the county. Goodwater is a great place to raise our kids."

Ciara already knew that Audrey had three, ranging from a two-year-old to a third grader. The two-year-old was currently at a playgroup, Audrey had told her.

"Are you waiting until fall to start Mark in school here?" she asked, her curiosity inevitable.

"Our school is small, but we've been really happy so far. Small is good when it comes to class size."

"I'll bet." Ciara smiled. "I'm homeschooling to finish this year. Then we'll see."

"Well, check it out—" She broke off. "Your intrepid workmen are coming in out of the cold."

Ciara, too, had heard the front door opening. Mark burst precipitately into the kitchen. "Mom, come see! We finished the steps already."

"Aren't you freezing out there?" Audrey asked in her good-natured way.

"Nuh-uh." He barely spared her a glance. "Mom, you got to come look."

Taking her cue, Audrey said it was time she should be getting home, and walked out with Ciara. They were immediately breathing in the pungent scent of freshly cut lumber.

They had to step around Daisy, who wagged her tail in apology but made no attempt to heave herself to her feet. Watson greeted them with his usual enthusiasm, which had Audrey laughing. Ciara's gaze was drawn straight to Gabe, who was crouched on the porch, apparently stabbing a screwdriver into a board. She couldn't help noticing his powerful thigh muscles with the denim stretched taut.

He rose lithely, his unreadable gaze flicking from Audrey to Ciara. "We're going to need to replace the porch boards, too."

She made a face. "Figures."

She said her goodbyes to Audrey. Gabe dipped his head and said her name. Both stood watching as Audrey descended the next steps and went to her car, accompanied by Watson. It was Gabe who whistled sharply when Watson started to give chase to the car.

"Thank God the road isn't busy," Ciara exclaimed, having a sudden vision of what Watson's new hobby would have been.

"If it was, you might have to keep him tied up," Gabe said. His tone was very restrained.

So restrained that she said cautiously, "Has he been after the horses again?"

"Yeah. They didn't seem all that disturbed, though."

"He wouldn't hurt them!" Mark insisted.

Gabe didn't say anything.

"You'll let me know…?" Ciara said.

"I will." He sounded rueful.

Her son reclaimed her attention, and Ciara duly admired the raw porch steps. "Did you do some of the cutting?" she asked Mark.

"I did all of it." He stole a glance at Gabe. "Well, almost all of it."

One of Gabe's faint smiles warmed his eyes. "He did."

"I hope you're being careful."

Not listening, Mark leaped down the steps with

his usual impetuosity, calling over his shoulder. "Can we keep working?"

Gabe's hesitation was brief but telling. "I don't see why we can't finish the job today," he said. "Your mom can decide whether she wants to stain the boards or paint them, but we'll need a little warmer weather for that."

For him, it was a long speech.

"Um…what's better?"

Apparently, there were pluses and minuses to each. She admitted to liking the look of paint, and he said it preserved the wood better than a semitransparent stain, although the wood didn't "breathe" as well through it.

Who knew wood breathed?

She told him she was planning to have the house painted once the weather warmed up a little, too. "I haven't decided what color yet. But definitely not white."

He gazed contemplatively across the pasture toward his own house. "You don't like white, huh?"

"I work with color." She was a little chagrined at having sounded as if she was denouncing his taste. "I won't go too gaudy, I promise."

He was definitely smiling. With that blasted beard, it wasn't always possible to be sure, but this time she was. "I'll consult you the next time I paint."

Would they stay friendly? She felt a funny little

pang she didn't quite understand at the idea of the years passing with him occasionally having dinner with her and Mark. Would she want to stay here, once Mark had gone off to college?

"How often do you have to paint a house?" she asked.

His eyebrows rose. "Haven't you had it done before?"

Having lost patience in the adults, Mark and Watson were wrestling and chasing each other on the rather ragged-looking lawn. Gabe had propped a shoulder against the square porch upright and seemed to be watching boy and dog. She kept her gaze on them, too, although she was awfully conscious of him beside her.

"Actually, I haven't," she said. "Well, my parents did when I was growing up, but I didn't pay attention. My husband and I—" She stopped, shrugged and resumed. "We'd only owned a home three or four years when we got divorced. I've rented since then."

"The divorce recent?" he asked.

Did he care, or had he felt civility demanded he ask?

"No, it's been almost seven years."

Lines seemed to have formed on Gabe's forehead. "Where's Mark's dad live?"

She could guess what he was thinking. She had

provisionally become the evil witch, keeping a boy from his father.

"He's in Seattle. The thing is—" She crossed her arms tightly, not looking at him. "He never had time for Mark anyway. I thought it might be less hurtful for Mark if he can't see Jeff, instead of knowing his father just can't be bothered."

"His loss," Gabe said after a minute.

The sting of tears took Ciara by surprise. "Yes," she whispered.

Laughing and backing away from Watson, Mark crashed into one of the sawhorses set up on the grass. It tipped over, him on top of it. In a ripple effect, the second sawhorse fell over, too.

Gabe didn't so much as twitch.

Mark scrambled up, his face suddenly stricken. "I'm sorry! I'm sorry. I'll put them back up. I didn't break anything, did I?"

"Doesn't look like it." With a barely heard sigh, Gabe straightened away from the porch support. "You need to be careful on a work site, though. You could get hurt if you don't pay attention."

"And you're letting him use a saw," Ciara mumbled.

With a low, rough chuckle, Gabe said, "Don't worry, I'm hanging right over him. Got to say, though, he's good with tools so far."

"Who'd have thunk?"

His second laugh sounded as rusty as the first, making her wonder if they came rarely.

"I'll make lunch," she said.

Mark put the sawhorses back more or less in the same position they'd been and picked up a hammer and pair of leather gloves that had fallen, too.

"Why don't you give us another half hour or so?" Gabe suggested. "We can get most of these floor boards pulled."

"Deal." She looked fully at him. "Have I said thank you?"

"As often as you're feeding me, it's the least I can do."

"You mean my bribes are working?" she teased.

His gray eyes met hers. "Is that what all those desserts are?"

"Maybe." Why was she embarrassed? "No," she said hastily. "They're more another way of saying thanks. I doubt you really wanted to take Mark on as a project."

"Can't say I realized he'd be a project, not that first day. But—" His expression had closed utterly, although clearly he was picking and choosing what he was willing to say. "He's a good kid," Gabe said finally. "Doesn't hurt to encourage someone as eager as he is."

"I wish his father felt the same." The words were torn from her.

"I don't understand a man not wanting to be

around to raise his son." The one next to her didn't give away the pain he must feel, but after hearing what had happened to him, she knew it was there. She had no doubt he'd have given anything in the world to be able to raise his daughter.

She smiled shakily at him. "Fortunately for us, we hit the jackpot in the neighbor stakes. You're a good man, Gabe Tennert. But that doesn't mean you owe us anything. If you ever want to back off—"

She'd have sworn a hint of color touched his cheeks above the close-cropped beard. "I'll tell you." He nodded and started down the steps.

Before she reached the kitchen, she heard the ripping sound of the first board being pulled up.

She wondered what Gabe would have done if she'd gone up on tiptoe and kissed his cheek. And whether his beard would be stiff and scratchy or silky under her lips.

And, oh God, what would have happened if he'd turned his head at that precise moment, and her kiss fell on his lips instead?

She hadn't felt this kind of honeyed warmth low in her belly in longer than she could remember.

It was foolish beyond words to let herself develop some kind of crush on her reclusive next-door neighbor, who would probably be appalled if he knew.

Thoughts jumping, she wished she'd asked

Audrey how long ago he'd lost his wife and child. Opening the subject again would make it sound as if she was interested in him. Ciara knew she'd never dare ask him, not when their conversations hadn't approached personal yet.

At least, not until today, when the word *divorce* crossed her lips.

Yes, but that had to do with Mark, not me, she told herself. So it didn't count.

Lunch. Think about lunch. Not the quiet, powerfully built man with remote gray eyes.

Who had said the astonishing words: *He's a good kid.*

This warmth seemed to envelop her heart.

"I'M SURPRISED MARK didn't want to come." His fingers flexing on the steering wheel, Gabe was careful not to look at the passenger in his pickup truck. It was a week later, his suggestion that they might combine planned trips to Spokane casual.

"I am, too," Ciara admitted. Then, "Normally, he hates shopping, but I thought he'd want to look at wood with you."

And, damn, but Gabe had been relieved when Mark decided to stay home. Because of the kid's nonstop mouth, he told himself, not because he'd wanted to spend the day alone with Ciara.

"You don't worry about him home by himself?" he asked.

"Why should I? He's twelve. He's not into par-
tying, drugs—"

"Rock and roll?" Gabe said, with a tinge of
humor.

Her chuckle was contagious. "Actually, he
likes late sixties, early seventies music. Grateful
Dead, Simon and Garfunkel, Cream. My mother
thinks it's a hoot. She grew up in the San Francisco Bay area, and went to concerts at the Fill-
more and Winterland. I, of course, rolled my eyes
at her music. Now here's her grandson, awed because Grandma actually saw Sons of Chaplin, Jimi
Hendrix and Jefferson Airplane before they became Jefferson Starship."

A smile tugged at his mouth. "My father would
have said something scathing about long hair and
draft dodgers. My mother would have called it hippie music."

"It was. I don't know if Mom exactly qualified as
a hippie, but there are pictures of her looking rag-
gedy, wearing ponchos and giving a peace sign."

The highway ahead was mostly empty. He let
himself glance at her. "And now?"

"She still mostly wears jeans and wears her hair
in a long braid, so maybe there's a little hippie lingering in her."

"Your father?" This wasn't like him, wanting
to know everything about another person. He pre-

ferred to believe he was just being polite, making conversation, but knew better.

She laughed openly. "Oh, he's a stockbroker. He was working on his MBA when they met at Berkeley. Mom swears he was wearing a white shirt and tie when a former girlfriend dragged him to an organic foods café where Mom worked part-time. She claims it was love at first sight anyway. Dad grunts but says, 'Maybe.'"

Gabe wondered if her parents' votes in major elections canceled each other out, too. The thought amused him.

"Where do they live?"

"Bellevue. Across Lake Washington from Seattle." The change in her voice was subtle, but there. The openness was gone. She'd been willing to talk about her parents past tense, but wasn't as happy about present tense.

Knowing he was pushing it, Gabe still asked mildly, "You didn't want to stay near them?"

"Oh, we mostly email and talk on the phone anyway." Her tone had become vague. "What about your parents? You sounded as if…" She hesitated.

"They're both gone." *Gone*. Nice euphemism. "Dad owned and managed a small airfield. He gave lessons, offered charters." Gabe had to swallow to say the bad part. "Mom liked to go up with him. There was a mechanical failure. Plane went down and they both died, along with another couple who was with them."

"Oh, my God," Ciara whispered. "I'm so sorry. And sorry I asked."

"It's okay." He shook his head. "It was a long time ago."

"Were you an adult?"

"Yeah, early twenties."

"Did you learn to fly?"

He shook his head. "Don't much like heights." His father, of course, had been disgusted. His son's unwillingness to face his fears head-on like a man and learn to fly anyway had been a major bone of contention between them. It hadn't been the only one. Gerrit Tennert had been a voluble man who was well liked by almost everyone. He'd never understood his son and only child's introverted nature.

"Bet that caused some conflict," Ciara said softly.

He grunted agreement.

"I don't actually like to fly very much, either. I haven't had occasion to have to very often, fortunately."

He'd like to think she wasn't offering that tidbit as a sop to his admission of an unmanly phobia, but knew she was kind enough to do just that.

He made a sound that, hell, was probably another grunt.

"You'll find plenty to do while I'm browsing?" she asked after a minute.

"Chances are you'll have to wait for me," he said honestly. "I like to handpick my wood, especially the accent pieces."

She smiled at him. "So you'll be fingering chunks of wood while I'm doing the same to fabrics."

"Guess there are some parallels," he admitted. Unfortunately, he could all too well imagine her stroking velvet or silk with a delicate touch. And damn, lately he'd caught himself a few times, when he ran his fingers over a finely sanded piece of wood, wondering if her skin would be even silkier. It would certainly be warmer, more giving. The curves softer, less predictable. And shit, he was getting aroused, thinking about her skin and her touch. He hoped she didn't glance toward his lap.

"Woodcraft has some specials right now on woods I like to have on hand in my lumber room."

She coaxed him into talking a little about what woods in particular he was looking for. He told her how Chechen had gotten the secondary name of Black Poisonwood, and that boxwood castello wasn't really boxwood at all. She liked the names: Zapote, Granadillo, Brownheart. By the time they reached the outskirts of Spokane, he was sorry they were splitting up until lunchtime, after which they'd agreed to go to Costco before going home.

When he dropped her in front of Hancock Fabrics, Ciara gave him a cheeky smile and said, "Have fun," before hurrying toward the entrance.

He carried a funny feeling under his breastbone as he made his way across town to his own destination, and even as he began shopping. He still didn't know what impulse had made him ask yesterday if she had any errands in Spokane to do this weekend, but the drive had seemed to pass a lot faster than usual, and he was already anticipating sitting across a table with her while they ate lunch. Talking some more on the drive back to Goodwater. Not like this was a date, of course, but…it was something. Friendship, maybe, although if that was what it was going to be, he'd have to quit thinking about how much he'd like to see her naked.

By the time he helped her pile bags and bags of fabric and what she called "notions" into the canopy-covered bed of his pickup, Gabe had admitted to himself that they were already friends. He'd had half a dozen meals at her house now; he fed her kid lunch several days a week, and even his solitary meals were much improved these days, given the home-baked goodies that wrapped them up. If he didn't watch it, he was going to have to let his belt out a hole or two pretty soon.

Yeah, and her food wasn't the only reason his pants fit a little too tightly some of the time lately. And that was something he needed to think about.

He already knew the perils of trying to conduct a sexual relationship with a local woman. With Ciara, he'd have to triple or quadruple the risks. She lived right next door. He was spending a lot of time with her son. Worse yet, instinct told him she didn't have casual sexual encounters. Sure as hell not so close to home, not with her such a dedicated mother.

Besides—how would they ever get away from Mark?

Not happening, Gabe told himself sternly, knowing he should have obeyed his first inclination, which had been to keep his distance from these neighbors. Now— Damn, now it would be hard to start making himself unavailable. All he had to do was picture the pride on Mark's face when he'd told his mother he'd sawed all the boards for their front steps, or the bewilderment and hurt on Ciara's face when she said, *I wish his father felt the same.* Or the soft glow in her eyes when she told him he was a good man.

He struggled most with the realization that he wanted her to keep thinking he was a good man. He wanted to see a time when Mark took for granted that he felt pride in himself. He wanted—

He wanted a hell of a lot he'd sworn he would never try for again.

No, he wasn't willing to go there. He'd meant his vow. But…maybe he didn't have to live a life as solitary as he had been. Maybe he could enjoy feeling almost as if the three of them were a family, without investing himself too much in these two other people.

And maybe he was a goddamn fool to risk even that much.

He tuned in to her happily telling him about her shopping expedition—the triumphs, the disappointments, the women she'd talked to, the ideas that had been sparked by unusual fabrics she'd snapped up.

They weren't running as late as he'd expected, so they stopped for lunch at a café he liked instead of opting for fast food. While they ate, she asked how he'd done, and he found himself telling her about some of his upcoming jobs and about the furniture he made as time allowed.

"I have a couple of outlets for it, one here in Spokane, another in Coeur d'Alene." Coeur d'Alene, across the border in Idaho, had a beautiful setting on the lake of the same name and was an upscale resort town. The gallery that carried his furniture thrived, and, as a result of what he showed there, he'd had some commissions from customers as far away as San Francisco. The rocking chairs and coffee tables and desks he made were still just a sideline for him, though. Almost a hobby. He wasn't sure he wanted to change the balance.

"I'd love to see your furniture," Ciara said, her attention entirely on him. "Do you have a website?"

He snorted, and she smiled.

"No, I guess not. You don't need to, do you?"

Gabe swallowed a bite of his burger and shook his head. "I turn down as much work as I take. I work regularly with contractors who recommend me both for historic renovations and for new construction. I'm not interested in expanding to the point where I'd have to take on employees. The last thing I need to do is advertise."

"I can see that," she said thoughtfully. "Me, I'm new at actually trying to make a living at what I do. Before, it was just something I did for fun that seemed to be taking on a life of its own."

"I suppose you can live cheaper over here, while you get the business off the ground." So, sue him— he was curious why she'd chosen to make such a drastic move. He'd hinted at the deeper question before, but she'd shied away from answering it.

"It really wasn't that." She bent her head as if concentrating deeply on the remaining half of her chicken-teriyaki sandwich, leading him to suspect she was avoiding his gaze. "I had in mind a rural lifestyle. And, like I told you, I was trying to put some distance between us and Mark's dad. Once I started browsing real estate online, I was intrigued by this corner of the state."

He reached for a French fry. "Spring seems to be taking you by surprise, though."

Her head came up so he could see that cute nose-crinkling thing she did. "Reading about it is one thing. Discovering it gets down close to freezing in April is something else. I guess I should think about buying a cord of wood or so before winter, shouldn't I?"

The weather was hinting at spring now, in early May. He hoped she wouldn't be too shocked when next winter rolled around. The climate was a whole lot milder in the Puget Sound area, where she'd come from, than in this part of the state far from the moderating effects of an inland sea.

He educated her on some of the practicalities of life in a harsher climate than what she was used to, warning her to expect, come winter, to lose power now and again, and suggesting she consider adding some insulation as she had work done on the house. "Might make it more comfortable."

Eventually, he decided she was just picking at the remains of her lunch and asked if she was ready to go.

She looked surprised. "I'm in no hurry if you want some of that pie."

The array of pies in the glass display case as they came in had been impressive.

Gabe usually did indulge when he was here, but

he shook his head. "Can't compete with your desserts. You've spoiled me."

"Oh." She blushed. "Well, thank you."

Instead of splitting up again when they got to Costco, they pushed their carts side by side, him watching as she picked out some jeans and socks for Mark. "He's growing like a weed," she grumbled. "I don't quite dare buy shoes without him trying them on, but these jeans should be safe." In turn, she eyed some of the frozen dinners he put in his cart along with practicalities like batteries, lightbulbs and an industrial-size box of bandages.

"I nick my hands a lot," he explained. He held out a hand, which was battered enough to make his point. "Don't want blood dripping on raw wood."

Anxiety infused her expression when she looked up from his scarred knuckles. "You won't let Mark—?"

"We're careful," he said gently. "Won't be the end of the world if he bashes his knuckles a few times, will it?"

"Just so he doesn't cut a finger off."

Gabe grinned. "I haven't done that yet, and I've been woodworking for—" he had to think "—twenty-three years now. Since I learned in shop class."

She waited until they had checked out and loaded their purchases in the bed of his truck along with everything else they'd bought. Not until they were on the road did she ask any more questions.

"Was your house your parents'?"

"Yeah." He frowned at having to make the admission.

It bothered him sometimes, sleeping in his boyhood bedroom, living with fleeting glimpses of his parents' ghosts. But at the time, keeping their house and property rather than selling it had seemed to make sense. He had been working for someone else, dreaming about going into business for himself. The barn here had been perfect for a workshop. After selling the airfield, he'd had enough to set up his business. Having already met and married Ginny, he'd been grateful for the bigger house. After she and Abby were gone, he'd given thought to moving. In the home he'd shared with them, they were everywhere. In the end, though, he hadn't wanted to lose that last, tenuous connection with them. So he'd stayed put, not sure if he was comforting himself or if it qualified as torture. The one thing he'd done was move out of the master bedroom he'd shared with Ginny. He'd given away most everything that belonged to her and stripped the room, but he didn't like stepping foot in it anyway.

He guessed from the sidelong way Ciara was eyeing him that Audrey had told her about his family, but she was tactful enough not to say anything, and it wasn't anything he wanted to talk about.

The light in front of them turned green, and he accelerated, glad to have to concentrate on his driving in the busy city traffic. Glad, too, to be leaving it behind. Visits were fine, but after a few hours, he started craving the silence and solitude of his spread.

Which was neither as quiet nor as solitary as it used to be. It occurred to him that he ought to mind more than he did.

Truth be told—he'd been happier today than he had been in a long time. Unease rippled through him. Now, that should worry him.

CHAPTER SIX

"THAT'S IT. NICE and easy," Gabe reminded Mark. He watched critically as the boy steered Aurora in a wide circle at a walk. "Remember how sensitive she is to commands. Now, slowly ease back on the reins."

The quarter horse obediently stopped. Flushed with triumph, Mark grinned. "Can I trot now? Huh? I think she likes me. Don't you?"

What Gabe thought was that Aurora was being exceptionally patient. When he'd put Mark up on her Monday for the first time, he hadn't known how she'd handle a novice rider. He'd been more willing to bet on her than Hoodoo, though. In fact, Hoodoo was currently confined to a stall in the barn to keep him out of the way. He'd trumpeted his annoyance a few times, but eventually settled down.

Although Gabe leaned back against the fence, one booted heel hooked on the lowest rail in a pantomime of confidence and relaxation, he'd made sure he was inside the fence, ready to leap to the rescue if needed.

Or, at least to *look* as if he was ready, in order to placate Mark's mother.

From outside the fence, Ciara watched today with considerably more tension than Gabe felt. She was keeping her mouth shut, but her fingernails appeared to be biting into the wood of the top rail, as tightly as she gripped it.

"All right," Gabe agreed. "What are you going to think about?"

"Staying relaxed," the boy said obediently. "Back straight, don't tighten my legs too much, let myself move with her."

"Good." Gabe reinforced his message with words and tone. Easy does it, he worked to convey. "Loosen the reins just a little…"

"I remember."

"Are you sure he's ready for this?" Ciara asked, voice as taut as her posture.

"He trotted the other day and did fine." Nonetheless, Gabe didn't take his eyes off the boy and horse.

"What if he falls off?"

Gabe shrugged. "Sooner or later, he will. And then he'll get right back on and try again. That's how you learn."

"Oh, God," she whispered.

He found himself grinning and hoped she couldn't see.

They both watched as Mark gently tightened his

legs. Aurora started forward, her walk lengthening into a trot. He kept her moving in a wide circle, just as Gabe had earlier instructed him. He was bouncing high enough from the saddle to raise bruises on that skinny butt and make Gabe wince, but the horse seemed to be taking it in stride.

"She's trotting," Mark called as they passed close to Gabe. "Look, Mom! I'm trotting."

"I see," she said, waving, then lowered her voice. "He's not very athletic, you know."

"I've seen that," Gabe agreed, "but he's good with his hands when he focuses, and riding is a different skill set than playing soccer or baseball. Balance is important. Centering yourself. The ability to control your movements."

Her laugh broke. "Mark?"

He took his eyes off the horse and rider long enough to see the genuine terror on her face. Funny, until these two came along, he hadn't bothered trying to reassure anyone in a long time. Now he did a lot of it.

"This is good for him," he explained. "I was clumsy at his age, too. Riding, you learn to make small movements. If he sticks to it, I'm betting you see him doing better on his feet, too."

She gave a small, tight nod.

He raised his voice to reach the boy's ears. "All right, Mark. *Gently* steer her into a figure eight."

The boy's face showed the same intense concentration Gabe saw on it when Mark used tools in the workshop. He was still flopping around some in the saddle, but less so.

Aurora obediently turned more tightly, crossing the circle of the invisible arena, turning again, all signaled by her rider. The fact that she changed leads the way she should had to do with her training, not her rider, but reminded Gabe that was something they'd have to talk about during a future lesson.

"Back into the wider circle," Gabe called.

A look of intense concentration on his face, Mark did as commanded.

"Now tighten your legs just a little. She'll canter."

Mark nodded, gripping the saddle horn with one hand. A moment later, Aurora broke into a canter, a smoother gait than the trot.

Ciara moaned. "I can't bear it."

"He's doing fine. Watch him. His body is starting to move with the horse."

Gabe let them canter for a good ten minutes before calling for a trot then a walk. "All right," he said, "walk her around the pasture for a few minutes to cool her off, but don't let her take a bite of grass."

Gabe removed his booted foot from the rail and turned to face Ciara, resting his forearms atop the fence. "You know, maybe we should put you up next. Best way for you to get over being scared to death every time he gets up on horseback."

"Me?" She tore her gaze from her son to stare at him in shock. "You're kidding."

The blue of her eyes had never been as rich as it was now, outside on a sunny day. It wasn't quite warm, but the mercury had climbed into the high fifties in a nod to spring. Ciara wore a nubby sweater over jeans, her hair loosely captured in some kind of knot at her nape. Fine moment to discover he liked long hair, something he'd never thought about one way or another before. Ginny had kept her fine blond hair in a kind of pixie do that suited her, but left nothing for him to run his fingers through or spread over the pillow. Ciara's hair caught fire in the sunlight, too. He imagined sifting through it in search of all the myriad colors that made up that distinctive shade of reddish-brown.

He waited to be hit with guilt because the comparison hadn't been in favor of his pretty wife, but all he felt was a faint echo. Ginny was long gone. If she'd been here, he wouldn't have even noticed this new neighbor as a woman. That wasn't the kind of man he was.

Disconcerted, he thought, *There's nothing for me to feel guilty about.*

It was the first time he'd ever admitted as much to himself.

"I don't know," Ciara said, and he had to struggle to remember what she was expressing doubt about.

Oh, yeah. Getting up on a horse.

"If Mark can do it, you can, too," he said.

"Well… It might be fun." She didn't sound so sure, but he smiled.

"As soon as Mark brings Aurora back, you can have a turn. Just a walk," he said, before she could protest.

Her gaze fastened on his. "Will you stay close? Until I say otherwise?"

"You have my word."

Mark had reached the far fence, turned Aurora and started back.

"I'm going to a local cutting-horse competition Saturday," Gabe heard himself say. "I thought you and Mark might like to come. He'd enjoy watching it. I didn't want to say anything to him without your okay, though."

"Are you riding in it?"

"Not to compete," he said. "I'll be one of the riders in the arena helping control the herd of cattle while the competition is going on. So I can't be with you all the time, but you might like meeting some people." He worked to keep his voice neutral, a little surprised at how much he wanted her to say yes, even though he was suggesting the outing for Mark's sake, not his. "There'll be a junior division, so it'll give him a chance to meet kids his own age, too," he added.

"That sounds like fun," she said without hesitation. "And you know he'll be thrilled."

He nodded. "Good." Mark reined Aurora to a stop in front of them, already begging to keep going, but when Gabe said it was his mother's turn, he dismounted readily. "It's really fun, Mom," he enthused.

She didn't seem eager to move. "Do I climb on from the fence?" she asked.

Gabe took hold of the reins right below Aurora's chin as Mark dismounted. "Nope," he told her, "come on in here."

After a minute, she bent and slipped between the rails but kept her back pressed to them. "She's so big."

Gabe had to coax Ciara into taking the two steps to the horse's side. Once she'd gotten that brave, he bent, hands cupped, and waited until she placed a foot on his hands. Lifting her, he instructed, "Leg over her back."

With her arms raised, her sweater rode up to expose a strip of creamy skin. *Damn,* he thought, relieved when she settled into the saddle and seized the saddle horn in a death grip, the sweater regaining full coverage.

Seeing the way she was holding on, Gabe tried to hide his amusement, but from her glare, wasn't sure he'd succeeded. She turned it briefly on her son, too.

"Not a word out of you. And if you laugh, I swear I won't make manicotti again until you turn sixteen."

Mark pretended to zip his lips.

Gabe cleared his throat to disguise his chuckle as he shortened the stirrups and adjusted Ciara's sneaker-clad feet in them. "Heels down." Gripping her ankles, he positioned her feet. "You'll need boots, too," he said. Just yesterday, after the first lesson, she'd bought Mark a pair of cowboy boots at the general store in town. His walk had held some extra swagger when he'd arrived in them today.

Gabe pried one of her hands off the horn and showed her how to hold the reins.

Her entire time in the saddle passed with Aurora ambling slowly, her eyes sleepy. Gabe walked right beside her with a hand resting casually on her shoulder.

"You're doing fine," he said a couple of times, just as he did to Mark, and out of the corner of his eye, he saw Ciara gradually relax until her body began to sway with the movement, and her knuckles didn't show white.

They circled in the pasture for a good ten minutes before he had her ease back on the reins and bring Aurora to a stop by the gate where Mark waited.

"Put your weight on this stirrup and swing your

leg over," he instructed Ciara. "That's it. Now ease your foot out of the stirrup and let yourself slide down. I've got you."

He wrapped his hands around her waist and lowered her until she was on her own two feet. They stood so close, Ciara pinned between him and the horse, that he could have bent his head and rubbed his cheek on her head. Neither of them moved for a moment that stretched longer than it should have. Sitting atop the fence, Mark was chattering away, but Gabe couldn't parse a word. Over the familiar horsey scents, he smelled something tantalizing that had to be uniquely this woman's. His nostrils flared, and his fingers flexed slightly, finding bare, silky skin beneath the sweater. Sensations seemed heightened. He felt the warmth and give of her flesh and then her quick breath.

God. If they'd been alone—

But they weren't. It took everything he had to release her and step back. She turned slowly, her eyes meeting his, and he saw awareness to match his as well as wariness and curiosity in them.

His heart gave some hard beats that made him momentarily lightheaded. *Think about this later,* he ordered himself. It was lucky they *weren't* alone. He'd have done something stupid. He knew he would have.

Gabe made a conscious effort to behave normally. "Mark, you can unsaddle her."

"Cool!" He launched himself from the fence, and Aurora flung her head up and danced in place.

"Easy," Gabe reminded him. It was becoming one of his most commonly spoken words, along with *slowly* and *gently*.

"Oh. Yeah." As he unbuckled, his mother ducked between the rails again, putting the fence between her and Gabe.

Just as well, he tried to convince himself.

Nothing happened. Keep it that way.

Ciara started talking, her tone extra bright as she told Mark about the cutting-horse competition. He was as excited as she'd predicted.

"How come you aren't riding in it?" he asked Gabe, who shrugged.

"We all take turns. I only do it for fun."

"Do you think someday I'll ride good enough to be in one?"

"Maybe," Gabe temporized. "What you'll see Saturday is how important the horse's training is. A good cutting horse is smart. It all comes down to how well he and his rider work together."

Mark was tall enough to handle the saddle without help. He slung it and the blanket over the fence then applied curry comb and brush to Aurora's sleek brown coat. Her skin shivered in pleasure, making the boy laugh.

Once Mark unbuckled and slipped off the bridle, releasing Aurora, Ciara seemed anxious for them to get home. After they left, Gabe went into the barn and opened Hoodoo's stall door, giving him an affectionate slap on his rump as he trotted by.

Hoodoo was a hell of a cutting horse, possessing both the smarts and the razor-sharp reactions to have gone far if Gabe had been interested enough to compete at a regional or even national level. He'd turned down a number of offers for the young gelding from more serious competitors. He couldn't imagine selling either of his horses.

Leaning on the fence, he watched Hoodoo tear around the pasture once just for fun, bucking and kicking as if Watson was nipping at his heels—as he sometimes still did. Gabe had concluded that the dog was only having fun, too, and that Hoodoo didn't mind the company. Aurora seemed more irritated in her matronly way.

Reluctantly, he let his mind circle back to his intense physical reaction to Ciara Malloy, and to the discovery that his invitation to the competition hadn't been the casual thing he'd imagined it to be.

If he brought a pretty woman and her son along with him, there'd be talk, thanks to his notoriety as a loner. That was one of the many things he hadn't thought through in advance.

He grunted. When had he ever paid attention to gossip? Hell, if he was lucky, friends would conclude he'd moved past his grief, and they'd ditch the pity.

Good plan—if that had been the plan. If there'd been a plan at all.

No, Ciara and Mark Malloy had just *happened*, and he still didn't quite know how and why.

WHEN CIARA OPENED the door to Gabe, the first words out of his mouth were, "Where's Mark?"

It was Friday night, a couple of days later. Mark had been at his place that morning for his usual woodworking/math lesson. He had conveyed his mother's invitation to dinner, and, once home, reported that Gabe said, "Tell your mother thank you. That sounds good."

It was starting to feel less like a big deal to ask him, although Ciara wasn't letting herself analyze the relationship or number of times a week she, and not just Mark, now saw Gabe.

Another thing she tried not to think about was the impact his presence had on her, every single time she saw him. She prayed he had no way of guessing that the sight of him was enough to make her feel like a teenager in the throes of her first mad crush. Right this minute, heat tinged her cheeks, and she felt breathless.

"Hi, Gabe," she said, and congratulated herself at her blithe unconcern. "I think Mark and Watson went down to the creek. Why?"

His gaze steady on her, he stepped across the doorjamb, his height and broad shoulders dominating the entry. "First time I've been here he hasn't raced out to meet me."

"Well, he did see you this morning. Here, let me take your coat."

He shrugged out of it and handed it to her. The sheepskin lining at the neck was warm from his body. She was embarrassed to realize she'd have buried her face in the soft fleece to inhale his scent if he wouldn't have seen. Her fingers momentarily tightened on the coat before she hung it on the rack she'd found at a Spokane antiques store to make up for the fact that the house had no closet anywhere near the front door.

She suggested he come back to the kitchen and then led the way, her nerves jumping with her awareness of him so close behind her.

"Smells great," he said the minute he stepped into the kitchen—like he always did. Tonight she'd made a chicken and broccoli dish strongly flavored with curry. Just before the doorbell rang, she'd removed it from the oven to make room for the sourdough biscuits.

In Watson's absence, Daisy was allowed in the kitchen, and Gabe bent to greet the dog, his voice gruff and yet gentle, while Ciara went to peer unnecessarily into the oven. The biscuits hadn't been in there long enough even to be tinged with gold. "How'd things go today?" she asked over her shoulder.

"Fine." A pause, as if Gabe was trying to decide whether he was supposed to say any more. Apparently, he concluded that he should, because he continued. "Mark's a smart kid. Doesn't really need my help with the math."

"At least you understand what he's working on," she muttered.

"I do." His gaze held kindness. "You must have done this stuff in school. I'm sure you could do some review if you had to."

"I plan to this summer. I can't expect you to tutor him forever."

He frowned. "You aren't putting him in school come fall?"

"No, I intend to homeschool him until he's ready for college achievement tests."

"I didn't realize that," he said slowly. "I figured you didn't want him to have to start in a new school so late in the year."

She faced him, chin jutting. "I told you. I wouldn't dream of expecting you to help with his math long-term. I'm sure I can do it. He's thriving with independent study—"

They both heard the back door open.

"Mom, is Gabe here yet?" Mark bellowed, appearing in the kitchen an instant later. "You are!" He didn't even look at his mother. Instead, he focused with typical intensity on Gabe. "That's cool, because I looked stuff up online about cutting horses, but I don't understand some of it."

He was off and running, not even noticing he'd interrupted a conversation or doubting that Gabe would want to jump right into talking about the subject that currently preoccupied him. Gabe's eyebrows flickered, but without displaying anything like annoyance, he answered Mark's questions patiently.

Not wanting to admit to herself that she was relieved at the interruption, Ciara occupied herself setting the kitchen table instead of asking Mark to do it. After the first couple of times Gabe had eaten with them, she'd switched from the dining room back to the kitchen table. Watson still wasn't happy to be excluded, but he was less distressed to be one door away from his family than he'd been shut in a lonely bedroom an entire floor away from them. He only whimpered instead of howled.

By the time she'd put out butter, poured drinks and set the still-hot casserole dish on a hot pad in the middle of the table, the biscuits were browning nicely, and she was able to order Mark to wash his hands and sit down. The biscuits went in a basket lined with a cloth napkin.

She offered them to Gabe first.

"I haven't smelled anything this good in…years." The hesitation was almost infinitesimal.

Ciara couldn't fill in the blank, but she knew

what he was thinking. He hadn't had anybody else to cook meals for him on a regular basis since his wife died.

He took two biscuits and immediately split one open, reaching next for the butter, his expression reverent.

Barely pausing to dish up, Mark wanted to know what a "tiedown" was and why it couldn't be used in cutting-horse competitions.

Gabe obligingly talked about the straps that kept a horse from throwing his head back, and the possible risks of injury for the horse. "A lot of what judges look for in the competition," he explained, "is a horse that works quickly and efficiently without needing much input from his rider once they've committed to a cow. Physical restraints suggest a lack of training or control."

Next thing Ciara knew, the topic had shifted to other equipment: curb chains, split boots, skid boots. Lord. It sounded like equipment for logging, not horses. Gabe had to be getting bored.

"Kiddo, that's enough," she intervened in the briefest of pauses when Mark was catching his breath. "You'll see all this stuff in action tomorrow. That's soon enough. Give Gabe a chance to eat, okay?"

Her son stared at her in bewilderment. "But I want to understand everything *before* I see it. 'Cuz then it'll be more interesting."

Gabe had managed to clean his plate and now took a second helping of the chicken. "I'll explain when I'm outfitting Aurora in the morning."

Mark's mouth fell open. "You mean, you're not taking Hoodoo? I wanted to see you ride Hoodoo."

"Hoodoo is the better cutting horse, and he doesn't like playing a supporting role," Gabe said patiently. "He'd be antsy the whole time, wanting in on the action. Aurora is less excitable. I use her when I'll be a turnback man or herd holder."

"I read about those, but it sounds kind of boring just sitting there." Mark didn't hide his dissatisfaction. "Which one are you doing? And how come you don't get to do the cutting?"

"Locally, we tend to take turns. I could have done both, but that would have meant taking both horses, both of them having to take turns tied in the trailer for hours. I don't want you and your mom to be stuck there the entire day if you get bored, either."

"You mean, we don't get to stay all day?" he demanded, expression indignant. "Mom, did you say we couldn't stay?"

"No," she said, "but you're not listening to Gabe, either. I'm betting everyone involved in these competitions takes turns doing things besides riding in the competition."

"That's true," Gabe agreed. "There have to be judges, various people take turns bringing the cattle, ranchers offer the use of their places, plus during every moment of the competition you need two herd holders and two turnback men." He held up his hand when Mark's mouth opened immediately. "No, that's just the terminology. Those riders aren't always men. Around here, we have quite a few women and girls active in the sport."

"Girls?" Mark said in obvious shock.

"Excuse me?" Ciara said. "Girl here."

"You're not a girl." He looked at her like she was crazy. "You're Mom. Plus, you don't even ride."

"But she's going to learn, isn't she?" Gabe's mouth curved. "Who knows? Maybe we'll get chaps and cowboy boots on her, and she'll decide to try cutting."

"I thought girls barrel raced at rodeos."

Ciara's eyes narrowed at the way her son said *girls* a second time. But he seemed impervious, his gaze fixated on his hero.

Or had Gabe tarnished his status by declining to compete tomorrow on Hoodoo? she wondered in amusement. *And* supporting the right of mere girls to compete equally.

"That's the traditional rodeo event for women," Gabe agreed, "but times are changing. No reason a girl can't rope as well as a boy, is there?" He nodded toward the basket that held the biscuits. "You mind handing me that, son?"

"Huh? Oh." Mark pushed it across the table.

"How about if you quit asking questions and eat instead?" Ciara suggested.

Silencing him for long was impossible. He was at his most…well, excitable and persistent tonight, and worry began to stir along with the beginnings of a headache. Had he talked and demanded answers non-stop while he was at Gabe's this morning, too? She'd seen this plenty of times, when he became fixated on a particular enthusiasm until it became something close to an obsession. It had been one of his problems in school. Most people found his single-mindedness disconcerting. He could drive Gabe away without meaning to.

Gabe had showed up to dinner, not called with an excuse, she reminded herself, so probably Mark hadn't been as annoying this morning.

Her son was becoming sulky by the time the meal was over. He didn't like being thwarted.

Needing a break from him, Ciara said she'd clean the kitchen. "You go do something else. Remember we'll be leaving pretty early in the morning."

"Eight should do it," Gabe said. "It's not that long of a drive."

"Oh. Okay." Mark got to his feet and pushed his chair in but then just stood there. "Are you going home?" he asked Gabe.

"I'll stay and help clear the table, at least."

"Can't I stay, too, Mom? I'll help."

"No." The pressure in her head was building. "I want to talk to Gabe about contractors."

"Why do you have to do that? It's boring."

"Mark." She put enough snap in her voice to let him know she was serious.

Mumbling under his breath, he hung his head and dragged his feet as he left the kitchen. They heard a yip of pleasure from Watson, and a moment later, the sound of Mark trudging up the stairs accompanied by the skitter of claws.

Ciara couldn't help the sigh that slipped out.

Gabe's eyes rested on her. "He's pretty wound up tonight."

She forced a smile. "Just excited."

"I hope he isn't disappointed."

"If there are plenty of horses to look at, I doubt if he will be," she said drily, reaching for the casserole dish.

Gabe pushed back his chair and gathered the dirty plates.

"You don't have to help," she said, flustered. "You're a guest."

"I want to."

Faced with such a simple answer, she didn't have any choice but to accede. She found a plastic bowl to hold the leftovers and then reached for ClingWrap.

"What questions do you have?" Gabe asked from right behind her.

She jumped. "Oh. I don't really have any. Although I suppose I should move ahead with some of the work."

"What work do you intend to have done?"

She dreamed aloud while he ferried the rest of the dirty dishes to the counter, and she rinsed them and put them in the dishwasher. It, at least, was relatively new.

"Ephraim's son insisted on installing one as his health failed," Gabe said, after she'd said as much. "He'd never had a dishwasher. Not sure he actually used it when they weren't staying."

"No wonder it's in such pristine condition."

He set down the basket and leaned a hip against the counter. Ciara dried her hands on a dish towel. "You're welcome to the leftovers."

"There's enough for you and Mark to have another meal."

"It's not one of his favorites, in case you didn't notice." She'd had to scrape half his helping off his plate into the garbage, which meant he'd be wanting something else to eat about an hour from now.

"I thought it was just his excitement."

"Nope. Much to his dismay, I refuse to cook nothing but his limited list of favorites."

A smile lit Gabe's eyes.

"Coffee?" she suggested, flustered.

"Thought you'd never ask."

Mugs. She turned too quickly, before he could step back, and bumped into him. Then she stumbled as she tried to retreat.

His hands gripped her upper arms to steady her. His heat and strength penetrated the thin cotton sleeves of her shirt, and for a moment she froze, not looking any higher than his strong brown throat. Then she gabbled, "I'm sorry."

"Ciara." His voice was deep, even hoarse, when he spoke her name. Instead of releasing her, he gently squeezed her arms.

Slowly, she raised her gaze to his face. His eyes were dark, compelling.

Ciara's mouth and tongue shaped his name, but no sound emerged. Head swimming, she knew she couldn't have looked away from him to save her life. Legs weak, she seemed to be swaying toward him.

The next sound came from him: a groan.

Please let him kiss me, she thought in panic and exhilaration, even though she knew how terribly this would complicate everything.

He bent his head slowly. At the same time, Ciara rose on tiptoe to meet him. She felt his beard first, springy and not quite scratchy, then his lips. They brushed hers softly. Her eyes fluttered shut as she waited breathlessly for more.

CHAPTER SEVEN

EVEN SLAMMED INTO full-blown arousal, Gabe managed to hesitate.

You weren't going to do this, remember?

But now he knew the plump, soft texture of her lips, the heady scent of her hair, the pleasure of having her pushing up eagerly to meet his kiss.

A second groan was torn from him, and this time he dove deep. His tongue sampled the warm, silky depths of her mouth, and one of his hands clamped over her ass to lift her higher and pull her tight against him.

His back to the countertop, he separated his legs enough to tug her to stand caged between his thighs. His other hand plunged into her hair, cupping the back of her head to hold her so he could kiss her harder, deeper. He had gone blind and deaf; all he knew was the intoxicating taste of her, the sensation of full-length contact with that long, lithe body he'd been watching since the first time he set eyes on her.

Somewhere in the back of his mind, he knew this couldn't go any further. Spinning her around to set her on the counter, stripping her jeans off, burying himself inside her here and now wasn't an option, however desperately he wanted to do exactly that. Shock tugged at him. Where had that idea come from? He'd never in his life had sex anywhere except in his truck or in a bed.

Ciara cupped his jaw, rubbing her fine-boned hand in circles as if savoring the texture of his beard. He turned his mouth from hers long enough to kiss her palm and then nip her thumb.

"Gabe," she whispered, and pressed her lips to his neck. He'd have sworn he felt the damp flick of her tongue. The damp touch felt like an electrical shock.

God help him, he hurt.

Can't have her. Not now.

Why?

A faint rattle penetrated his intense absorption in her body, her scent and his own aching need.

Dog tags. The old dog, giving herself a shake.

The kid and the other dog were in the house. They could come downstairs and burst into the kitchen at any minute. That's why he couldn't make love to her right now.

Her mouth sought his, and he couldn't help kissing her again, but this time he kept it lighter. Teasing. A brush, a nip. He gently sucked her lower lip.

He'd never wanted a woman the way he did this one.

The thought was like a bucket of icy water. That was crazy. What about Ginny? He'd loved his wife.

He'd never wanted her so damn much he hadn't believed he could make it as far as the bedroom.

No. He'd forgotten, that's all.

"Ciara," he said roughly, against her lips. "We can't."

"Can't…?" Her body went rigid in his arms. "Oh, God," she exclaimed, and wrenched herself free. "What am I *doing*?"

"Same thing I was doing." His voice sounded like sandpaper.

They stared at each other in mutual shock. And no, he didn't like seeing *her* shock. What was so wrong with him? *He* was the one who had real reason to pause. With the scream of ripping metal, a shout of terror, he'd lost his family in one instant and sworn never to risk being devastated like that again. Divorce wasn't the same.

She hadn't liked responding to him the way she had, though. There was no mistaking it.

"I'm sorry," he said. "I didn't mean to do that."

"Oh!" She whirled to turn her back on him, hugging herself.

Suddenly sure that had been the exact wrong thing to say, Gabe felt like a shit. But it was the simple truth. He couldn't lie.

"Please go," she whispered.

"No." Damn. He scrubbed a shaking hand over his face. "Wait."

She didn't move. He looked at her narrow back, her shoulders hunched, the delicate nape of her neck beneath the bundle of richly colored hair.

"I don't want to leave things like this," he said, the words clumsy but true. "I usually keep to myself, but with you and Mark—"

She gave a ragged laugh. "We didn't give you any choice?"

"It's not like that. I could have said no."

At last, Ciara turned to look at him. Her face was drawn and set. "Why didn't you?"

"I don't know." That was a partial truth. How could he say to her, *Because, looking at your kid, I'd have felt like I was kicking a starving stray puppy?* "I've enjoyed Mark," he said again. "And you. These dinners here."

Her eyes searched his, making him fear she was seeing deeper than anyone had in a long time. Or maybe ever. He shifted uncomfortably.

"You just don't want to get any more involved than you already were," she said. It wasn't a question.

The answer should have been, *Damn straight. I don't.* Gabe was stunned to realize he wasn't so sure anymore.

"I want you," he said. "But you don't seem like a woman who has casual sex."

Her expression changed, and he thought, *I've blown it again.*

If anything, her crossed arms tightened around herself. "You're right. I'm not."

"My wife died."

She nodded, no surprise apparent. If she hadn't heard about the accident from Audrey, she had from someone else. That was a small town for you.

"Since then..." He moved his shoulders uneasily. The couple of times he'd tried to have a sexual relationship with a local woman, he hadn't struggled like this for the right words. He'd just laid it out. Said, *I'm not going there again. Moving in with me, marriage, those aren't on the table.* He knew what Ciara would say to that. On a squeeze of something like anguish, he imagined having no contact with her and Mark. Him living across the pasture, seeing lights in their house, the dog tearing around the pasture, but no eager boy showing up at his workshop, no invitations to dinner. Not doing errands with Ciara, God, never seeing her except from a distance.

Compassion stole over her face when he didn't continue. "I understand. I...have issues of my own. And you're right. If we had sex, things would blow up sooner or later, and that would make it difficult to stay neighborly. Mark wouldn't understand if anything changed. So let's...let's just forget this happened, okay?"

He was baffled by the tumult he felt. Wasn't that what he wanted her to say?

"I don't know about forgetting," he said.

Her eyes widened. He couldn't look away from her.

"I might not be able to forget, either," she said, so quietly he had to lean forward to hear. "I haven't… I don't usually…" She shook herself. "Do you still want that cup of coffee?"

Relief infused him.

"Sure." This time he stepped back to allow her plenty of space to reach into the cupboard where she stored mugs without accidentally brushing against him. He'd have broken if her body had come into contact with his again so soon.

"I'm surprised Mark hasn't thought of an excuse to reappear," she said, in a carefully friendly tone. *Let's share our amusement.*

"You lied to him," Gabe said, remembering.

"Lied?"

"About what we were going to talk about."

"Oh." Pink touched her cheeks. "Even mothers need a break sometimes, you know."

"Goes without saying."

While she spooned sugar into her mug, he reached for his. He took his coffee black.

"Mark hasn't said why you pulled him out of school."

He'd have sworn she stiffened. After a moment,

she put the lid back on the sugar bowl and turned to face him. Her jaw seemed to have an extra jut to it.

"He was being bullied. We lived close enough to the school, he walked instead of riding a bus. The last straw was when three boys cornered him on the way home and beat him up. He had two black eyes and a cracked rib. School officials claimed to feel regret and sympathy, but the *incident*—their word—had occurred off school property and wasn't really their responsibility. I'd had it."

He read his newspaper, watched the evening news. "I thought schools were pretty sensitive about bullying issues these days."

"They pretend to be." There was suddenly fire in her eyes. "But I guess that's only when they can't blame the victim."

Gabe mulled that over for a minute. "They thought it was Mark's fault the boys went after him?"

"Yes!" Vibrating with outrage, it was obvious she'd forgotten the earlier tension. "They suggested counseling. For Mark!"

"So what is it with Mark?" he asked without thinking it through first. "I wasn't sure it was my business, but I could tell something was wrong."

Ciara drew herself up. *"Wrong?"*

Oh, shit, he thought, and slammed the gears into Reverse.

THE PICKUP TRUCK bumped and swayed across the uneven pasture. Despite the seat belt, Ciara jolted against Mark on one side and Gabe on the other. It was the unintentional contact with Gabe's big, solid body that had her self-conscious.

Not that she hadn't been self-conscious since the minute she'd said hello to him that morning. She didn't know which was worse—thinking about that kiss, or remembering the way she'd blown up at him after he asked about Mark.

As Gabe beat a retreat last night, her parting words were, "And I thought you were different."

He had paused on the porch and looked at her, deeper than usual lines carved in his forehead. "Can't say if I am, since I don't know the background."

"You don't need to know it," she had snapped, and, childishly, slammed the door in his face.

She had almost told Mark this morning that they weren't going with Gabe, after all. Her mother had called yesterday evening after Gabe left, but Ciara hadn't said anything about the argument. Mom wouldn't understand why she'd flipped out over one word. Instead, she spent half the night trying to think up excuses her son would accept, but none of them were very good. And the truth was—she wanted to go. She wanted a chance to apologize.

All she could do was hope Gabe would give her that. Unable to sleep, she had bolstered her belief that he would. Gabe was the one to back away from the kiss because he didn't want to risk ruining this new, precious friendship, after all.

He liked Mark. He kept saying he did. So she could forgive his ill-chosen word, couldn't she, as long as he'd forgive her for going off the deep end like that.

She had packed a lunch this morning, as promised, and she and Mark had driven down to Gabe's place so that he didn't have to navigate her driveway pulling the horse trailer.

Face unreadable, he'd nodded when they appeared, seeming unsurprised, but scarcely said a word to her during the drive.

Not that he'd have had much chance no matter what, she thought ruefully. Totally wired, Mark had been as bad as he was last night at dinner.

Honestly, by the time they arrived, Ciara felt as if she had to get out of the pickup before she either screamed or burst into tears. She felt intense gratitude when Gabe pulled in at the end of one of two lines of parked pickups and trailers forming an L that, along with a barn and small set of bleachers, boxed in a large fenced arena. Already a herd of cows milled aimlessly in the arena. Gabe had told them the county fairgrounds hadn't been available this weekend; a swap meet was bravely setting up in defiance of temperatures Ciara still thought were on the chilly side for any outdoor activity. She'd

insisted Mark bring his parka and gloves, as she had, although looking ahead through the windshield she could see that most of the people here wore faded jeans and equally faded denim jackets as well as cowboy boots and hats. Only a handful that she could see had added sheepskin-lined coats. A few wore down vests over Western-style shirts.

Gabe set the emergency brake and turned off the engine. Without being obvious, Ciara straightened so she was no longer touching him.

After he got out and settled a dark brown Stetson on his head, Ciara heard voices calling greetings, and Gabe's laconic answers. Behind them, Aurora trumpeted her own greetings.

Mark's head turned as he gaped. "Look! An Appaloosa! And there's a palomino."

There seemed to be horses present of just about every color and pattern, from mottled gray to dingy white, black with white spots decorating the rump to huge brown-and-white spots that even Ciara knew meant the horse would be described as a pinto. The majority were some shade of brown, sorrel like Hoodoo or the darker red that, with a black mane and tail, was called a bay, according to Mark.

Nervous for all kinds of reasons, Ciara waited until Mark clambered out then hopped out herself, wobbling momentarily on the rough ground with tufts of grass.

"I wish *I* had a cowboy hat," he said wistfully.

Apparently, they were de rigueur. She and Mark looked positively naked without them, Ciara had to admit. Even middle-aged women wore cowboy hats here.

They found Gabe already backing Aurora down the ramp. He looped the lead rope through a metal ring attached to the trailer and disappeared inside again, emerging a minute later with a saddle and pad.

"Mark, will you grab the bridle?" he asked. "Oh, I have a spare hat in there. You might see if it fits."

Ciara smiled tentatively at him. "Thank you. He was just noticing how he'd stand out without one." The last thing she wanted to say was that Mark rarely paid attention to anything like that. Normally, she'd have said he didn't notice what anyone else wore, or realize that complying with an unspoken dress code was part of social conformity.

Not that there was anything *wrong* with his indifference to appearances. Not everyone was a fashion plate.

It seemed to her Gabe's face relaxed. "I'm costing you money here, you know."

"I've noticed, and we haven't even put a horse and tack on our shopping list yet."

He smoothed his hand under the pad he'd laid over Aurora's back, adjusting the lie of it. "Then come the hay and feed, the vet bills, the farrier's bills. Yeah, and you'll need a trailer, and I doubt your van would pull one."

"So I trade it in for a pickup truck like everyone else is driving." She rolled her eyes. "I should have looked for swimming lessons."

He laughed, the flash of white teeth startling her.

Her heart skittered. She'd have said she didn't like a beard on a man, but she was getting used to his. She'd have liked it better if it didn't make his expressions even harder to read.

"Hi," a young voice said behind her. "I don't know you."

Ciara turned to see that the speaker was looking at Mark, not her. The girl might have been Mark's age or even younger, although since she was skinny and didn't have much of a figure yet, it was hard to tell. A blond braid flopped over her shoulder, and her jeans and boots were well-worn.

"Hi," Mark said. He handed the bridle to Gabe.

He'd adjusted the battered black felt hat to an angle that mimicked the way Gabe wore his. It was somewhat large for him, making him look young and scrawny, but the girl wasn't old enough to care.

"I'm Jennifer Weeks," she said. "Mr. Tennert knows me."

Gabe tipped his head as he slapped Aurora's rib cage hard then tightened the girth. "Yes, I do. Jennifer, Mark Malloy and his mother, Mrs. Malloy, are my new next-door neighbors."

Not that new, she couldn't help thinking. It had already been over a month since they moved in. The next second, she found herself marveling. Only a month? How had Gabe become so much a part of her and Mark's lives so fast?

"Are you riding today?" the girl asked.

"No." Mark's awkwardness resurfaced. "I'm just learning."

"I am," she declared. "You can cheer for me. Do you want to meet my horse?"

His eyes widened. "You have your own?"

"Well, of course I do," she said matter-of-factly.

"Which one's yours?"

"You have to wait to see."

"Can you tell me why stuff happens? Gabe said he would, but he won't be able to once he goes in the arena."

Ciara cringed.

"I don't mind," the girl said cheerfully. "Come on, let's go."

"Um…sure." He looked uncertainly at his mother and Gabe.

Gabe grinned and made a shooing gesture with one hand.

Mark and Jennifer took off, Ciara staring after them.

"It's okay." Gabe wasn't looking at her, but she'd noticed before that he didn't seem to need a visual to sense her worries. "So long as he shares their

enthusiasm for horses, the kids he'll meet here are friendly."

"But he's barely a beginner. What if they make fun of him?" Taunt him? Isolate him? She'd seen it happen over and over.

"He's knowledgeable. You must know that. He's done a lot of reading."

"That's not the same thing," she argued.

"Not if he was to be put on horseback, but he won't be." He disappeared back around the trailer, not reappearing for several minutes. When he did, he wore chaps. He nodded down the line of trailers. "Walk with me."

"But how will he find me?" Even Ciara knew that was a dumb thing to ask. This was a ranch, and a modest one at that, not a huge fairground. All that was here in the way of buildings were the couple of barns and a simple farmhouse, painted white like hers and Gabe's. Whoever had painted this one had gotten wildly imaginative, though, trimming it with black.

"Not a big place," he said mildly.

She had enough self-control to drop the subject before she came off sounding even more neurotic than she already had. Mark knew enough not to walk too close behind a horse that might get startled and kick him. And if one of the oh-so-friendly kids here was a shit to him, well, that wouldn't be anything new. He'd find her, and she'd know immediately from the familiar bewilderment and hurt on his face.

Instead of swinging up on Aurora, Gabe led her as he walked beside Ciara behind the row of trailers. He exchanged a few words with everyone they passed still tacking up a horse. She stayed silent most of the way.

"You know everyone?" she asked finally.

"Some better than others." His shoulders moved. "We don't get a lot of new folks."

"That's why they're all staring at me," she realized.

He didn't say anything, but she saw his jaw tighten. Oh, Lord. Was this the first time he'd brought a woman along to one of these get-togethers?

"There's Mark," he noted.

Ciara followed his gaze to see her son surrounded by a good-size group of other kids of varying ages. A couple had to be upperclassmen in high school, and one boy both smaller and skinnier than Mark couldn't be more than nine or ten, at a guess. Several held the reins of their patiently waiting horses. Mark was currently stroking the nose of the palomino he'd admired when they arrived. It appeared that he—she?—belonged to Jennifer Weeks.

"They're mostly nice," Gabe remarked, as if he

felt her anxiety. "This gives him a chance to start making friends."

Mark had never had a real friend. Sometimes there were other boys he ate lunch with or paired up with for PE, always the nerds like him. Unfortunately, they tended to have their own passions that rarely intersected Mark's. She remembered one time when she was driving carpool, listening to Mark and another boy in the backseat. The other boy—Edward—was fascinated by space exploration. He went on and on about the space station and walking in space. Mark had lectured him in turn on the species that made the Galapagos Islands home. She hadn't been able to tell if they even listened to each other.

"That's why you suggested this, isn't it? So Mark could meet other kids." It was absurd to feel hurt. She'd known all along the invitation had been extended for Mark's sake, not hers.

"Partly," Gabe agreed. He was looking straight ahead and frowning, as if something she'd said had bothered him.

"I'm sorry," she blurted. "I mean, about last night. It's just…a hot button of mine."

"I noticed." There might have been a tinge of amusement in his tone. He lifted a hand in response to another greeting. A good minute passed before he said, "It was my fault. I'm not always good with words."

Her feet quit moving. "I was awful."

"No, Ciara." That deep, quiet voice had never been so tender. It affected her as powerfully as a touch. His touch.

She lifted her gaze to his, to see…she couldn't quite tell. Understanding? Kindness? Something more that made her chest ache?

"I'm being called," he said suddenly. A moment later he was on horseback, looking completely natural. He wouldn't have been out of place riding into town in Tombstone, she thought.

Except for the lack of holster and gun, she amended.

Ciara took a couple of cautious steps back when Aurora pranced, apparently anticipating entering the arena.

Gabe looked down at her, the Stetson shadowing his eyes.

"Maybe this wasn't such a good idea."

She felt a spurt of panic. He regretted bringing her?

"I invited you, and now I'm deserting you."

Past a lump in her throat, Ciara said, "I'll be fine. Go have fun."

After a moment, he touched one finger to the brim of his hat, and, in response to some invisible signal from him, Aurora broke into a trot. A moment later, he'd joined several other horsemen beside the arena. Someone on foot opened a gate, and five riders entered the arena.

The cows began to low.

CIARA WASN'T ON her own for long. She'd barely found a place on the bleachers when two women climbed to her row and sat beside her.

The rawhide lean one with weather-beaten skin and graying brown hair stuck out a hand. "Nadine Shreve. This is my husband's and my place."

"Oh. It's nice you're hosting the competition."

"We train cutting horses professionally," she explained. "We have something like this going on about once a month, weather permitting. Gives us a chance to work our horses and show 'em off, too."

The second woman, probably in her thirties, leaned forward and smiled. "I'm Leslie Weeks. My husband's the other herd holder. With Gabe?"

"You're Jennifer's mother," Ciara said with interest.

She smiled. "That's right. I suppose she nabbed your boy right away. Not a shy bone in her body, that girl."

Ciara laughed. "I could tell. But that's good. Mark was feeling shy. He's barely learning to ride, so he was afraid he'd be a fish out of water today." *Like he always is,* she didn't say.

"You two came with Gabe, didn't you?" Nadine asked.

Both women waited with unblinking interest.

"Yes. I bought the place next door to his. He's been really nice to Mark," she told them cheerfully. For his sake, she'd better make it plain right away that their relationship was not romantic. "He's giving him some woodworking lessons, and now putting him up on one of his horses, too." Out of the corner of her eye, she saw activity starting in the ring. "I've never seen a cutting horse work. Will you explain what's happening?"

She had a suspicion they weren't done grilling her, but proved willing to give her some history of the sport and tell her what Gabe and the other three riders posted around the arena were doing while the competitor rode quietly into the herd.

None of it was what she'd expected, which resembled more a sort of mini-stampede. Instead, the cattle seemed to hardly notice the horse moving among them. The activity didn't pick up until the rider apparently selected an individual cow and began edging him out of the herd. Even then, the rest of the herd mostly remained calm at one end of the arena. The only panic was on the part of the young steer that had been separated from the others. She was reminded of Watson when they shut him away by himself.

Leaning forward, fascinated, Ciara saw immediately what Gabe had meant when he talked about the horse's training being all important. The poor cow was desperate to get back to the safety of the others and kept trying to race by the horseman. As far as she could tell, the rider did nothing from that point on but sit in the saddle as his horse spun on its haunches, leaping explosively forward just enough to keep the steer isolated. After what was obviously a set amount of time, he backed off and let the steer go. Then he rode back into the herd, chose another victim, and the dance started all over again.

Nadine explained that, to get good points, the rider had to select a cow from the center of the herd, not the edges. It was called a "deep cut," she said.

"Rafe will be marked down some now," Leslie added. "See how he's getting the herd stirred up? Gabe and Larry are having to work to keep them together and at that end of the arena. Needing that kind of help from the herdholders brings a penalty."

Indeed, Aurora was doing some dancing of her own, Gabe a still center as she effortlessly outthought her opponents.

"Rafe's new at this." Nadine sounded forgiving. "Bought his horse from us."

The competitor drove a black steer out, and the herd settled down. Ciara looked away to locate Mark, who stood at the fence with several of the other kids, watching. Just as he'd seen Gabe do, he'd crossed his arms casually on the top rail.

A lump formed in her throat. Was there any

chance he really would make friends around here? That these kids were less judgmental, maybe less inclined to join cliques? She had trouble believing that; human nature didn't vary that much. But cultural values did, she reminded herself, and Goodwater and its environs were an entirely different world than the busy Seattle suburb that was home to endless strip malls and every chain store in existence, as well as close-packed apartment complexes and neighborhoods filled with homeowners who disappeared every day to work, many at the nearby, huge Boeing plant. Maybe the differences had to do with the effects of crowding. There were so few people here. She'd have guessed that made them less tolerant, but maybe she was wrong.

This wasn't like school anyway, she reminded herself. These kids weren't doing much talking. Mostly they were watching.

Every so often, in a down moment between riders, Gabe's head turned, and she realized he was keeping an eye on both her and Mark. A couple of times, looking at her, he did that almost-salute thing with the brim of his hat. Of course, that intrigued the women around Ciara.

As competitors came and went in the arena, the crowd around her grew. She'd never been the object of so much curiosity. She couldn't tell entirely whether being a newcomer was enough of a draw, or whether her connection to Gabe Tennert gave her the equivalent of a flashing neon light on her forehead.

"He's never brought anybody to one of these things," a woman named Marcia Wright said, adding with something like awe, "Not once."

Ciara was incautious enough to say, "But he must have brought his wife."

"Well, yes, but that was a long time ago. It's been, what, five years?" She looked to the other women for confirmation. General nods and murmurs of "About that" settled the question.

So now she knew, Ciara thought. That was a long time to be by himself.

She'd read that men were more inclined than women to go straight from one marriage to the next, although admittedly most had been divorced rather than lost their wives to a shocking death.

Daughter, too, she reminded herself. Of course that would have magnified the tragedy beyond imagining.

She could tell no one bought her repeated explanation that really Gabe was being kind to Mark, so after a while she quit bothering to make it.

Fortunately, the women were polite enough to accept that their raging curiosity wouldn't be satisfied, not today. Conversation went a hundred different ways. They asked questions about her business. Several quilted, which gave them a common interest. She learned about a number of active community groups, a rock club with adults who loved to encourage interested kids, as well as some summer happenings that might interest Mark. She learned even more about cutting horses and the skill of riders, as one performance after another was critiqued in a kindly way.

Some of the women absented themselves only to appear in the arena as competitors themselves. Eventually, Gabe and the others drove the herd of cattle out of the arena and into a stock trailer backed up to the gate. Another trailer took its place and a fresh herd entered the ring, lowing and trotting around in confusion.

Gabe and the other three riders left through a hastily opened gate and were replaced. So he wasn't going to be in there all day. Or maybe this was just a lunch break.

She excused herself and followed him back around the row of trucks and trailers to his, where he was unsaddling Aurora.

"Bored yet?" he asked.

"No, it was interesting. I admit I'm hungry, though."

He smiled. "Me, too. I kept thinking about those cookies Mark mentioned."

Today's were snickerdoodles, apparently another favorite of Gabe's. She hadn't yet hit on anything he didn't like.

Mark arrived, begging for them to stay so he

could watch the junior division. It developed that Gabe had brought a couple of lawn chairs, which he carried around in front of his truck, where they could sit and watch while they ate, their view only slightly impeded by the fence rails. Truthfully, Ciara didn't mind. Without an educated eye, one rider and horse were beginning to look an awful lot like the next.

Gabe's comments about performances were few and laconic, and essentially kind. A few participants either showed or bred cutting horses professionally, but for most people here, this was fun.

The kids were noticeably less skilled—a couple actually fell off their horses, but got back on and continued. Red-faced, of course. The first time, Mark started to hoot, but Gabe silenced him with a hand on his arm.

"Got to learn somehow," he said quietly. "You won't want anyone laughing at you."

After finishing his lunch, Mark took off to rejoin the crowd of other kids. Gabe asked if she'd prefer to sit on the bleachers.

"Whatever you'd like," she said. "I'm happy here, but if you want to visit with friends—"

He shook his head. "I'm not much for visiting."

Except with her and Mark, Ciara thought with a funny squeeze of pleasure as she realized how completely he had broken the mold once he met them.

This feels *right*, she acknowledged, sitting beside

him, listening for his dry humor, feeling content just because he was there.

Pleasure became something else as her heart constricted. She was in such trouble. Gabe wouldn't want her and Mark full-time, forever. He'd made that plain. She couldn't make the mistake of letting herself dream.

"Mark's green with envy," Gabe commented, and she followed his gaze to see that Jennifer had just ridden into the arena on her palomino. It wasn't hard to spot her son watching, his expression easy to read.

She closed her eyes on another stab of pleasure/pain. Gabe was still keeping an eye out for Mark, as if doing so came naturally to him.

As if he was Mark's father.

It won't last, she told herself. Mark had had teachers before who started the year positive but lost patience with him. This wouldn't be any different. She couldn't expect any different.

Gabe chuckled low in his throat, and she opened her eyes to see cow and girl face off with near identical expressions on their faces.

Ciara took a deep breath. Damn it, she could revel in the moment, couldn't she? Was that too much to ask?

A few minutes later, Jennifer was grinning in triumph as she backed her horse off and let the steer trot back to the herd. Mark was applauding like mad right along with the other boys beside him.

Like one of the guys, she thought in bemusement.

CHAPTER EIGHT

IT WAS MARK who gave Gabe the opening he guessed he'd been subconsciously waiting for.

After the little skirmish with Ciara over his poor choice of words, Gabe had made up his mind to back off. He wasn't making any long-term commitment to either her or her son, which meant the boy's issues weren't his business. He sure as hell had no right to judge her decisions.

But damn, the itch to know more about these two people didn't go away. It was just there, a constant irritation that got more and more insistent until it was rubbing itself raw like a saddle sore. What would drive a woman like her to change her life so drastically? Given the limited formal education she had admitted to, he couldn't imagine she'd ever expected to turn her back on the public schools and educate her own kid. And the move over here, so far from her parents as well as her ex, not to mention from malls and movie theaters, fast-food restaurants and friends, indicated motivation that had to go deeper than feeling Mark wasn't being adequately protected at school.

He resisted the impulse to scratch that itch during the next week, though. For one thing, he didn't want to endanger a relationship that was coming to mean too much to him. For another…well, it was his way to think long and hard before he formed an opinion, never mind made it known to someone who might not want to hear what he thought.

But today he'd "borrowed" Mark with his mother's permission to help install kitchen cabinets at a new construction in Post Falls, Idaho. He didn't mind spending the day with the boy, and Mark had shown enough aptitude for woodworking and interest in cabinetmaking, Gabe thought he might enjoy seeing how it all came together on the job site. Sure, the contractor would provide the help Gabe needed, but there was no reason he couldn't bring his own labor, was there?

The drive passed quickly enough. Mark never ran short of things to say. For long stretches, all Gabe had to do was grunt now and again. He couldn't say he was bored, though; the kid had a quick mind and a bottomless sense of curiosity.

Once they arrived, Gabe did his best to turn the job into a classroom for Mark while still accomplishing his own goals. Mark learned how to locate studs, and already understood why Gabe measured and marked carefully before he so much as touched a cabinet. Being perfectionists was something they had in common.

The carcasses of solid wood cabinets were damned heavy, even without drawers and doors. Mark proved to be stronger than he looked when it came to helping hold upper cabinets in place as Gabe drilled pilot holes, set the first couple of screws in place and then meticulously made sure the top was level and the front edge plumb before continuing the installation.

As usual, they hung the upper cabinets before starting on the lower ones. Despite the best measurements and planning he had been able to do, he still had to tap some shims into place to achieve the results he wanted. No drawer in one of *his* cabinets would stick because of a subtle skewing. He was paid to produce the best, and he did.

Mark's focus as he worked wasn't that different from Gabe's, and the boy fit in just fine with the construction workers at the house. The two of them finished and left right on time to get home for dinner, to which Ciara had invited Gabe.

Man, he was getting spoiled. He hadn't stopped for a solitary burger in weeks now. This almost felt like—

He stopped himself before he could complete the thought. *Not going there, remember?*

They hadn't been on the road more than a few minutes when, out of the blue, Mark said, "Were you always good at math in school?"

Wondering what inspired the question, Gabe

said, "In math, I was. It came easily to me." He hesitated only briefly. "Reading was different. It still doesn't come easy. I'm dyslexic."

Mark kind of knew what that meant, but they talked about Gabe's particular form of it. The boy had a little trouble imagining how letters could reverse themselves to Gabe's perception when really they stayed right where they were supposed to be on the page.

"Means I didn't do real well in school," Gabe admitted. "I still read slowly." He glanced at Mark. "You haven't said much about your other lessons. You do okay in social studies and the like?"

"Yeah, it's mostly really easy." He grimaced. "Some of it is awfully boring, though. I mean, it's just, like, reading and worksheets. Mom thought we could do more with some really cool websites."

"Until you found out we have only dial-up."

"Yeah. And I don't *care* about stuff like government. I'm more interested in sciences. I wish I had a real lab. And Mom *says* we'll go on field trips, but then we never do 'cuz she's always working."

"You didn't move that long ago," Gabe pointed out. "It must be tough for a parent who has to work full-time to homeschool, too."

Slumped low in his seat, Mark grimaced.

"You miss school?" Gabe asked after a minute. "You must have had teachers you liked. Maybe a counselor."

"My math teacher was okay, but the science teacher had us do really stupid projects like make up animals that would live in a certain environment. It was like creative writing," he complained. "I wanted to learn *real* stuff."

"I can understand that."

"English class was dumb. I don't like *stories*. Anybody can make things up. Kids do it all the time. They were always saying I—" He applied the brakes.

Gabe wondered if he wanted to hear this, but how could he resist now? "You?" he prodded gently.

"I don't know," he mumbled. "That I'm weird or something."

"You must have had friends."

He shrugged, head down, voice still subdued. "Not really. So maybe I am weird."

Well, yeah, Gabe thought, but not necessarily in a bad way. Asperger's was his best guess.

"You're a smart kid. I'd expect you to be a good student."

"I guess my grades were okay. But Dad—"

Gabe had a really bad feeling he was going to detest Mark's dad even more than he already did as soon as he heard what the guy had had to say. Maybe he should stop with the prodding. Instinct told him some things had to be spoken aloud, though, and that those might be the very things Mark wouldn't tell his mother.

So he went ahead. "What did your dad say?" he asked, as gently as he could.

Mumble, mumble.

He had to have misheard. "He said what?"

"That I'm some kind of retard!" Mark yelled. "Okay?"

The steering wheel creaked, Gabe's grip on it was so tight. His molars were about ready to crack, too. "No," he said, "it's not okay. You *are* smart. You must know that."

The slouching posture had gotten downright sulky now. Mark's shoulders jerked.

"He said that to you?" Gabe asked.

"Nah."

"Then what makes you think—?"

"I heard him tell Mom."

Gabe flinched. "Bet she was mad."

"Yeah, but—" Those skinny shoulders jerked again. "She probably thinks so, too. 'Cuz I can tell teachers and everyone think, you know, that I'm weird, too. And probably dumb."

Through his icy rage, Gabe managed to come up with a tone that was almost matter-of-fact. "I guarantee you, nobody thinks you're dumb."

"Dad does."

"I don't think that's what he meant, either."

Another shrug. Mark had his face averted now.

Not paying much attention to the passing land-scape, Gabe still let a mile or two pass before he spoke again. He had to stop at a red light, which allowed him to glance at the boy. "You spend much time with your dad?"

"Nah."

The traffic light turned green, and, very conscious of having a passenger, Gabe took a careful look each way before he started forward. On his own, he'd gotten so he could go through busy intersections without remembering, but it was different when he had Ciara or Mark with him. They probably thought he drove like a little old lady.

Better than the alternative, he told himself. And it wasn't as if he was having flashbacks. Just…a prickle of anxiety.

"You miss him?" Gabe asked finally.

Not usually slow to speak, Mark took his time before answering. "I dunno." Another pause. "Sometimes."

"I'm sorry." Gabe hesitated. "I didn't always have a great relationship with my father, either."

"Really?" Mark looked at him again, surprise on his face. He'd probably never imagined Gabe had been a boy with a father and mother. Kids didn't tend to think of adults that way. "How come?"

Gabe brooded about that for a minute. "He was always hard on me. Couldn't understand why

I struggled in school." He frowned. "My father owned an airfield. Have I told you that before?"

"I think so."

"Well, he had a flight school, too, and offered charter flights. Me, I never liked flying. Heights scared me. Dad couldn't understand that, either."

"Really?" Mark's voice rose in surprise. "You were *scared*?"

"Don't you think we're all scared of something?"

"Most kids don't act like they are."

Gabe half smiled. "They just don't want to admit to it. Most adults don't like to, either. Especially men."

"How come you told me, then?"

He had to think about that. "I don't see you making fun of me because you know I'm scared of heights."

"You wouldn't care if I did, would you?"

Gabe smiled. "Probably not anymore." He paused, feeling clumsy. "I told you because you need to know that nobody is perfect. Most people have things they're good at, things they're not. That's the way it is."

"I don't know anything Dad isn't good at," Mark muttered.

"What's he do for a living?"

"You mean, for work? I don't really understand it. Mom says he's called a financial manager."

Gabe nodded. "So he's good at math, too. He passed that ability on to you."

Mark looked perplexed at the concept, but then his expression cleared. "Because Mom *isn't* good at math. So I didn't get it from her."

"Right. But don't tell her I said so."

They exchanged a grin.

Time to change the subject. "So…do you know what your mother is making for dinner tonight?"

"You really like her cooking, don't you?"

"Yeah. I really do." He didn't say, *I like sitting at the table with the two of you, too. Laughing. Hearing Watson whine from the other side of the door. Looking at your mom. Imagining my fingers slipping through her hair. Kissing her. Seeing her naked.*

Nope, there was a lot he didn't say.

"So, YOU HAD a good time today?" Ciara asked as she hung up the dish towel and Mark sat down in front of the computer that sat on a small desk in a nook of the big kitchen.

Gabe had left after dinner, and Ciara was thinking about settling down with a good book while Mark prowled the internet—an exercise in patience. She paused behind him and watched as he logged on then swiveled on the chair to face her.

"Yeah, it was super cool," her son declared enthusiastically. "He really let me help. When we were done, he took some pictures with his phone. Next time he's here I'll have him show you."

"That's great. I'll bet the cabinets were beautiful."

"He said thank you for the sandwiches."

She smiled. "He told me."

"Usually he goes to Subway or something. Or he doesn't eat lunch at all, 'cuz once he starts working he doesn't like to stop."

"I can understand that," she agreed.

She asked about the town of Post Falls and learned next to nothing. It was lots bigger than Goodwater.

Of course, almost every town was.

Sure, the river was pretty. The cabinets went in a *big* house. Lots bigger than this house.

Her son was not destined to become a travel writer.

"Did you two find enough to talk about?" she asked, indulging her curiosity. She only hoped Mark had let Gabe get a word in edgewise.

"Yeah." His forehead pleated. "On the way home he asked me a bunch of questions."

She slowly straightened. "A bunch of questions?"

"About school and stuff. Why I don't go anymore. You know. And he wanted to know about Dad and why I don't see him."

A giant hand squeezed her rib cage. "Did he?" she said grimly.

"Yeah. Usually he just talks about what we're doing. When he talks at all," Mark said. "He's kind of quiet. This was different."

What was different was that he'd gotten her son away from her long enough to grill him, and she knew damn well what conclusions he'd come to.

"Speaking of," she said, keeping her tone casual, "there's something I forgot to ask Gabe. I'm going to run down to his place right now."

"Really?" He gazed at her in bemusement. "You're going to run? You never run, Mom."

She faked a laugh. "I'm going to drive. Not run. You're right. I never run if I can help it."

"Okay." He turned back to the computer, and she sensed he'd dismissed her from his mind. "I'll see you later."

She grabbed a down vest on her way out the door, even though she was mad enough to be steaming.

Lights shone in the windows of Gabe's house, but no porch lights were on when she pulled in. She leaped out, went to the back door and rapped hard on the glass inset.

A moment later, he appeared, a big man whose solid body usually offered reassurance and a shiver of excitement she'd forgotten she could feel. Not tonight. Tonight she was too mad.

He flicked the porch light on then opened the door. "Ciara. Is something wrong?"

"Yes," she snapped. "Something is wrong."

"Come on in." He backed up, letting her storm across the threshold. His expression changed when he got a good look at her face.

She pushed the door shut behind her hard enough to make the glass rattle. "Mark told me you asked *a bunch of questions* today. About school and why he doesn't see his father."

"We talked," Gabe said slowly.

"You don't approve of me homeschooling him, do you?"

He looked stoic. "Did I say that?"

"I could tell you were shocked when I said I mean to keep on doing it."

"I admit I've been wondering why you would."

Her skin prickled with anger. Something else, too, but she couldn't think about that. Protecting Mark was her first priority. Nothing else could be allowed to interfere. "Then you should have asked *me*. Not him. How dare you interrogate him the minute you have him alone!"

Gabe's gray eyes narrowed. "I did ask you, but your answer didn't make a lot of sense."

"So you went behind my back?"

"We talked. That's all."

"You think I should have let him be bullied for five more years of public school?" she yelled. Oh, God. She probably sounded like a crazy person, blaming him instead of the vicious little thugs who'd persecuted Mark, the teachers and administrators who wouldn't protect him, but she couldn't seem to help herself. The sense of betrayal was huge.

Gabe stood four square in the middle of his kitchen, irritation setting his jaw. "I didn't say that."

"Then what?"

"Nobody in Goodwater has bullied him."

She spun away then back to face him. "Oh, like the school here will be any different."

"Why won't it?" he said softly.

So softly that, too late, she realized he had set a trap. He wanted her to say, *Mark is why it won't be any different.*

The fact that she so much as *thought* anything like that scared her to death.

I don't think it. I don't.

She glared at him. "I'm not willing to take that chance."

"He told me kids think he's weird."

"Which you totally understand, since *you* think there's something wrong with him." She crossed her arms tightly, and her fingers bit into her own flesh. Why had she ever let things between them get to the point where this *hurt* so terribly? But she couldn't let those feelings matter. Nobody was judging Mark, she thought fiercely. Not if she had anything to say about it. *Nobody.*

"I apologized for my choice of word," he said. "But Ciara, you have to know he's not quite normal."

"That's a horrible thing to say!"

"Why?" he asked in a voice of reason. "What's normal anyway? Hell, what's wrong with not being normal?"

There. He'd said it again. *Wrong.*

"Not normal." Her laugh sounded hysterical. "Isn't that nice. A polite way of saying *weird*. Full circle. You know what?" She was yelling again. It was that or throw something. Or cry. "He thinks he's weird because of people like you!"

Now he leaned forward, his sheer bulk suddenly menacing. "By God, you won't tar me with that brush, lady. I don't deserve it."

A rational part of her mind knew he was right. Except for her, nobody had ever been kinder to Mark, more patient, more understanding. Something else she couldn't let matter. The temper driving her, the fear that was at its heart like the eye of the storm, kept her from backing down.

"But you think I have no business homeschooling him. Why don't you just say it?" she goaded. "It's not a secret, is it?"

He swore harshly. "All right. I'll say it. You're making a mistake. You're a fool if you think it's healthy for him to be locked up in that house with no friends and his mommy his only teacher."

He might as well have hit her. Stricken, Ciara

backed up a step, then another. She saw his expression change to dismay, maybe even horror at what he'd said, but shock gripped her in cold talons.

"I don't know why I ever thought I could trust you." She shuddered at what she was saying, what it meant, but couldn't seem to stop herself.

"Ciara. Damn it, you know I didn't—"

"I'm sure you thought you were doing the right thing." She fumbled behind her for the doorknob. "But my decisions about how I educate my own son are none of your business. Thank you for what you've done, but Mark won't be back."

They stared at each other. On a distant plane, she thought he looked as stunned as she felt. The next moment, he wiped his face clean of expression.

"Fine," he snapped. "I have better things to do than let some kid hang around talking nonstop."

She fled, all but falling down the two steps from his back door, scrambling into her van. Grateful she'd left the key in the ignition to make her getaway quicker.

She turned the key with a shaking hand and then looked to see that he'd closed his door and turned out both the porch and kitchen lights. He'd meant it.

I have better things to do.

Not until she was safely at a stop in front of her own house did she let herself collapse forward, forehead pressed to the steering wheel, and think, *What did I do?*

JUST AS GODDAMN WELL, he told himself. The woman and boy both had thrown a curve into the life he'd carefully built. The one that suited him, that protected him from ever again having to face utter devastation.

Feeling the need to get away, the next morning he loaded Hoodoo into the trailer and hauled him to the Coeur d'Alene area to a favorite trail. He refused to let himself remember that he'd intended to bring Mark this time. Solitary was good. Solitary was how he'd chosen to live since he was left alone by fate.

An hour into his ride, he realized he wasn't settling like he should have been into the beauty of the wooded land studded with lakes, the sunny day with the bite of spring in this northern part of the country. The closest he came to any human contact was when he nodded brusquely as he reined Hoodoo to one side of the trail to let a couple of other riders pass.

Maybe he should have called around, found someone else who felt like a trail ride today.

He made a sound in his throat that had Hoodoo's ears swiveling.

Sure, he thought, but then he'd have had to make at least occasional conversation, and he didn't much feel like that.

Good thing he *hadn't* brought Mark Malloy then, he thought savagely. The kid would have talked the whole way. Peace was what he was looking for, not a chat fest.

An hour and a half into the ride, he realized he was getting hungry. He hadn't brought a lunch; he never did. Between one blink and the next, he saw himself sitting down at the table in Ciara's kitchen. Before he could feel the keen edge of anticipation, he blanked the picture out. He'd get a burger on the way home. He hadn't had a good, greasy cheeseburger and fries in weeks. Couldn't think of a better meal.

Once he'd trailered Hoodoo, he stopped on the Idaho side of the border at a familiar hamburger joint. Got his lunch to go so the quarter horse didn't have to stand around unnecessarily. His stomach rumbled as he took a first bite, but by the time he stuffed the last fry into his mouth, he felt queasy.

Fine. It went with the sick feeling he'd been carrying beneath his breastbone all day.

When he passed the old Walker place, his foot lifting from the gas to start slowing for the turn into his own driveway, he didn't so much as glance that way. None of his business whether they were home or not.

Poor Mark. Would the kid ever work up the nerve to articulate to his mother how isolated he felt?

Frowning over the fact that his mind had taken a forbidden pathway, Gabe nonetheless followed it. He was aware of the irony that he, of all people, should be championing someone else's need for companionship. But he thought all kids needed friends, and in his quiet way he still enjoyed riding in cutting-horse competitions partly because he was able to share that enjoyment with other people. Sometimes he went out to a tavern to watch a Mariners or Seahawks game because there'd be other people around to groan at a bad call or hoot and holler at a home run. He worked with contractors he considered friends. When he'd been alone for too many days, he looked forward to an installation where he'd be working with some other men. Even a loner like him needed other people.

Mark might have been miserable in school— but look how he'd leaped to join the group of kids at the ranch.

After parking in front of the barn, Gabe let down the ramp and backed Hoodoo out then led him to join an impatient Aurora in the pasture. He fed the horses, spent some time leaning against the fence listening to them whuffling and crunching, but brooded the entire time.

When it came down to it, Ciara was right. What he thought didn't matter. She had a right to make the important decisions about her own son. He'd overstepped. The why didn't matter, either.

Give him a couple of days, he decided, and he'd quit thinking about Ciara and Mark at all. He might really *be* glad to regain his former solitude. If anyone was the loser here, it was Mark.

Not my business, he reminded himself, and set about backing the trailer into the barn.

CIARA HEARD MARK'S footsteps stop in the doorway to her workroom. A jangle of metal tags told her Watson had come, too. Even without having heard Mark coming, she'd swear she could *feel* him hovering.

Her back to him, Ciara continued ironing open, newly stitched seams, even though she tensed, knowing what was coming. They'd had the same conversation repeatedly in the intervening days since her confrontation with Gabe.

"I wish I could go to Gabe's," he said wistfully.

Yep. Here they went again.

"I don't understand why I can't."

She pressed down hard. Too hard. Steam burst from the iron, and she hastily lifted it. "I explained."

"I was making something. It was going to be really great."

Hearing his sadness, she closed her eyes but felt her face momentarily convulse. She had to take several slow, careful breaths before she could speak.

"I'm sorry, honey. I know you don't understand, but I'm trying to make the best decisions I can for both of us. Gabe was—" Oh, Lord, that sounded

as if he was dead. "He's probably a nice man."
Probably? "But I didn't like the way he asked you
all those questions when he had you alone. Those
were the kind of things he should have talked to
me about."

Mark shifted from foot to foot. Claws clicked
on the wood floor. "It wasn't like that, Mom. We
were just talking. I'm the one who told him stuff."

She unplugged the iron and set it on the stand
then turned to face him. "About?"

"Just…stuff," he mumbled. "You know."

She waited.

"It makes you sad when I—" He screeched to
a halt.

Alarm flashed through her. Were there things
he wasn't telling her, because he thought she'd be
upset?

Stupid thing to think. Of course there were. He
was almost a teenager. And a boy. What boy told
his mother everything? Heck, she hadn't told her
mother everything, not by a long shot. Mildly chagrined, she thought, *I still don't.* She talked with
her parents weekly, but had been very careful to
make any mention of Gabe casual. She sure hadn't
said anything about an earth-shattering kiss.

But to Mark… What had he told Gabe but not
her that had him looking so appalled right now,
after his near-slip?

Find the right words. "Of course I'm sad when

I find out someone hurt your feelings, but that doesn't mean I don't want you to tell me. It's easier for me to make the right decisions for you when I know how you really feel about a particular teacher or school or friend."

"You mean, like how I feel about Gabe?"

Oh, dear God, no. Not about Gabe. She was too afraid she knew.

"Sure," she said, crossing her arms in a relaxed way. "I have to warn you, though. I won't swear to change my mind about him because of what you say. Sometimes there are factors you don't know about."

His chin jutted out in a way she recognized from her own mirror. "How come? If it has to do with me, shouldn't you tell me?"

"When you're a parent, you'll understand." Oh, boy—how many times had she heard her mother say that?

"You don't want to hurt my feelings," he said. "That's why you won't tell me everything."

It struck her, suddenly, what a startling conversation this was to be having with her son. His heart was always in the right place—he'd never hurt her feelings on purpose—but he definitely wore blinkers. He never noticed what anyone else thought or felt. She'd have said he had never had an insight into someone else's behavior or motivations in his life.

But apparently, she'd been wrong.

"Sometimes that's true," she admitted.

"Like when Dad said I'm a retard." He shot it at her like a bullet, and she reeled as the words struck, her hands falling to her sides.

"You heard?" she whispered.

He looked down at his too-large feet and shrugged.

"Oh, Mark. I'm sorry you heard. Especially since he didn't mean it. Not the way it sounds."

He lifted his head, and his eyes looked older than his years. Too old. "How did he mean it?"

"Only that—" The words stuck in her throat. "That—"

His shoulders jerked again. "It doesn't matter."

"It does." Damn, she had to blink hard to hold back tears. That bastard, she thought viciously. How could he do this to his own son?

"He didn't mean he thought you were dumb," she managed finally.

Still in the doorway, Mark slouched, head down, body language saying, *I'm not listening, and I don't believe you anyway.*

"Really," she tried, scrambling for a convincing yet nonhurtful way to explain. "The thing is parents always assume their kids will be like them. Especially since you're a boy, he expected you to share his interests and abilities."

"Gabe says I kind of *am* like Dad," Mark surprised her by saying.

"What?"

"The way I'm good at math. 'Cuz you're not. So I must have gotten it from Dad, right?"

"I…" She blinked. "I guess that's true."

"*He* might have been bored by social studies and units on government, too."

"Actually…I think he was," she said, groping for memories of Jeff talking about school.

Mark lifted wounded eyes to her. "So why doesn't he think I'm like him?"

The pain in her chest made it hard to sound thoughtful instead of furious, but she'd had lots of practice. "Well, you know how big he is into football."

Mark nodded. Jeff could have accepted almost anything about his son, if only he'd loved watching NFL games with him and dreamed of playing himself. Mark being Mark, he'd never even pretended.

"Your dad is a people person." She explained what that meant. "It makes him uncomfortable when you don't always say the right thing to his friends, or when we had teacher conferences because you were having trouble with other kids." *Trouble.* A euphemism, in this case.

"Gabe doesn't mind when I don't say the right thing."

Ciara closed her eyes. "Gabe is…" Oh, no. Had she been about to say *different*? Yes. Heaven help her. Gabe *was* different. *And I told him I couldn't trust him. I didn't listen to what he was trying to tell me because I was afraid he might be right.*

Because she was afraid of *him*, and what he made her feel?

"He's different from Dad." Mark sounded sad again. "He listens to me, and he doesn't mind when I'm, I don't know, dorky. You know?"

She knew.

Her throat tried to close, but she pushed an "I'm sorry" through anyway.

"So…why can't I see him?" He stared beseechingly at her.

Ciara felt like the worst mother in the world.

You're a fool if you think it's healthy for him to be locked up in that house with no friends and his mommy his only teacher.

But…what else could she do?

"Don't you miss Gabe?" Mark asked in honest puzzlement.

Yes. Desperately. Waking in the night with a rock in the pit of her stomach kind of missing.

What had she done?

Made us miserable, that's what, she admitted, especially when she remembered Gabe's last, brusque words.

Fine. I have better things to do than let some kid hang around talking nonstop. And…he hadn't wanted to be friendly with them, not when they first met. He'd made no secret of it. Maybe he really had been relieved that she'd given him an out.

But…she had to try. She knew she could make him understand if she were willing to tell him things about her family, her childhood.

She shivered at the mere thought. *I can't.* No. If she did, he'd come to the same conclusions Jeff had. There was a reason she had such complicated feelings about her family and was glad, at least for now, to have distance as a really good excuse for *not* seeing them.

"I do miss Gabe," she admitted. "Let me think about this, okay, Mark?"

He opened his mouth to argue, took a long look at her face and closed his mouth. His restraint stunned her.

"Okay, Mom. Can we have lunch?"

Her smile trembled but was real. "We can."

"I gotta take Watson out."

"I'll put lunch together while you do that. See if Daisy wants to go, too."

He agreed and bounded down the stairs. A thud suggested he'd tripped on one of the last few steps and fallen, but then she heard his voice talking to the dogs and figured he was all right.

Now tears did sting in her eyes as she realized she wouldn't want Mark to be any different from who he was, even if she could wave a magic wand.

How many times had she told herself that? But

she had an awful suspicion that she might have been lying to herself, while now she knew she meant it.

Halfway down the stairs, she stopped, her hand tightening on the banister.

Was there even the slightest possibility that her mother felt the same about Bridget, despite everything?

As clear as a bell, she heard something else Gabe had said: *What's normal anyway? Hell, what's wrong with not being normal?*

CHAPTER NINE

"WHAT THE HELL?" Gabe lifted his hand, holding the sandpaper away from the maple board, and scowled at the gouge he'd just put in it.

That was what happened when he didn't pay attention to what he was doing. He had let himself brood, and the more upset he got, the more pressure he put on the sandpaper.

He swore and flung the sanding block away in a fit of temper unlike him. It hit with a clunk, bounced and rolled out of sight. Now he might as well put the beautifully grained board in his firewood bin. What a waste.

Growling under his breath, he sawed it into two pieces that would fit in his stove and carried them toward the big double doors.

That was when he heard a vehicle coming down his driveway, but not the familiar sound of a UPS truck. He didn't remember ordering anything anyway.

By the time he stepped out of the barn, he knew who was here, but not why. Without even looking toward Ciara's red Caravan as it rolled to a stop, he strode toward the woodbox by his back steps, lifted the plywood lid, dumped the chunks of maple in and let the lid drop.

Straightening, he braced himself and turned to see her getting out. No Mark, which meant she didn't want her kid to hear what she had to say.

He had the fleeting wish that he'd trimmed his beard. These past few days, he hadn't expected to see anyone. Why bother?

Not that long ago, he'd even been thinking of shaving the beard off. Lucky he hadn't. He'd have had to start all over with the damn stubble that caught on his pillowcase.

Gabe stood where he was and watched Ciara walk slowly toward him. She had her emotions tamped down tight; all he could read was wariness.

But damn, she looked good. She didn't walk like a woman who was trying to get men to notice her, but somehow that stride made him think of a model sauntering down a catwalk anyway. Leggy, loose, with just enough swing of her hips. Faded jeans fit snugly, and her sweater draped over a slim rib cage and breasts that were just the right size and shape to make him take notice whether he wanted to or not.

Her hair caught fire in the midday sun, and her eyes were a deeper blue than the sky.

He still didn't move, not so much because he was deliberately being a jackass as because he was paralyzed by everything he felt at the sight of her.

By hope.

She wouldn't have driven over here just to tell him she'd really meant it about never setting eyes on him again, would she?

She stopped a few feet away and nibbled uncertainly on her lower lip.

Gabe tore his gaze away. Out here in the bright light of day, she'd notice if he got aroused, and damned if his body wasn't already stirring. He pretended to ponder the open door of the barn behind her.

"Ciara."

"Gabe." Her voice came out a little shaky. Her breasts rose with a deep breath. "It's probably too little, too late, but I came to say I'm sorry. I…don't think I meant most of what I said."

"Sure sounded like you meant it." It was the hurt speaking. Had to be.

"No, I—" Her gaze slid from his, until she made an equal pretense at concentrating on the boring white clapboard siding of his house. "There's some backstory you don't know."

He didn't say anything.

"I…some of it doesn't matter." She squeezed her hands together. "The thing is, I guess I kind of blow up when anyone suggests Mark is different, because he's not! I mean, he's smart, and kind and— He's a good person." She sounded desperate now. "Just because he's smart…"

Well, that was one explanation. And to a degree, Gabe thought she might be right. Mark *did* focus on interests that were more academic than the usual preoccupations of kids his age. But that wasn't all of it, and he thought she knew it.

"He is a good kid." Gabe's voice came out gravelly. "You've heard me say that."

"Yes." She stole a look at him, a world of hurt and confusion in those beautiful eyes. "I got scared," she said, really fast. "Sometimes I'm afraid I'm not doing the right thing for him. I feel like I'm fighting the rest of the world. Everyone who dealt with him at the school, and then there was his father. But I don't know what else I *can* do."

"Ciara." He couldn't help himself. He reached out and gently pried her hands apart. "It's okay. You were right. I should have kept my mouth shut. Some of what I said... Well, I didn't mean it, either. You made me mad."

She gave a twisted little smile. "I'm good at that. I think everyone at Mark's last school did one of those end-zone dances when I pulled him out."

Man, the relief he felt seemed to fill his chest until there wasn't any room left. Not until this minute had he let himself acknowledge how wretched he'd been. Self-defense.

"Where is Mark?" he asked.

"Home. I...told him I was going to the grocery store."

"Are you?"

"I suppose I have to." She wrinkled her nose. "He'll notice if I don't come home with anything. But I didn't want him to know I was stopping here in case—" Her eyes shied from his again.

In case he said, *Go ahead and homeschool him, but leave me out of it.*

"You tell him we'll take up where we left off tomorrow morning. Usual time."

"Really?"

He'd never seen eyes that conveyed so much. Eyes were just eyes. But hers… He found himself staring into them, feeling like the oracle gazing into the water. Seeing more than any rational person would believe was there.

"Really." Damn, but he wanted to touch her. Just because she'd said she was sorry didn't mean anything more than that, though. He cleared his throat. "I missed you both." And cursed his discovery that a once satisfying life was now lonely.

A smile trembled on her lips. "We missed you, too. Will you come to dinner tonight, Gabe?"

His stomach growled, and he gave a low, rough chuckle at the same time as she laughed. "Thank you. If you're sure."

"I'm sure."

Their gazes locked as seconds ticked past. What if she wanted…hoped…? *No,* he told himself sharply. *Don't blow it again. Take it for what*

*it is—a casual friendship. He was doing her and
her son a favor; she tried to balance the scales
by giving him something he didn't have: home-
cooked meals.*

Part of him hoped she didn't guess how much
he looked forward to those meals, and not because
of the food.

"Ciara," he heard himself say, and at the exact
same moment she said, "Well." Already she was
backing away. "Um…six o'clock?"

Staying rooted where he was, Gabe said,
"Sounds good."

"Okay. Well, then…" She backed right into her
van, kind of bounced off it, blushed and grabbed
for the door handle.

When she drove away, he was still standing
where he'd started, right in front of the wood bin,
but he felt a hundred pounds lighter. So buoyant
he was ready to play a superhero.

Wincing, Gabe fingered his beard, grown
scruffy this week, and decided he'd better at least
trim it before dinnertime. Superheroes were always
clean cut, weren't they? Not that he'd shave it off,
he decided; not yet. That would be too obvious.

MARK DIDN'T EVEN notice the constraint between the
two adults, and his ebullience gradually relaxed it,
to Ciara's relief.

"I can work on my box tomorrow, right?"

Gabe agreed he could.

Next thing she knew, Mark had not so subtly worked the topic around to birthdays. Specifically his. Which wasn't far away.

"It's real soon. Huh, Mom?"

July 3, he would officially become a teenager. Thank God there were as yet no signs of puberty, beyond the deepening voice that frequently cracked. Or maybe she shouldn't be grateful; his being among the youngest in his class could have contributed to his social problems. Especially this last year, when a lot of the middle school students looked like teenagers, he'd been left behind.

"And here I'd forgotten it," she teased.

He, of course, took her seriously. "You never forget my birthday."

She just laughed.

She didn't have to face the awkwardness of being left alone with Gabe. He didn't offer to help her clear the table, and Mark and Watson walked him out to his truck, both bouncing in excitement.

The last thing she heard was, "Can I ride tomorrow, too?" She couldn't make out Gabe's quiet rumble, but had no doubt of his answer.

How could she have thought, even for a minute, that Mark was better off without Gabe Tennert in his life?

Mark had barely come back inside when the phone rang. Ciara dried her hands and answered.

"Ciara?" The voice was her ex-husband's. "Just, uh, realized I hadn't called in a while."

Jerk.

"Mark will be glad to hear from you," she said.

"Wait," he said urgently. "You've got to tell me what to send him for his birthday."

At least he remembered that his son *had* an upcoming birthday. Of course, if he actually *knew* him, he wouldn't need suggestions from her. She gave a few nonetheless, and he said, "Yeah, the software sounds good. Uh…you two are doing okay in…what's it called? Backwater, Washington?"

"You know perfectly well it's Goodwater."

"What is it with you? You can't laugh at a joke?"

His jokes always came with a barb, the kind that tore into her skin. Even in the early days, he'd reacted as if she was the one lacking when she didn't find some crack of his to be funny.

"Ha ha. We're fine, Jeff. The move was good for us."

"How can it be?" He sounded incredulous.

"We have a neighbor who is spending time with Mark." On a rush of warmth, she thought how good it felt to be able to say this. To picture the self-contained man whose eyes were nonetheless so kind…when they didn't heat with an emotion that wasn't kind at all. Like they had when she backed away from him today and almost fell over her own feet.

She knew what he wanted, and she wanted it as much. If only the complications didn't scare her so much.

"Spending time with him?" Jeff said suspiciously. "Why?"

"He's a cabinetmaker. He's teaching Mark to work with wood. He's also giving him horseback riding lessons."

"And you don't wonder, just a little, what's behind this? I mean, let's face it, nobody without some ulterior motive wants to spend time with Mark. Count on it, this guy's either got his eye on you, or on Mark."

Both angry and sad, she shook her head. How on earth had she ever imagined she loved this man?

"Don't you dare say anything like that to Mark. I'll get him for you." Refusing to hear another word, she pressed the phone to her stomach.

When she called up the stairs for him, Mark galloped down. "It's Dad?" His face was alight with hope.

She managed a smile. "Yep."

He took the phone outside, already talking a mile a minute about Watson and Daisy and…

SHE DELIBERATELY HADN'T asked Gabe to dinner the next evening. Two nights in a row…well, that would make it seem as if, oh, he *belonged* here. A couple of times a week was enough, she assured herself. Maybe three times. Or, if there was a special reason, four times.

But she was so hungry for someone to talk to, she regretted not asking him again.

Mom would understand if she wanted to grumble about Jeff, of course, but…it wasn't her mother she wanted to talk to. It was Gabe.

She kept remembering how he listened and seemed interested. If he really wasn't, he wouldn't keep making time for Mark, would he?

So she waited until Mark had said good-night and disappeared into his room, then went downstairs to the kitchen where he wouldn't hear her voice. From the window over the sink, she could see lights still on in Gabe's house.

He answered on the third ring with her name. "Is something wrong?"

"No. I just, oh, wanted to grumble for a minute, and I hoped you wouldn't mind."

He chuckled. "Everyone needs to grumble."

Absurdly, that was all it took to lessen the anger she'd been carrying around since she'd seen Mark's face yesterday, after he talked to his father.

"Did Mark tell you his dad called last night, after you left?"

"No." He paused. "Now that I think about it, he was a little quieter than usual this morning."

"*Quiet* isn't a word I usually associate with Mark."

He laughed again. "No, he's a talker."

"Why can't his father be anything like you?" she burst out with and then gulped. *Oh, no. Did I say that?*

The small pool of silence had her clutching the phone and staring through the dark to the golden square of what she knew to be his kitchen window. She couldn't see even a shadow that suggested he was looking out toward her, but she imagined he was. What must he be thinking?

"I mean, you seem to understand Mark," she said hastily. "Jeff won't even try."

"What did he say?"

"Mark won't tell me. But when he handed me the phone, he was…really subdued." He'd looked crushed. "When I asked what was wrong, he just shrugged."

"You want me to see if he'll talk about it?"

"You'd do that?" Then she shook her head. "I can't expect you to do counseling along with everything else. It was…" Oh, why not tell him? Wasn't that why she'd called? "Part of what made me so mad was that when I talked to Jeff briefly and mentioned you, he couldn't understand why you'd want to spend time with Mark. God knows, *he* doesn't want to."

She hoped he didn't read between the lines and guess what Jeff had insinuated.

"I'm sorry," he said, in that gentle way he had.

"Mark said you pointed out that he does take after his father in some ways."

"He told me his father is in finance."

"Yes, he has an MBA. He was never a reader."

"Mark said once he doesn't like fiction."

She smiled, relaxing again. "Nope. He's only interested in things that are real. And…not so much in human motivations, which are big in novels. I mean, 'whodunit' is really 'who would have had reason to do it', right?"

Oh, she loved Gabe's laugh.

"I'm not sure a lot of stuff teenage boys read or the movies they see have much to do with human motivations. Think monsters from outer space or bionic superheroes, and you'll be more in the ballpark."

She laughed, too. "Okay, you have a point."

There was another silence. At last Gabe said, "Would Mark be better off if he didn't talk to his father at all?"

She closed her eyes. "Sometimes I think so, but then— How would he feel, knowing his own father didn't care at all? Isn't some relationship better than none?"

"I don't know."

"I don't, either," she admitted. "I told you, Jeff is one of the reasons I moved to the other side of the state."

"I hope it turns out to be a good decision for both of you."

So did she. So far… She trembled at her realization. So far, it might be the best decision she'd ever made—because of Gabe. All because of Gabe.

He couldn't know. She shouldn't have called him. She couldn't even imagine what he thought, when this woman next door called late at night as if…as if they were best friends.

Or more.

I want to be more.

She didn't dare let more happen, not when her first priority was Mark. Gabe was good with him, but he wouldn't want to take him on full-time. Even assuming *he* was thinking about her that way.

She was getting *way* ahead of herself. And she needed to get off the phone now.

"Thanks for listening to me," she said, trying to sound a little amused at herself. "I saw your lights on and hoped you wouldn't mind if I vented for a minute. I won't make a habit of it, I promise!"

"I don't mind." His voice was quiet and serious. "I…like that you called me."

Her heart thudded as if she'd raced down to his place and back. "Thank you for saying that," she said softly.

"Good night, Ciara."

Her "Good night" was barely a whisper.

She stayed at the window for a long time, unable

to look away from the lights on in his house, trying to picture what he was doing, whether he still wore his usual casual garb and work boots, or instead padded around at night in socks or even bare feet. Maybe she'd caught him already getting ready for bed—she knew how early he started work in the morning. Did he wear pajamas? Or…not bother with anything at all when he went to bed?

Her mind immediately leaped into new fantasies. She let out the tiniest of whimpers and knew she should try to distract herself with a book. She sure wouldn't be falling asleep in the near future, not with the honeyed warmth of arousal making her whole body feel alive in a way it hadn't in forever.

CIARA SMILED OVER her shoulder at Gabe as she reached into a cupboard for mugs. "It's warm enough tonight, why don't we sit out on the porch?"

He could think of a reason that wouldn't be a really good idea, but felt sure the idea of the two of them using the darkness for privacy to go at it hot and heavy hadn't even crossed her mind.

"Sure," he heard himself say. "Moon's near full." He'd noticed last night how fat and round it was as he stood out on his back stoop.

Once the two adults had started talking about subjects that didn't interest him, Mark had sat down at the computer in a corner of the kitchen and immediately become engrossed, seemingly forgetting Gabe and his mother were even there.

Ciara had poured the coffee and handed Gabe his then touched Mark's shoulder. "We're going out on the porch."

He didn't react in any visible way.

Smiling, she shook her head as she let the kitchen door swing shut behind them. "I've never known anyone who could concentrate like Mark does," she said. "I can see him as a surgeon, but not, oh, an airline pilot, where he has to pay attention to information coming from a bunch of different sources."

"I've noticed that about him." Gabe opened the front door, waiting until she slipped past him before he went out and shut it behind them. "It makes him easy to teach. He doesn't get distracted."

"No, that's safe to say." She looked around. "I should get a porch swing, or at least buy some Adirondack chairs, shouldn't I?"

"Porch steps work for me."

They each sat on the top one, a couple of feet between them. He rested his back against the sturdy post that supported the railing. He stretched out his legs, while Ciara put her feet on the stair beneath her and wrapped an arm around her knees. After taking a sip, she gazed out at the moon-silvered landscape.

"Look at the stars," she whispered. "Where

we lived before, we could hardly see them. Too many lights."

Gabe pondered that. He knew he never wanted to live anywhere he couldn't step outside at night and see the heavens brilliant above him. He didn't want to have to listen to traffic all night long, either. Most people didn't seem to share his taste for solitude, though.

Solitude? Is that really what you want?

Didn't seem as if it was anymore.

He wasn't ready to acknowledge what that meant.

"Did Mark tell you I'm dyslexic?" he asked abruptly, not sure why. Full disclosure?

Between moonlight and the gold square of the window behind her, he saw Ciara's head turn sharply. "No. Is that why—?"

"Why what? Mark *is* a good student. I wasn't."

"Then how is it you understand his math?"

He moved his shoulders in acceptance. "I did well in math. And shop. That was about it."

Her eyes searched his face, although he sat in more darkness than she did. "Did you hate school?"

He let himself think back, something he didn't often do. "I guess I did. Teachers were mostly helpful, and somehow they passed me on year after year, but—" The burn of humiliation was still there, even after so long. "The worst was elementary school, when we had to read aloud. I'd try to pretend no one was listening, but it didn't work."

He shook his head at the memory. "I'd stumble even over words I could have read on my own. Kids made fun of me. Not all of them, but some. And my father was convinced I was just being lazy. Mom helped, but Dad…" He took a swallow of his coffee. "Funny thing is he wasn't a reader. Liked TV news, but we took the newspaper for Mom."

"You wonder if he wasn't dyslexic, too," she said slowly.

"He might have been." He'd never before thought about things like this. He'd gone to high school with Ginny, and she'd known he was a slow reader. Somehow, neither of them had ever tried to find some deeper meaning behind his father's attitude. But now that his mind had started working on it, he found himself thinking, *Yeah, that could explain how much Dad didn't want to admit what was really wrong.* "Maybe," he found himself continuing, "if he had a problem, it wasn't as extreme as mine. But if he'd blocked out his own problem, having it rear its ugly head again in his kid might have poked at stuff he didn't want to admit."

"Or he felt guilty because it was his genes to blame."

Guilty? His father? He snorted. "If so, you'd never have known it."

She was quiet for a minute. "Why were you thinking about this tonight?"

"I got to wondering if your ex had some of

Mark's issues." Part of a kind of introspection he didn't usually indulge in. Gabe saw her jerk at what he said and then bend her head so her hair swung down to provide a veil. He continued anyway. "Might be why *he* couldn't handle it."

"No," she said, so softly he tilted his head to hear her. "He's…not much like Mark."

Gabe watched her, guessing he'd upset her but not sure why. Did she believe her son took after her instead? She'd said she hadn't gone on beyond a high school education. Had she had difficulties in school? If so, he had to believe they'd been academic, not social. From the beginning, he'd been attracted to more than her looks. Her friendliness was so natural. Her warmth shone through. Okay, Mark was friendly, too, Gabe had to give him that, but otherwise he was…awkward. No, more than that. Unaware of how people responded to him.

While he sorted through possible ways to change the subject, she stayed curled forward as if protecting her midsection. He didn't like seeing her in pain, however it had been inflicted.

"I didn't mean—" he started to say.

At exactly the same moment, she straightened and burst into speech. "What you said about normal. I keep thinking about that."

"I've been sorry I said it," he admitted. "I upset you."

"Yes, but you were right. I started asking myself

who really is *normal*, and I don't know. Were the boys who ganged up on Mark normal? If so, who wants to be?" She spoke fiercely. "Are the computer geeks? The jocks? My ex-husband?"

"Hard to call an Albert Einstein or a Mother Teresa *normal*," he agreed.

"Extraordinary has to be better, right?"

"I'd say so."

"Well, then."

He smiled into the darkness. Well, then. Nice conclusion.

"What Mark doesn't do well is…conform." She said it like a dirty word.

"A lot of kids don't," he agreed.

A lot of adults, too, come to think of it. Nobody would have accused Ephraim Walker of being a conformist.

Gabe thought he wasn't himself.

The difference between Mark and everyone else, though, was that they knew what the standard was and just chose not to meet it.

Mark…well, odds were he hadn't bothered to notice that there were spoken and unspoken social rules at all, or what kind of behaviors it took to meet them.

That might have changed, though. Watching him the day of the cutting-horse competition, Gabe had seen the kid try a few times to mimic what the others were doing. Might be the age, a stirring of hormones. He wondered if the onset of puberty had anything to do with the boys assaulting him. Testosterone in action. Might there have been a girl serving as the trigger? Wouldn't surprise Gabe.

He and Ciara sat in silence that felt remarkably peaceful. Having reached a conclusion that satisfied her, she had relaxed. She flattened her hands on the porch boards to each side of her and tilted her head back, either admiring the stars or savoring the night air on her throat. Unfortunately, the position arched her back and pushed her breasts up.

He wondered what she'd do if he scooted over a little bit, enough to put his lips to that long, smooth throat. Nibble his way down her chest, or up to her jaw. Find her lips.

He forced himself to look away. He'd kissed her once and— Well, he still didn't know if that had been a mistake or not. But he had no idea if she was ready for anything like that—or if he was.

Damn, he wanted her in bed, or on the kitchen counter or anywhere else. But he didn't let his hormones rule him. Making love with her, there'd be consequences. Huge, life-altering ones.

His way was to think long and hard about any action that was outside his usual. Preferably when he *wasn't* within touching distance of her.

"Guess I should say good-night," he said, making rising motions.

She was flustered enough, he wondered what

she'd been thinking about—or whether she'd for-gotten he was there at all.

He'd walked up earlier, and now after she, too, said good-night, he crossed her lawn and ducked between the fence rails into the pasture, met by his horses, who seemed pleasantly surprised to have his companionship. What he knew was that Ciara stayed outside until he must have been long since swallowed by the darkness. He had to be halfway down the long slope before he heard the soft sound of her front door closing.

CHAPTER TEN

FEELING LITTLE ZINGS of panic, Ciara stood for a moment, her phone in her hand. The next moment, almost without thinking, she called Gabe. It alarmed her how readily she was doing that, but…they were friends. Right? It was so hard to believe she'd only known him for—what?—six or seven weeks?

He answered after a couple of rings, saying calmly, "Ciara."

"I'm sorry. You're probably working."

"I am," he agreed, but not sounding put out. "You must have had a reason for wanting to talk to me."

She wanted to talk to him about everything. Not like she was going to say that.

"Leslie Weeks just called. Jennifer's mother?"

"I know Leslie."

"Jennifer wants Mark to go with them on a trail ride tomorrow. He's not ready for anything like that!" she wailed. Oh, wonderful. Hysterical mommy. "Is he?" she asked, timidly.

He chuckled, a low rumble that soothed her as nothing else could. "Sure he is. The Weekses know he hasn't been riding long. Chances are they'll hardly break into a trot. Depends where they're going."

She told him, and he said, "That's a good choice. Lots of meandering, some up and down, a few creeks to cross. They offer to put him up on one of their horses?"

"Yes."

"I could let him take Aurora." He sounded thoughtful. "She's used to him. He's familiar with her. He'll want to start getting up on different horses eventually, but if you'd feel better about it now…"

"You mean that?" Her voice shook.

"Of course I do." A smile was in his voice. "Jennifer will be good for Mark."

"Do you think he'll do okay?" she begged. Oh, boy. She hadn't realized she was more nervous about how he'd do with the Weeks family than she was about him riding an enormous animal that could toss him in any momentary fit of pique then trample him into a bloody pulp. And her plea was an open admission to Gabe that she knew Mark was…different.

What's normal?

"She's a nice girl," he said in that easy way he had. "Mark hung out with her for a good part of a day already."

"Yes, but they were mostly watching what was

going on in the arena. And there's another family going, too. She said something about a boy, but I don't know how old he is."

"Remember, they'll be mostly riding."

She took a deep breath. "Okay. Shall I tell her they have to come by your place to pick up Aurora?"

"No, I'll trailer her over and drop them both off. What time?" She told him, and he said, "I don't hear Mark begging in the background. Doesn't he know about the invitation?"

"No, I took the call, and I wanted to talk to you before I said a word to him."

Another chuckle. "Have you been up to Colville yet? None of the restaurants there are real fancy, but we could keep going after we drop him and have lunch."

Her heart added a few quick beats. Was he suggesting a date? "What," she said, "are you afraid I'll come home and wring my hands if you don't distract me?"

He laughed.

"I'd love to have lunch. Thank you."

"Good." And there was that smile again. She could see it as if he was here in the kitchen with her. "See you in the morning."

Leaving her phone on the counter, she went to the back door. She'd heard Mark go out with the dogs ten minutes or so ago. When she called his name, he appeared around the corner of the house.

When she told him that Jennifer wanted him to go riding with her and her family, Ciara saw something on his face that shook her: vulnerability and…hope?

Oh, God, she thought, Gabe is right. *He does need friends his age. He needs more than I can give him.*

But…why would kids here be any different than the ones in his last school?

Suddenly, she dreaded seeing his face tomorrow afternoon, *after* the outing.

TALKING TO CIARA was easy. Too easy, Gabe had begun to think. There were times he felt like a tractor long abandoned in a field, buried in snow all winter, gears rusting until they locked, only now they were grinding into motion. He kept pulling up memories from so deep, he hadn't known they were there. The only thing he hadn't talked about yet was his wife and daughter. A couple of times he'd used Ginny's name as part of a story, and Ciara obviously knew who he was talking about, but that's as far as he'd gone.

He guessed she must wonder, but she hadn't directly asked about them, for which he was grateful. He kept expecting she would, since she was willing to talk about her ex-husband, but then he noticed something: Ciara never talked about her childhood. When he asked about her parents, he got a terse answer.

Her dad was an investment counselor. Mom? No, she didn't work. No mention of sisters or brothers, which led him to think she didn't have any, but he couldn't be sure. Pushing wasn't his way, although he'd made an exception for Mark, for reasons Gabe still didn't fully understand. The curiosity he felt about Ciara...well, he was afraid he did understand that. It might as well be a flashing red light.

Stop.

But he was beginning to think he wasn't going to.

Over lunch in Colville, she invited him to dinner the following evening, and he said, "That's nice of you, Ciara, but I'm thinking it's time I have you two over to my place instead."

She went very still, and her eyes widened. "You do so much," she said finally. Carefully.

"Is having me to dinner strictly payback?" he asked.

"You know it isn't."

He nodded.

"You're sure?"

She said that a lot. In this case, he knew she wasn't asking the obvious: *Do you really want to cook for us when you've been working all day?* No, she was asking whether he really wanted to let them deeper into his life. Share a home where he never had guests.

"I'm neat," he said, answering indirectly. "I won't have to frantically hide the empty beer cans and pizza boxes."

He loved the tiny dimple that formed in one cheek when she smiled widely. Along with the scattering of pale freckles over her nose, it gave her a puckish look.

"If you had pizza boxes, I'd want to know where they came from. If there's one thing I regret about Goodwater, it's the lack of pizza delivery."

He chuckled. "Maybe we should open a pizza parlor in town. Make our fortune."

Too late he heard himself. *We. Our.*

But she only laughed. "I think you need a slightly larger population than Goodwater has, if it's a fortune you have in mind." And then, smile slowly disappearing, she gazed into his eyes as if searching for something. He had no idea if she found it, but she nodded. "Mark and I would love to come to dinner. If you'd like me to bring a dessert—"

"I would love for you to bring a dessert," he said fervently, making her laugh again.

He professed himself willing to kill the afternoon shopping. He didn't admit that he most often worked seven days a week only because he didn't have anything else to do. He could afford the day off, and many more like it, if he could spend them with her.

When he told her he wanted to buy a Western hat for Mark for his birthday, she helped him guess at size to pick one out at the farm and ranch supply store. They browsed appliances because she thought she was going to have to replace her washer, at least, and maybe dryer, too. Unlike the dishwasher, those Ephraim had used, and although they weren't as ancient as he'd been, they weren't any spring chickens, either.

She peeked at a fabric store but didn't linger, to his relief. They had fun checking out antiques and secondhand stores and then stopped at a coffee shop. Before they finished their cups of coffee, her phone rang. It was Leslie Weeks, letting her know they were fifteen minutes or so out from the trailhead.

He couldn't help noticing that Ciara was really quiet during the drive, her body tense. Gabe finally couldn't help himself.

"Something wrong?"

"Wrong? What would be wrong? I've had a lovely day."

He knew fake when he heard it, but didn't say anything.

After a minute, her shoulders slumped. "I want so much for him to have had a good time. I can tell the minute I see him if somebody has snubbed him or said something mean."

"I've never known Jennifer to be mean, and her parents wouldn't allow it if she was."

"There's the other family."

He knew them, too. "Haven't seen the Saunders boy as much as I have Jennifer, but he's only ten or eleven. He'll probably be in awe of a kid Mark's age."

"You think?" she said doubtfully.

He did. It hadn't occurred to him before, but Mark might do well spending time with kids who were a little younger. There wouldn't be any of the boy/girl dynamics, for one thing.

"Having horses in common will be a big help. It's not like at his old school, where his interests weren't the same as the other boys'."

"That's true." But the doubt was still there, and her hands were clasped tightly in her lap.

He laid a hand over hers. For a moment she froze, and he started to withdraw his hand, then she grabbed hold as if he were a lifeline. At least this way she wasn't strangling the blood flow from her own hands, he thought philosophically.

And…he liked holding hands with her. Hers were so smooth and delicate compared to his. Not entirely free of scars—he'd noticed a few burns on her fingers, which she said were from being careless with the iron. And once the sewing machine needle had stabbed right through one of her fingers, missing the bone, fortunately. He had nodded his understanding. Whatever your tools, you couldn't let your mind wander when you were using them.

He had to retrieve his hand to pull into the packed dirt parking area. "Looks like our timing is perfect," he noted. A string of riders was heading down a long slope toward them, and he recognized the Weeks girl's palomino before he could make out faces.

The kids were all in the middle of the group, he saw with approval, the adults, experienced riders all, sandwiching them in. The Saunderses were out in front, Leslie and John Weeks bringing up the rear. He and Ciara got out and walked past the Weekses' pickup and trailer. As the riders came within earshot, Gabe's hello was enthusiastically returned.

When he saw Mark grinning and waving, he relaxed a little himself.

"See?" he murmured to Ciara. "Who can be sour when they're on horseback?"

Her own relief was in her laugh. "The Old West is better known for violence than it is for goodwill between all, and they were mostly on horseback, weren't they?"

"Then a horse was just a form of transportation. Now…" He didn't quite know how to articulate the pleasure he took in sitting astride one of his two quarter horses.

"You're right." She reached out suddenly and squeezed his arm. "Thank you, Gabe."

He frowned. "Nothing to thank me for. You came for a new start. That's what Mark's grabbing on to."

He felt her scrutinizing him but didn't let himself meet her eyes. Gratitude wasn't what he wanted from her.

Not that he knew what he *did* want. He might decide on nothing but a neighborly relationship, he told himself and then grimaced at the untruth.

As the group emerged from the trail, horses and riders milled around, raising dust.

The Saunders family rode past Gabe and Ciara, offering friendly greetings. Even the boy grinned. Over her shoulder, Wendy Saunders asked, "You going to make it to the quilt group?"

"You talking to me?" Gabe said with a grin.

They all laughed.

"Yes, I think so," Ciara said. "It'll be fun to meet everyone."

"Quilt group?" he asked in an undertone.

"Oh, everyone shows off what they're working on. They make crib quilts for babies in foster homes, too."

"And they gossip."

She smiled. "Best part."

Mark beamed as he reined Aurora to a stop in front of them. "That was fun! I bet I'm going to be really sore tomorrow, huh? Aurora was awesome! She did everything I told her to do. We cantered and trotted and scrambled up and down steep places and—"

Sweat was drying on his mare's strong brown neck and shoulders. They'd have walked the last distance to be sure the horses were cooled off before they had to stand in trailers for the trip home.

Gabe cut into Mark's long, hyper recitation of everything they'd done. "You're the rider," he said. "What're you going to do next?"

"Unsaddle her," Mark said promptly.

Gabe nodded in satisfaction. "Good."

Of course Mark kept talking while he unbuckled the girth and slid the heavy Western saddle off. For a minute Gabe thought the weight would bring him down, and he grabbed the horn to bear some of it, but Mark straightened.

"I can do it. My legs are just wobbly. I've never ridden anywhere near that long," he marveled.

"Mom says we can go again in a couple of weeks," Jennifer called from where she was sliding the saddle pad off her own mare. "You'll come, too, won't you?"

"Sure," he said confidently, before his gaze slid sidelong. "I mean, if it's okay with Mom. And..." He hesitated.

Gabe nodded at Ciara, who said, "Of course you can."

She looked almost dazed, he realized. She really had expected the worst. He wanted to tell her the worst would never happen to her son again, but couldn't. When he was growing up, Goodwater had had its share of cruel kids, but he had a suspicion there was less of it in such a small community. Parents heard really quickly if their kid had been a shit. And, in general, around here people were decent to their neighbors whether they liked them or not. As he aged, Ephraim had done his damnedest to alienate most people, but Gabe hadn't been the only one to bring him meals, do repairs on the place, give him rides to appointments. Gabe did believe Mark would be treated with more kindness here in Goodwater than he would have been in a huge, urban school.

His jaw squared. By God, he'd be talking to some parents himself if it came down to it.

Frowning a little at the strength of his reaction, he watched Mark lead Aurora up the ramp into the trailer and loosely tie her. He liked the way the boy's hand slid along the horse's back and down the slope of her rump as he came back out. There was assurance in that touch, and affection, too, telling Gabe he'd been right to trust Mark with his horse.

He slapped the boy on the back then helped

him slide the ramp into place and close the double doors.

"Time to get on home."

He wished he'd be going to the Malloys' for dinner, but thought it was just as well he wouldn't. Spending too much time with them, he'd take to imagining too much.

CIARA HOVERED IN the kitchen. "Are you sure I can't do anything to help?"

Tenderizing steaks, Gabe shook his head. "You brought dessert. Wander around if you want."

"I'm afraid Mark already is," she said ruefully.

He shrugged. "He's been in the house before."

She hadn't thought about the fact that, when Mark stayed for lunch, the two of them must have come into the house. "Oh. Okay," she said, feeling awkward because she wanted so much to poke her nose in every room and...well, *be* nosy.

Gabe's farmhouse was as basic as the old Walker place she'd bought, but larger and in better repair. She'd been surprised to see what had to be original kitchen cabinets, dating as far back as the 1940s, at a guess. The countertop was equally ancient, edged with metal. Somebody had updated the appliances, but otherwise...she was willing to bet this kitchen hadn't changed since he'd been a boy, waiting for his mother to put dinner on the table. Hadn't his wife wanted to put her stamp on the house? Hadn't *he* wanted to build beautiful cabinets for his own house?

She had no idea where Mark was, but she decided not to worry about it and stepped into a living room as dated as the kitchen. The walls were papered in gloomy stripes of tan and dark green. The wood floors gleamed; probably Gabe hadn't been able to stand seeing good wood go uncared for. A massive sofa looked like it might have belonged to his grandparents. Heck, he probably headed straight for the single recliner that faced an aging television set.

It was the framed photos on the fireplace mantel that drew her, although she almost tiptoed as she approached. He'd given her permission to look—in fact, wasn't that what his invitation, followed by a suggestion that she wander, was really about?—but the minute she saw the woman and little girl in the photos, Ciara felt as if she was intruding anyway.

His wife had been…maybe not beautiful, but pretty. Petite, fine-boned, with a chin that was just a little pointed and fine, pale blond hair cropped short. From the way the woman's smile glowed, Ciara had to guess it had been Gabe behind the camera. That smile made Ciara's heart cramp with pity and sadness for the quiet, guarded man she knew.

She felt even more reluctance when she turned her gaze to several pictures that included his daughter. The first looked as if he'd taken it when he and his wife were bringing their new baby home from the hospital. His wife—Ginny—looked so happy. In another, Ginny had probably been the photographer. He was holding a blonde, laughing toddler high above him, and was laughing himself. It was hard for Ciara to look away from that one. His face was so open—and beardless.

He wasn't hiding, not then.

For a moment she studied his face, like the Gabe she knew and yet not. That face was angular and very male. But the laugh displayed creases in his cheeks she hadn't known were there.

With some reluctance, she transferred her gaze to his daughter, who was darling. She might have been three or four in what looked like a studio portrait. Dressed in green velvet trimmed with lace, she looked like a tiny elf, taking after her mother with that pointy chin and blond hair captured in a side ponytail and carefully curled. Ciara knew how much she must have loved to twirl with that full skirt and shiny, patent-leather shoes.

She heard a footstep behind her.

"My wife and daughter," Gabe said.

She turned to see that he was looking past her, at the row of pictures he couldn't avoid seeing every time he walked into this room.

"They're so beautiful."

"I thought so," he said gruffly. After a moment—

she thought it required an effort from him—he looked at her. "Ginny and Abigail. We called her Abby."

"Audrey told me what happened."

"It was so damn fast." His jaw muscle spasmed. For a moment she thought he wouldn't go on, but then he did. "We'd been to see the touring production of *The Lion King* in Spokane. Abby was singing one of the songs from it. She knew them all from the movie already." A faint, reminiscent smile curved his mouth. "She couldn't carry a tune, but that didn't bother her."

Struggling against tears, Ciara nodded, unsure if he was even seeing her.

"A traffic light turned green. The nearest vehicle on the cross street was a ways off. Plenty of time for the driver to see his light had turned red and stop. Police say he accelerated instead. He was drunk as a skunk. Slammed into Ginny's side of our pickup." He hesitated. "It was an extended cab. Abby was sitting behind Ginny instead of behind me. I'd…left a box of tools on the seat behind me." He turned again to look at the pictures of his family.

Oh, Lord, Ciara thought, seized by pity. As the driver, he'd have felt responsible no matter what, but he must have gone over and over the decision not to take the toolbox out of the truck. If he had, his daughter might have lived.

He couldn't have known. And maybe she'd have decided to sit behind Mommy so she could see Daddy better anyway.

"Abby was—" His throat worked. "Ginny lived in a coma for a few days, but I knew. I wasn't sure she'd want to wake up and find out— But it didn't happen. Next thing I knew, she was gone." Pause. "They were both gone."

"I'm so sorry," Ciara whispered.

"You don't expect—" He kept looking at the photos for a moment and then faced Ciara. "It's been a long time."

"But you must look at them every time you come in here."

"I wanted to hold on to what I could," he said simply. "But time passes. I sit in my chair—" he nodded toward the recliner "—read the paper, turn on the TV, don't always give them a thought."

She wasn't sure she could imagine. If Mark— No, the concept was unimaginable. Except it wasn't, because this man had suffered that loss, the most terrible of all.

"Neither of them knew. They were both happy when it happened. Maybe there are worse ways to go," he said.

"Oh, Gabe," was all she could manage.

He looked fully at her, his forehead creasing. "I didn't mean to make you sad."

"It's you I feel sad for." She wanted quite desperately to put her arms around him. She saw something in his eyes to make her think he wanted the same, so she stepped forward and his arms closed around her, even as she wrapped hers around his torso and laid her cheek against his chest.

They stood there for what felt like a long time. He rubbed his face against her hair. She shed a few tears but let his Western-style shirt soak them up. Eventually, she realized one of the pearl snap buttons was embedding itself in her cheek.

Finally, self-conscious, she stepped back, her gaze flicking guiltily to the mantel, where his wife smiled at the man she had loved.

Gabe followed Ciara's gaze then shook his head at her. He had an odd expression on his face. "It's been a long time," he repeated, his voice so sure she knew what he was telling her.

The thought brought a lump to her throat along with a buoyant sensation of hope.

But…he couldn't mean what he was suggesting, could he? Unless all he wanted was a lover. If he was thinking about having other children…

He won't want them with me, she thought, ice weighing down that hope. *Not if he knew.*

Did he have to find out?

Not if, well, they went on the way they were. Or even if they did become lovers. Maybe she could have that much. He hadn't kissed her again; he'd hardly touched her since the night in the kitchen.

But she knew he wanted her. He couldn't always hide the appreciation and the heated need in his eyes.

"You didn't have a beard," she blurted out.

"No." He lifted a hand to his jaw, rubbed it over his brown whiskers. "I quit shaving then thought, what the hell. Truthfully, though, I'm not sure it isn't more work than shaving is."

But saving work hadn't been the point, she knew.

"I might shave it off one of these days," he said, watching her.

Was he really asking a question? Ciara smiled tremulously at him. "I like you either way."

His eyes warmed. "Good." He kissed her, the merest brush of his mouth against hers, but enough to make her shiver. Then he said, "I came to say the steaks are ready to go on the grill. Mark wants to help."

"Lucky you," she said, her laugh *almost* genuine.

CHAPTER ELEVEN

USUALLY GIVING GRAIN to his horses in the evening was a solitary activity. Not usually. Always. Since Ginny and Abby died, and then he'd only had Aurora. Ginny had been as hesitant about riding as Ciara was, but they agreed that Abby, growing up with horses, would be a natural. She had loved being led around or sitting in front of him clutching the saddle horn, safe within the circle of his arm, when he let Aurora canter. In one of the photo albums, he had pictures of his little girl laughing in delight, begging for him to go faster. *Faster, Daddy!* The voice was barely a whisper now, but he still heard it.

He'd already bred Aurora when the accident happened. Hoodoo had been born only a couple months later. Part of his instant attachment to the gangly colt had to do with knowing how fascinated Abby would have been. They'd talked constantly about what color the foal might be, whether it would be better if it was a colt or a filly, whether eventually she'd ride Aurora or Aurora's son or daughter.

Abby wouldn't understand if he didn't love Hoodoo. Selling him was never an option, even though Gabe didn't need a second horse.

How many times had he had to justify to himself feeding two? Now, it was a good thing he did have both. Mark wasn't far away from getting into more serious riding. Gabe had no idea if Ciara could afford a horse for him.

She was getting more comfortable on horseback, too. He didn't see her taking up cutting, but thought she'd enjoy trail rides. The time might come when they'd need three...

He shook his head as he walked back to the house after seeing them off. He could hear a soft crunching sound coming from around the side of the barn. Mark had happily measured out the grain and fed Aurora and Hoodoo. All three of them had leaned against the fence, even Mark seemingly content with the quiet.

With Ciara to one side, Mark to the other, Gabe had become aware of the strangest sensation. It was as if he'd become hollow, and now life was pouring back into him. It felt damn good at that moment, but these past weeks he'd felt plenty of discomfort, too. Two months ago, he'd told himself he never wanted a close relationship with another human being again. Now he knew he couldn't help himself. It wasn't a matter of coolly weighing risks versus benefits. His heart seemed to be opening despite himself.

After locking the back door for the night, he went straight through to the living room, wanting to see his wife's and daughter's faces again. Earlier, with Ciara, he'd been stunned by the truth of what he said to her: *It's been a long time.*

Another thing he'd have told anyone a few months ago was that the wound was as raw and open as it had been the day he buried the only two people he loved. He guessed he'd known on some level that wasn't true. When he'd heard himself inviting Ciara to dinner, he understood that he was ready to tell her about them. But not until he'd stood there beside her, seeing her expression and the familiar photos on the mantel, had he realized how much time had healed.

She was alive and vivid. What he felt when he looked at the photos had become muted. Softened into sadness instead of tearing grief. Gentle affection. Memories. The ability to smile at the happy ones, like Abby singing joyfully if tunelessly. The glance he and Ginny had exchanged just before—

His throat tightened. Oh, the grief was still there. Still sharp on occasion, but not the same. He had looked at their pictures, looked at the woman beside him who carried wounds of her own, and known he was ready to try again.

Something he wasn't sure would have happened if those two hadn't moved in next door. If Mark wasn't such an odd duck, so impossible to rebuff.

If Ciara didn't have this need to balance the scales, or maybe just a need to feed people.

If she wasn't such a good cook.

He chuckled, low in his throat. He picked up one of the framed pictures, this one of Ginny beside Abby at three or four years old, both sitting on the fence with Aurora grazing in the background. He gently touched each of their faces with his callused fingertip, then carefully set it back in place.

He wondered if the day might come when he'd want to display other photographs on the mantel. Put some of these away in albums.

For the first time in five years, he thought it was possible.

CIARA JUMPED WHEN she heard the doorbell ring, even though she'd been expecting it. She'd invited him, for Pete's sake! She hadn't seen him in three days, since dinner at his house, and she'd been really looking forward to tonight, even before the change in plans that had her ridiculously nervous.

She made herself take a few slow, deep breaths before she went to let Gabe in, frustrating Watson, who was barking frantically and spinning in circles in front of the door.

I should have called. Not...not set Gabe up like this.

It wasn't like that.

They could have dinner, if he offered to help

clear the table she'd let him, then he'd say good-night and go. Same as always.

Unless…

She gulped again and opened the door, letting Watson shoot past her. All he wanted was to greet Gabe, who immediately reached down to stroke his head and tug at his ears.

He looked so good, wearing his usual jeans, boots and a long-sleeved, dark blue T-shirt. His gray eyes were friendly, a contrast to the first time she'd met him when she and Mark stopped by to introduce themselves. Was it possible he'd trimmed his beard? she wondered. She would swear she could see the bone structure better than before, the hollows beneath his cheekbones. Or maybe it was only because she had seen the picture and now knew what he looked like beneath that close-cropped beard.

"Where's the rest of the greeting committee?" he asked.

Moment of truth. "It's just us this evening." She tried for light, almost amused. "I almost called, but…we both have to eat."

His expression shifted. "Mark's not home?"

The very quality of the air she breathed changed. "Believe it or not, he's with the Weekses again. Seems he has a new best friend." His first best friend? She didn't want to admit that. "Jennifer didn't have any homework. Heck, with the school year so close to over, teachers probably aren't bothering to assign any. So, even though it's a school night, Leslie let her rent *The Lone Ranger*. She picked up pizza in Colville and they're going to have ice cream and unlimited soda."

His mouth quirked even as he stepped inside. "They're ready to party."

"Apparently. Except...*The Lone Ranger*?"

"I don't see many movies." He sounded apologetic.

"I do because of Mark, but we skipped that one. The reviews were pretty awful."

"Might be just right for an eleven-year-old and a twelve-year-old."

"Is that how old she is?" What a relief, to have something so normal to talk about. "I hadn't thought to ask."

"I think so." He sounded doubtful. "Could be twelve, too, I guess."

"You don't think—?" She was horrified, although she knew she shouldn't be.

His smile deepened. She would swear she could see the crease in his cheek along with crinkles beside his eyes. "I don't think so, Ciara. She still strikes me as pretty childish."

"Mark, too." Except she realized she wasn't positive. Mark would be thirteen in only a few weeks. Girls were definitely boy crazy by then. The way she remembered it, seventh-grade boys weren't all that interested in girls, but were getting more so by eighth grade.

But there was no way Mark was going to be suave with the girls. What kind of girl would ever be interested in *him*? Not that there was anything wrong with him. He just wasn't…

Ciara gave up, aware of Gabe's gaze resting on her face. She imagined he was reading her mind. She often had the suspicion he could.

"Come on back to the kitchen."

Conversation remained general as she dished up a chicken in wine sauce flavored by marjoram that Mark didn't like very well. She had impulsively decided to cook it as soon as he hung up the phone and said eagerly, "Can you drive me over there right now, Mom?"

Gabe told her about an enormous table he was crafting out of cherry and inlaid with some other woods for a wealthy man in Coeur d'Alene. She talked about a couple of recent projects. She was making several pillows for a woman who had been a Peace Corps volunteer in West Africa twenty years ago. She'd brought back some distinctive fabrics and never done anything with them. After stumbling on Ciara's website, she'd sent them to her to design and sew pillows.

"She said she made one herself, but it was awful, and she wanted something classy. It's fun. The fabrics are amazing. These will be a different look for me. I'm thinking I might see if I can find similar imported fabrics to use for the pillows I sell through boutiques."

"It's like my furniture making," he said with a nod.

"Yes, except—" Was it bad to ask? "You didn't seem to have anything in your house you've made."

Gabe took his time about answering. He helped himself to more brown rice and then chicken. "I actually do have a couple pieces," he said. "A rocking chair. And there's a dresser in my bedroom." He didn't say where the rocking chair was. In his daughter's room? "But you're right. I meant to replace the kitchen cabinets first. Put it off because the commissions kept coming and then—" He shrugged. Didn't have to finish. "Not a lot of reason to change anything, I guess."

Ciara nodded. There was comfort in the familiar. It would be painful to build the cabinets he knew his wife had wanted, and painful in another way to leave those plans behind and do something different.

"I wish I could afford you," she said ruefully. "I'll bet your customers don't have to brace their feet to yank open their silverware drawers."

She loved the way his eyes smiled before his mouth did.

"I do try to prevent that." His voice became a little huskier. "I can give you the good neighbor discount."

"Ten percent?" she joked.

"Closer to eighty." He sounded serious.

"I couldn't let you do that," she said, shocked.

"Sure you could. But I don't suppose it's at the top of your remodeling list."

She followed his gaze to her very old-fashioned kitchen with inadequate storage and counter space, then sighed. "No. I think the bathrooms might come first. And getting the floors refinished before the wood is too damaged."

They talked about that a little, but she began to wonder if he was as distracted as she was. She didn't have much appetite. Most nights Gabe would take a third helping when she offered, but tonight he shook his head. She couldn't quite tell what he was thinking, but he was definitely thinking hard.

About her?

She pushed away from the table and leaped up. "Dessert?" she said brightly. Oh, didn't she sound like the perfect hostess? "Lemon meringue pie."

"Why don't we wait for a bit," he suggested. The husky undertone was there again. Very slowly, he rose to his feet, too. "I'd sure like to kiss you again."

His directness got to her as flirting wouldn't have. Her breath froze in her lungs. She gripped the back of her chair, not sure if her knees would otherwise have held her up. "Yes," she whispered, knowing this was what she'd wanted, why she hadn't called to suggest he come tomorrow night instead.

In two steps, he closed the distance between them. With one big hand, he lifted her chin. His eyes were stormy, intense.

"You're so beautiful."

Any other time, she'd have argued. Said, *Don't pretend. Of course I'm not.* But…she really believed he did think so. There'd been electricity between them almost from the first. She remembered thinking he wasn't anywhere near as handsome as Jeff, then the next second realizing how little that mattered. He was pure male. He didn't need to put on the charm for her to find him compelling.

She reached up and laid her hand against his jaw and cheek. The scratchy/soft texture of his beard against her palm was unbearably sensual. Her skin tingled as she imagined him rubbing his face against her breasts. She had a bad feeling her nipples were already tightening.

Gabe made a ragged sound and bent his head. Just like the last time, she met his mouth with need she didn't even try to disguise. The kiss was almost instantly explosive.

Even so, Gabe was still careful. Almost gentle. His tongue stroked, but it didn't stab. The sensation of being savored was astonishingly seductive.

She teased him with her tongue and the edges of her teeth, reveling in his shudders of reaction, the way the muscles in his shoulders bunched, the involuntary sounds he made. A few slipped from between her lips, too, when he kissed his way across her cheek to nip her earlobe and then explore the sensitive skin behind it.

The feel of his mouth along with the soft brush of his beard on her neck had her shivering, letting her head fall back. One big hand enclosed her breast and gently squeezed and rubbed. Her knees became rubbery.

"Gabe. Gabe."

He groaned and lifted his head. Dark color ran across his cheeks above his beard. "I want you, Ciara."

"Yes. Please," she added.

The assessing look he cast toward the counter shocked and intrigued her, but she'd left everything from crusted pans to spice jars scattered all over it. There wasn't *room* for... Well. She'd never done anything like that, but she couldn't help imagining him standing in front of her, her legs locked around his hips...

His gaze went back to hers. "Upstairs?" he asked hoarsely.

She nodded, grabbed his hand and led him.

Through the swinging door, Watson greeted them with delight. Even Daisy heaved herself to her feet. Ciara ignored both. She didn't look at Gabe as they mounted the stairs, but didn't let go, either.

Don't chicken out. Then, *Don't let him change his mind.*

He was so close behind her, she could feel the heat of his strong body as they entered her bedroom. He closed the door firmly before the dog could follow them.

The room wasn't very big; none of the bedrooms in a house of this era were. She had only a double bed, which wasn't really large enough for him. He didn't even look toward it. His eyes, molten and intense, never left her face.

"I want to see you." He pulled her shirt up, and she lifted her arms so he could pull it over her head. He looked his fill. "Pretty," he said hoarsely, his hands wrapping almost all the way around her waist, sliding upward and then cupping both of her satin-clad breasts. Shivers racked her. It wasn't long before he unhooked the front closure and groaned.

He picked her up as if she weighed nothing and laid her down on the bed. She heard one clunk followed by another as her clogs dropped to the floor. Gabe flattened his hands to each side of her, and his mouth closed over one breast.

The feeling was indescribable. Wet, warm, a tug that was both gentle and insistent. The sensual whisper of his beard. She arched to meet him and knotted her fingers in his unruly brown hair.

His tongue circled her exquisitely sensitized nipple, and then he moved to the other breast as small cries broke from her.

When he lifted his head at last, his eyes were ablaze. She yanked at his T-shirt, desperate to see and touch his bare chest.

The V of hair on his chest was the same shade as his beard. No red, no hint of blond. Plain brown, on a man she'd have said wasn't showy, until now when she saw the flex of powerful muscles. They quivered as she greedily ran her hands over his body, from his taut stomach to his bulky shoulders. He watched her as she explored him, but she saw the moment he broke.

"Ciara." The way he said her name had always shaken her, and never more than now.

The hands that lifted her hips so he could pull down her jeans had a tremor. She reached at the same time to unzip his jeans, but he'd backed too far away as he skinned the denim down her legs and over her feet, taking her socks with them. He paused to knead her feet until her toes curled, and she moaned.

Then he finished stripping himself, taking a small packet from his pocket before he discarded his pants.

"Can I—?"

His gaze flashed to her, and he shook his head. "Better not. It's been a long time for me."

The sight of those steady, competent hands shaking got to her almost as much as seeing the size and urgency of his erection. She was ready, so ready, when he came back down to her, his body pressing her into the mattress, his mouth closing over hers with stark need.

They kissed and touched, rolling once so she was astride him then over again. This time he was between her legs, and he pushed forward. Somehow, he was still being careful of her, giving her body time to adjust to an intrusion that felt new, even as she wanted it so much, holding some of his weight on his elbows. She flattened her feet on the bed and lifted her hips to draw him deeper, harder. Only then did he let go and begin to thrust.

Her fingers dug into his back as she tried to pull him closer, to hold on for a ride of astonishing gentleness and power and need like nothing she'd experienced before. She lost the rhythm, squirmed and fought. At some point he reached down and gripped her hip, pacing her movements, until the rising flood swept her away in a cataclysm of pleasure.

He drove harder, deeper, taking her through the pleasure and out the other side. And then his body went rigid above her, and he made a guttural sound that might have been her name. Ciara held on to him with everything she had, wanting never to let go or start thinking again, instead of *feeling*.

He came down with most of his weight to one side, but he held on tight to her, too.

OH, DAMN, WAS ALL he could think. It couldn't have been as good as it seemed. Guilt niggled. Of course it wasn't. He'd loved his wife. Making love with her had been everything he'd wanted. Satisfying.

It had been a long time, that was all.

He hadn't felt guilty other times he'd had sex since Ginny died. All he'd been doing was scratching an itch. She'd have understood. But this—

Face buried in Ciara's wealth of red-brown hair, he listened for his wife's voice, and then gradually relaxed as he knew again. It had been a long time. She'd want him to be happy.

I am, he realized. More completely at this moment than he had been in five long, empty years.

He rolled onto his back, tilting his head to see Ciara's face as he smoothed her hair back from it. "Bubinga," he murmured.

"What?" She tried to lift her head from his shoulder and apparently failed, a weakness he found amazingly satisfying.

"Bubinga," he repeated. "It's a hardwood from West Africa. The first time I met you, that's what I thought. Your hair is the color of bubinga. Beautiful."

"Oh." She laid a hand on his chest, her fingers flexing into the mat of hair there. The curve of her cheek told him she was smiling. "You didn't look like you thought I was beautiful. I was sure you thought I was annoying."

"Uh…that crossed my mind, too," he admitted, feeling amusement at how far he'd come. "I liked having Ephraim's house empty. Quiet, instead of kids, dogs, noise, people who wanted to be too friendly…" He moved his shoulders.

"And then Mark and I showed up."

"Yep." He lifted his head so he could really see her. "Took me a few weeks to know how glad I was you had."

"Really?" Her expression vulnerable, she searched his face. "Do you mean that?"

"Do you doubt it?"

She looked deep. Finally, she shook her head, her smile tremulous. "You do like my cooking."

He laughed. "And a few other things." His hand squeezed her butt.

Ciara wriggled. "Mark would be shocked." But she didn't sound too concerned about that.

"Is he thinking about sex yet?"

"If he is, I haven't noticed."

"No."

She rubbed her cheek against him, raising goose bumps of pleasure. He stroked her hair the way he did fine woods, savoring the texture, and loving that he *could* touch her.

"Did you ever think we'd end up, well, *here*?" she asked suddenly.

"In bed?"

Her head bobbed.

"Part of me wanted to from the beginning."

She giggled. He guessed she could probably see the part of him that had been enthusiastic from the get-go and was already stirring.

"In my head, though..." He wasn't sure whether he was actually talking about his head or his heart, but guessed it didn't matter. "I'd decided never again."

"Really?" Sounding surprised, she wriggled again so she could see his face.

He knew his smile was rueful. "What was I supposed to do? Go to singles bars in Spokane? Here in Goodwater..." He shrugged. "Women have expectations. Not the same as mine."

He couldn't tell what she was thinking. She sounded merely curious when she asked, "You think I'm an urban woman who won't have any?"

She had to be insulted. Didn't she?

"I guess I'm starting to have my own," he said simply.

"About...*me*?" The *me* came out as a squeak.

He chuckled. "Who else is here?"

She tucked her head back down so he couldn't see her face. She was quiet for a long time. Gabe only waited, feeling her tension, not understanding it. Bracing himself for something unwelcome.

"Can we…take this slowly?" she said at last. "I swore—"

"I did, too," he admitted.

"I didn't expect *you*."

At that moment, hearing her bemusement, he relaxed. He smiled a little, thinking it would be all right. She'd been burned by her divorce, but she'd get past it. She'd been as miserable as he had been after that fight. What's more, she wanted what was good for Mark, and Gabe knew he was. He'd have been offended if she'd decided to hook up with him for that reason, but her face was expressive, betraying more of what she felt than he suspected she'd like. Plus, he couldn't mistake her response to him tonight. In fact…

He let his hand stroke lower, down the delicate chain of vertebrae to the point where her hips flared. Her quick shiver encouraged him. With his other hand, he tugged at her hair until she lifted her face to him. Their mouths met in a slow, sweet kiss that gradually heated.

"How long do we have?" he mumbled.

She looked blank for long enough to gratify his ego. Then remembrance that she had a son spread across her face. "Oh!" She turned her head until she saw the bedside clock. "Um…I don't have to pick him up until nine-thirty."

He calculated. "An hour." He gently squeezed her nape. "Plenty of time."

"Plenty," she whispered, and kissed him.

IF THIS WASN'T June and they weren't in the last couple weeks of the school year, Ciara might have been desperate enough to enroll Mark in the Goodwater Middle School. She knew she didn't really mean that, but…how else were she and Gabe ever going to have any real privacy?

If her son wasn't with her, he was with Gabe.

When the next weekend came and Gabe invited her on another shopping expedition to Spokane, she crossed her fingers before asking Mark. Not that they could exactly pull off onto a deserted road and count on no one coming by, but—a motel room by the hour was sounding better and better. When Mark said, "Can we go out to lunch, too?" she almost groaned.

From Gabe's expression when he came to pick her up and they both popped out the front door, she suspected he'd been having similar thoughts. Stealing kisses on the porch at night wasn't enough.

This time, they did Costco again and then, after lunch, The Home Depot, before starting home with the bed of Gabe's pickup packed with a surprising number of purchases.

Before they reached her driveway, Gabe suddenly put on his turn signal. "You haven't met the Ohlers yet, have you?"

"No, but…"

He turned up a driveway she'd noted. "They have two kids. Horses, too."

"Really?" Mark hung eagerly forward between the seats.

"Might be good to get to know them."

She had caught only a glimpse of this house, the same era as hers and Gabe's, and also painted white, but shielded from the roads by a stand of evergreen trees. Their pasture was behind the house, sloping toward another loop of the shallow creek.

A skinny, gaping kid accompanied by two dogs appeared before they had even rolled to a stop. Gabe set the brake. "Let me introduce you."

Mrs. Ohler came out the front door, drying her hands on a dish towel, but beaming when she saw Gabe. She was a wiry, tiny woman with curly dark hair bundled at the back of her head and bright dark eyes.

"Well, who have we here?" she asked, clearly friendly. Once Gabe performed introductions, she apologized for not having come over to welcome them. "Truth is," she said, "Mason put his back out, and it's been all I could do to keep up with the store and the kids."

She and her husband, she explained, owned the

sporting-goods store in town, which Ciara had yet to enter. Mason had been lifting their older son to dunk a basketball when he'd herniated a disk. She shook her head in exasperation and obvious fondness at the same time.

Gabe chided her for not letting him know. "I could have mowed your lawn or taken care of the animals for you."

She smiled at him. "That's what I have two boys for. In fact, my oldest is back feeding the horses right now."

It was the magic word.

Mark's expression lit. "Can I see the horses?"

"Can he, Mama?" asked the younger boy, Will, who she'd said was seven.

"Of course he can."

The two boys took off around behind the house. After watching them go, she grimaced. "As you might have guessed, I'm expecting another. Just got over the morning-sick phase."

Ciara had wondered. The swelling wouldn't have been as obvious on a woman with more generous proportions, but Sabine Ohler didn't look big enough to carry a baby to term.

Appearing mildly alarmed, Gabe decided to follow the boys, leaving the two women to talk pregnancy and childbirth. Yes, Sabine said, she'd been half hoping for a girl this time, but she'd had an ultrasound, and, plain as day, this would be another boy.

"Do you plan to keep trying...?" Ciara asked delicately, and the other woman snorted.

"Wasn't trying this time. This is an oops baby. Not that I'm letting any of the kids hear me say that."

Ciara nodded her understanding.

Mason, Sabine finally said, had returned to work just last week, but wearing a back brace. He'd had some injections, and the doctors were hoping not to have to do surgery.

"Never rains but it pours," she complained, but good-humoredly.

The two women wandered back to the barn and pasture, too, where she introduced her oldest boy, Jacob. Jacob was only nine, but he and Mark were chattering away.

Even Ciara could tell the Ohlers' two horses were nowhere near the quality of Gabe's. But unless he'd already blurted out something tactless, Mark was making only admiring sounds. Jacob asked if Mark could come and ride with him, and his mother said friends were always welcome.

"Mason or I keep a good eye on them when they're on the horses," she said as an aside to Ciara. "They're placid as can be anyway. Ours will be like rocking horses compared to either of Gabe's."

"Can I, Mom?" Mark begged.

Gabe caught Ciara's eye and nodded with a faint smile. An intent gleam, too, that told her he'd set this meeting up for a good reason.

Excitement quivered in her belly as she agreed that she was sure Mark would enjoy that.

Monday after school, they agreed, since the Ohlers would be tied up with grandparents tomorrow. Sabine would be home to supervise since Mason was back at work. Once Ciara heard the school bus go by, she could send Mark on down. She seemed to take it for granted that Ciara would let him ride his bike on their deserted country road.

She expressed some surprise that Mark wasn't already enrolled at Goodwater Middle School, but obviously assumed he would be come fall. Ciara didn't correct her.

They departed on a wave of good feelings and expectations. Ciara had no doubt they'd made more friends. Once more, thanks to Gabe. She didn't let herself acknowledge the tiny flicker of resentment that accompanied the gratitude.

The two boys didn't really know Mark yet, but they seemed to like him. Horses made all the difference, she was starting to believe. Mark chattered the rest of the way home about Jacob and Will and how they'd said their bay was half Morgan and did Gabe think he really was?

Only as Gabe helped them unload and carry their purchases in did he and she exchange a look.

A promise.

Three o'clock the day after tomorrow?

Yes.

CHAPTER TWELVE

"Can Watson go with me?" Mark yelled up the stairs.

Ciara had her cell phone in her hand. She'd been standing by the window, waiting to see Mark pedaling down the driveway. "Well…" She set down the phone and went out into the hall, where she could see her son poised at the bottom of the staircase. "The Ohlers' dogs might not like him. What if there's a fight?"

"I asked. Jacob says they like other dogs."

"Call back. Ask Jacob's mother."

"Mo-om!" he protested, but disappeared into the kitchen. She almost slipped back into her workroom to phone Gabe, but refrained. Instead, she assumed a pose of complete relaxation, propping a shoulder against the wall.

The kitchen door banged as it swung back and forth. Jittering with impatience, Mark reappeared. "Mrs. Ohler says fine."

"Then fine. But take the leash just in case—"

He and Watson raced out, Ciara calling after him, "Watch him on the road—"

Slam. They were gone.

Pulse jumping, she hurried back into her work-room, where she could see her son tearing down the driveway on his bike, his dog loping beside him. Such a normal sight, she thought with a funny squeeze, before she remembered and snatched up the phone.

To her relief, Gabe answered right away.

"Mark just went to the Ohlers'."

"On his bike?" When she assented, he said, "Why don't you come down here? That way he can't surprise us."

"On my way."

This was downright pathetic, she thought, as she detoured to the bathroom to brush her teeth and stare anxiously at herself in the mirror. No makeup, her hair could use something—but the clock was ticking. And Gabe would be mussing up her hair the minute he got his hands on her anyway.

As she drove the short distance, she couldn't de-cide whether there was an illicit thrill in sneaking around to have amazing, fabulous sex, or whether she should be ashamed of herself.

Not that there was a choice. Of course she had to sneak around! She was the single mother of a twelve-year-old boy. She'd had a few clumsy talks about puberty and sexuality with Mark, but she wasn't about to let him know she was having extramarital sex, and with their neighbor, who happened to be his idol, besides.

Gabe was outside when she pulled up in front of his barn. He hustled her into his house and upstairs so fast, she was breathless and laughing when they got there.

This was her third visit there. In the two weeks since the first time they'd made love, Mark had once gone to the Weekses', and once to ride horses with the Ohler brothers. Unfortunately, he wasn't likely to stay at the Ohlers' more than a couple of hours, tops. And she didn't want him to come home and not find her there.

She'd speculated before about the bedroom, which was really cramped, even though all that was in it was Gabe's big bed and a truly gorgeous chest of drawers with contrasting woods in an Arts-and-Crafts style. No rocking chair. No room for a rocking chair.

No time to think about it today. Gabe stripped her with record speed, and her own urgency was such that she was ready for him before he shed his own clothes and donned the condom. He hardly had to touch her or kiss her before her body was on fire for his possession.

This time she pushed him back and slung her leg over him. Face flushed and intent, he watched her even as his hands engulfed her breasts and rubbed and squeezed and stroked. She teased him with her body until she couldn't stand it any longer and changed the angle, pressing herself down on him, groaning as he filled her.

At first she tried to go too fast, but Gabe's body helped her set a pace that had them rocking, him groaning…and her coming with record speed. As usual, her orgasm triggered his. He gripped her hips hard. She loved the feel of his muscles locking as he drove himself into her harder, deeper, even as he swelled and pulsed inside her.

This time, she was the one to collapse slowly on top of him, feeling boneless, sated and happy. Yes, *happy*, like she could never remember being before.

Gabe's powerful arms closed around her, and he nuzzled her forehead, his lips soft, his nose bumping her. Listening to the hard tattoo of his heartbeat, loving the soft, springy feel of his chest hair beneath her cheek, Ciara smiled.

He mumbled something.

"Hmm?" It was too much effort to formulate a word.

"I said," his voice was husky, a little slurred, "is this slow enough for you?"

Her forehead creased. What? "Slow? That wasn't exactly slow."

"You wanted to take it slowly." She could feel his lips moving against her temple. "That's what you said."

Oh. That kind of slow.

She mulled over what he'd said, and, more, some underlying tension in his tone.

Carefully, she separated herself from him so that she could push herself up enough to see his face. She was suddenly conscious of her nakedness in an entirely different way than she had been.

"You don't like it."

"I like everything about you, Ciara. Except I'm starting to wonder whether this is all you want." There were troubled lines on his forehead. "Sneaking over here in stolen moments. Pretending the rest of the time that we're nothing but friendly neighbors."

She grabbed a pillow and clutched it in front of her. "What do you suggest? I say, 'Hey, Mark, I'm running down to Gabe's for some sex?'"

"You know that's not what I'm suggesting." He took her hand in his. "I'd like for us to go out to dinner. To maybe kiss good-night in front of him. To let him know something is happening between us." He went quiet for a minute. "Unless you don't think anything is."

"Of course I do!" she flared. "What do you call this?" A waved hand encompassed the bed, them.

"Sex," he said, his jaw muscles spasming. "Although I thought we were making love."

Her heart pinched. "We are," she whispered. "It's

not like…like I just want a quickie. You don't have to make it sound—"

"I'm sorry." His voice had softened. "I'm pushing you."

"I don't even know what you want."

Those gray eyes took in her face, her doubt, her fears. "I think you do," he said gently. "I told you I had expectations."

She wanted what he was implying. She wanted it so fiercely, she almost doubled over from the pain.

"What's wrong, Ciara?" He was reading her mind. "What aren't you telling me?"

That made her stiffen. "What makes you think I'm hiding something?" she asked sharply.

He didn't say a word. He didn't have to.

"It's only been a few weeks."

Did that sound as weak to him as it did to her?

Yes, she saw in his eyes that it did.

The truth was, she'd been falling in love with him almost from the moment she saw him walking toward her and Mark that first day, big and closed off and unfriendly. When, despite the unfriendliness, he hadn't been able to make himself be unkind to Mark.

Sexy *and* kind. What could be more irresistible than that?

But…he was right. If he knew about Bridget, knew what she, Ciara, carried in her genes, knew her shame, he wouldn't want her anymore. She was the one to search his face now, hunting for hope.

Might not want her anymore, she tried to tell herself.

It was like falling off a cliff. One minute so happy, the next scared. Her pulse seemed to pound in her head, blurring her vision. He wasn't going to let them go on like this, snatching at small pockets of happiness. He was going to insist on the whole shebang…except she couldn't offer that without letting him see the stain on her character. And, oh, she didn't want to. She didn't.

I could tell him a little. It was the cowardice in her that had her begging. *See how he reacts.*

But he wouldn't understand, not unless he met Bridget. Bridget in the abstract was one thing, in the real, disruptive, disturbing *right there* reality, another.

Ciara didn't know which would be worse: Gabe horrified by her sister, repulsed by the possibility that, if they had a child together, he or she might be like her, or Gabe gentle and, yes, kind with Bridget, and stunned to find that Ciara wasn't as good a person as he'd thought her to be.

No, she knew which would be worse—and which was likeliest.

"I need to go home," she said, suddenly frantic. Still trying to hide behind the pillow, she scooted off the bed and snatched up her jeans and panties from the floor. Her shirt—there. Her bra lay half under the bed.

Gabe sat up. She felt waves of hurt coming from him. She was behaving as if she was afraid of him, and it wasn't that at all. But she had to show him she wasn't, she realized. Or—not physically afraid anyway. Fleeing to the bathroom to get dressed wasn't an option. After a moment, she let the pillow go and bent to step into her panties then her jeans.

Following her example, Gabe dressed, too. All the lines in his face seemed to have deepened. The sight of him, wounded by *her*, made her feel sick to her stomach.

"I'm sorry," she said at last.

Shirt in hand, he looked at her across the bed. "Sorry for what?"

"For freaking like this."

"I was pushy. Maybe I should apologize for that," he said slowly.

"No. You're not the one who should be apologizing. I'm just…" Just what? A coward? *Yes*. "There are things I haven't told you," she admitted.

He stiffened. "You aren't still married, are you?"

"No! I've been divorced since Mark was six. It's…nothing like that." She bent to put on her socks and shoes, hopping in place, wishing he did have that rocking chair in here.

"I need a chair in here," he said, looking around. It had to be obvious to him, too, there was no space.

She'd been tempted to ask before whether all the bedrooms in the house were this small, but hadn't, because she suspected she knew. He'd moved out of the master bedroom after his wife died. She wondered if he kept it as some sort of shrine. It and his daughter's bedroom. The wondering had hurt, so she had blocked it out until this fleeting pang.

"This is fine." She was done anyway. Thank goodness for clogs that didn't have to be laced.

Then they looked at each other across that bed, until the silence had gone on too long.

He was the one to say, "I can be patient, Ciara," although those little lines carving his forehead remained.

That felt like a blow. He was the most patient person she'd ever known. *She* was the one with flaws, deep, ugly ones. The kind that would have him tossing a chunk of wood away. She'd seen him do that, when he discovered the clear grain that showed on the surface didn't go all the way through.

"Can we talk about this another time?" she begged. "I really do need to go home."

"Sure."

He followed her out, but he didn't kiss her goodbye and disappeared inside his workshop even before she started down the driveway. That scared her, but who could blame him? If it had been the other way around—oh, there was no doubt what conclusions she'd have jumped to. *All he wants is sex. I'm handy, but he has no intention of acknowl-edging any kind of relationship in front of other people.* That's what she'd have thought.

She knew what she had to do, but the resolution felt like a huge, horrible bruise. An old one, maybe, with so many shades of color they couldn't be de-scribed. The pain of it was so familiar, she forgot about it for long stretches of time, until she moved wrong. Stretched.

Fell in love.

She'd always believed in peeling off bandages in one quick yank. So she'd just do it.

She would call her mother as soon as she got home.

"GRANDMA AND GRANDAD are coming!" Mark an-nounced as soon as he arrived for his woodworking lesson the morning after the scene that had Gabe on edge. "Did Mom tell you?"

One of those things she didn't want to talk about? Or had she talked to her parents yesterday, sometime after she left Gabe?

"No," he said. "This been in the works?"

"Uh-uh." The boy frowned. "I mean, Mom kept saying we'd have to have them someday, 'cuz they'd want to see our place, but not like she knew when they *were* coming. Aunt Bridget is coming, too," he added, as if the addition were a minor and rela-tively meaningless fact.

Gabe didn't miss the phrasing: we'd *have* to have them. A lot of enthusiasm there.

"Aunt Bridget?" he said. "This your mom's sister?" Not Mark's father's sister, surely.

"Yeah. She's…" Mark didn't often hesitate, but this was an exception. "She's…I don't know. You'll see."

So Ciara did have a sibling. Now, it might be chance she hadn't mentioned her before; maybe they were far apart in age or not close for some other reason. But Ciara's reticence when it came to talking about her family was so notable, Gabe's antenna quivered.

"When's this visit happening?" he asked casually, as he wiped clean a saw blade and put it away to clear a worktable for Mark's project.

Mark looked at him as if he was nuts. "They're coming for my birthday. That's next week, you know. Grandma said it was lucky she hadn't already mailed my presents. They'll be here Tuesday. Grandma said they might stay a whole week, if Aunt Bridget is okay with it."

Gabe translated that to whether Aunt Bridget could get that long off work.

"Now, where were we?" he asked, getting down to business.

"Don't you *remember*?" Mark looked shocked.

A smile tugged at Gabe's mouth. "I remember. I'm checking to see if you do."

"I get to stain my box today." The boy did the hopping from one foot to the other thing, as if standing still was impossible when he was excited. It reminded Gabe of a restive horse prancing. "And then as soon as it's dry, I can put the finish on. So then it'll be done."

"Except for hardware. I'm thinking hinges for sure."

"And a latch. Maybe one with a little lock."

"Good idea. Once you start getting notes from girls, you won't want your mom to be able to read them."

Mark's face scrunched up. "Why would *girls* write me notes?"

"Now, come on. You can't tell me you aren't starting to notice pretty girls."

Watching the way Mark's gaze slid away, Gabe thought, *Aha.* So he was.

"Well, they won't be writing *me*," he mumbled.

"Why not?"

"I don't know any, for one thing. Plus…you know. That stuff we talked about." He didn't have to say the word aloud: *weird.*

"You know Jennifer Weeks," Gabe pointed out. "She's only a year younger than you."

"She's my *friend*," the boy objected. "That's different."

Too often, that was true. Even so, Gabe said mildly, "Doesn't have to be. A girlfriend *should* be a friend." He shook himself. "What say we get to work?"

Staining didn't take long. Almost sorry that Mark had just taken—and aced!—the test to show mastery of seventh-grade work, Gabe asked if he was doing any math on his own.

"A little, but just fun stuff." He smirked. "When I said I might do more this summer, Mom said *she* wasn't doing any schoolwork until September."

"I suspect teachers of all kinds look forward to summer as much as kids do."

Mark's surprise suggested he'd never thought of his teachers as human beings before. Come to think of it, Gabe reflected, that probably hadn't crossed his mind, either, when he was that age.

Gabe didn't have much selection of miniature latches and the like—he built large, not small— but he let Mark look through what he did have and then browse a catalog.

"I was thinking," Mark said, in an ultra-casual voice. "It's almost Mom's birthday, too. Hers is in August."

Interested, Gabe waited.

"So, do I have to quit coming when I'm done with my box?" he asked in a rush. "Or do you think I could make another one? Because then I could give this one to Mom."

The thought was generous, even if it was clear

that, if there was to be only one box, Mark was keeping it.

"You can keep coming," Gabe said without hesitation, although with some bemusement. Not all that long ago, he'd assumed these sessions were of limited duration. Give the kid some basic skills, send him on his way. Now? Now he wanted this relationship to become something else—family— but Ciara's reaction to his hints suggested that possibility was somewhere between unlikely and not happening. "If you make a second box, you can work more unsupervised. Just ask if you don't remember how to do something. Or we can experiment using a different technique."

"Can we do dovetail corners?" Mark asked eagerly. "They're so cool-looking."

They could be shaped in different ways to add a strong decorative element, too. Gabe smiled. "Why not?"

Mark finally hopped on his bike for the ride home after saying with satisfaction, "Then I'll give this box to Mom. It'll be the best birthday present *ever*."

Gabe thought it would be, too.

Quiet settled in the old barn once the boy was gone, leaving Gabe to brood instead of getting back to his own work.

The next move had to come from Ciara. If she cared about him at all, she had to share whatever it was that ate at her, that kept her from talking about her childhood and family. His stomach tightened whenever he tried to imagine what that might be. Her marriage had obviously been no picnic, and the way her ex treated his son made Gabe feel violent in a way foreign to him. But she was willing to talk about all that.

Had she been abused? But if so, he couldn't imagine why she'd invite her parents to stay, or allow them to have a relationship with Mark. She would protect her son from anyone, tooth and nail. And Mark had sounded excited about having his grandparents here. So it couldn't be that simple, that obvious.

He swore out loud. Why wouldn't she trust him enough to tell him? After her initial wariness, she did trust him with her son.

Because she'd assumed the sex would remain casual? Gabe didn't believe it. Wouldn't believe it.

This time the word he said aloud was one he rarely used. Hearing himself, he shook his head. Work had always been his solace. Even in the worst of his grief, he'd been able to lose himself in the care it took to create beautiful cabinetry and furniture. The concentration required allowed him to block out everything else.

He'd done it before. He could do it again.

But the pain that felt like a fist beneath his

breastbone reminded him why he'd never wanted to let anyone into his life again. To *love* anyone.

He'd been stupid enough to do it, and was now suffering the consequences.

"YOU KNOW, THEY won't get here any faster just because you're staring out the window," Ciara pointed out. "A watched pot—"

Her son rolled his eyes. "Never boils. But why aren't they *here*? It shouldn't take them more than five hours, right?"

"Or six. We're north of Spokane."

"But they live in Bellevue," he argued, "so they didn't have to cross the bridge or anything."

"No, but you remember how Aunt Bridget is sometimes. If she got upset…" As an adult, Bridget was mostly calm if she was surrounded by the familiar, if her routine had no deviations. She would agree she wanted to go somewhere and then flip out five minutes after leaving home.

"They wouldn't turn around and go home, would they?"

"They might," Ciara said honestly. She wouldn't even blame them, although growing up she had bitterly resented the fact that whatever Bridget wanted, Bridget got. She'd known on one level that wasn't true, of course, because it wasn't as if her sister was a spoiled brat. She truly couldn't bear any kind of sensory overload. And an upset

Bridget was unbearable. If she threw a screaming fit halfway over Snoqualmie Pass—Mom and Dad would be crazy if they *didn't* turn around and go home. Only— "They would have called," she said, "and they haven't. They're probably just taking their time. They'll have stopped for lunch." And at every rest stop, and every park. Bridget's tolerance for confinement was shaky, too.

Suddenly intent on something outside the window, Mark stiffened like a bird dog that had spotted a quail. "I think that's them, Mom! They're here!" He raced for the front door and tore out, Watson barking and whirling around him. Even Daisy was stirred to rise to her feet and trundle out to see what was happening.

Ciara followed more slowly, apprehension balling in her stomach like a greasy meal that wouldn't digest. She wanted to see her parents; she'd missed them. But…there was so rarely quiet time when she and Mom could just talk, or when they could all, as a family, joke and laugh. Part of her—the petty, childish part of her—thought Bridget sensed when attention wasn't on *her*, and made sure it was.

And Ciara knew that wasn't true, she really did, but so many years of her life had been dominated by a sister whose needs always came first, who was an embarrassment Ciara had kept hidden from friends.

Since Mark had been a toddler, she had *hated*

seeing her sister side by side with Mark, in case—
No, that was ridiculous, of course, but Jeff had said
enough to make her look anxiously for comparisons that didn't exist.

Now she felt as if she didn't really know Bridget
anymore.

An unfamiliar SUV was rolling to a stop in front
of the porch steps that Mark and Gabe had painted
just last week. Dad had told her they'd traded in
their van for a Toyota Highlander. She'd teased him
about going for stylish this time. He drove a Lexus
himself, but only, he always assured her, because
with his job, maintaining an image was important.
The family's second vehicle had always been something roomy and often aging. Buying new furniture
or a new vehicle wasn't done lightly in the Malloy family, not when Bridget was likely to throw
multiple tantrums until she adjusted to the change.

Ciara followed Mark down the steps as the doors
opened. Her father got out on his side, stretched
then grinned and grabbed Mark for a quick, one-
armed hug. After releasing his grandson, he held
out his arms, and Ciara threw herself into them.

She hugged him back, tears burning in her eyes.
"Daddy," she whispered into his chest.

And he said softly, "Ciara girl. You don't know
how much we've missed you."

He gave her another squeeze, which she returned
then stepped back.

Mark, of course, was talking a mile a minute. Her mom was trying to get a word in edgewise, not trip over an excited Watson *and* open the back door to let Bridget out.

"Hi, Aunt Bridget," Mark said. "This is Watson. He's my dog. Mom has her own dog, but she's waiting on the porch 'cuz she's old, and she doesn't go up and down stairs very well. But she'll like it if you pet her. And look! There's horses in the pasture. They're the neighbor's, but we get to ride them. Aurora is the brown one, and Hoodoo is her son. I'll bet you can give them carrots, too, if you want."

Ciara hugged her mother, too, whispering, "Motor mouth," and her mom laughed. And then she faced her sister, who had her arms wrapped tightly and was darting looks around as if she expected small explosives to go off. Which they were, in a manner of speaking, thanks to dog and boy.

Seeing Bridget, Ciara felt a little shock. It was easy to forget how much they looked alike, how obviously related. Her hair, more brown than auburn, was short, because she had no patience for the care longer hair required; she was a couple inches shorter than Ciara and a little plump, but her eyes were the same color, and then there was the shape of her face, even the freckles.

"Hi, Bridget," Ciara said, keeping her voice soft.

"This is my house. I'm glad you could come for a visit."

"This isn't your house. I've been to your house."

"Mark and I moved. We wanted room for dogs and maybe, someday, horses."

"Okay." Bridget looked at her mother. "I want to go home now."

"We're here to stay for a few days, honey. Remember us talking about it? It takes so long to get here, we can't visit and go home the same day."

"I want to go home," she repeated, her voice rising. "Goodbye, Ciara. We have to go home." She had begun to rock.

Ciara braced herself. Bridget would start screaming any minute. Maybe throw herself on the ground. Have to be restrained so she didn't hurt herself.

I can still call Gabe and tell him tonight isn't good, she thought in panic. *Bridget is tired. He'll understand.*

It was hard enough for Bridget to accept new surroundings, never mind to have a stranger sprung on her. One with a beard. The beard might scare her. Tomorrow would be better.

But the coward in Ciara was thinking Bridget might be so upset, tomorrow Mom and Dad would apologize but say they had to take Bridget home, and when Gabe came to dinner it would be just the three of them, like always.

"Come inside and see Ciara's house," Mom said calmly. "Don't you need to use the bathroom?"

Still rocking, Bridget stared at the house. "I do have to use the bathroom."

Whirling by, Watson bumped into Bridget, and she recoiled. "I don't like dogs! You know I don't like dogs, Mom!"

"You do like dogs," Ciara said. "Do you remember Charlie, the golden retriever that used to go for walks with us?"

Charlie had belonged to a neighbor who tried everything from six-foot board fences to a collar that gave an electric shock to keep the dog in his own yard. Eventually, he had to give up. Charlie was such an extrovert, he just wanted to be with people. Whoever barbecued outdoors had a temporary dog. He waited for the school bus with neighborhood kids, went for walks with anyone, looked both ways before crossing streets and lived a long, happy life. Ciara hadn't thought of him in a long time, but maybe Charlie explained why she'd always wanted a dog for Mark.

Bridget crimped her lips and glared at Watson, still racing around and letting out an occasional bark. "I liked Charlie," she agreed grudgingly. "That's not Charlie."

Although Ciara tried to explain, she doubted her sister understood the concept of Watson being young and not very well-behaved yet. Their mother coaxed her into climbing the porch steps, however. She balked at the sight of Daisy, but relaxed when Daisy didn't get up. Her tail thumped as she gazed at the visitors with her milky eyes.

"I like this dog," Bridget declared at last.

Ciara smiled. "Me, too."

Bridget used the downstairs bathroom and then announced again that she wanted to go home. Somehow Mom kept distracting her. Every so often she remembered that she was glad to see Ciara, and she'd say, "Hi, Ciara. Bye, Ciara. We have to go home now."

But she was hungry, and Ciara had been careful to make a meal she knew her sister liked. The last time she remembered Mom trying a new casserole, Bridget had screamed and thrown handfuls of it, making a truly awful mess and burning her hands, besides.

In the kitchen she paced restlessly while Mark set the table and Mom took salad makings from the refrigerator.

"Six places?" her mother murmured.

Ciara knew her cheeks were heating. "I invited our next-door neighbor to dinner, so you could meet him."

"Is this the Gabe we've heard so much about?" Mom said in amusement.

"Motor mouth at it again. Yes, it's the famous Gabe. He's been amazing with Mark."

"I see," her mother said, and Ciara was afraid she really did.

"Bridget," Ciara said, "a friend of Mark's and mine is coming to dinner. He's a nice man. The horses you saw outside are his. His name is Gabe."

Bridget looked alarmed. "I don't have to talk to him, do I?"

"No. He'll understand if you don't want to."

"Besides," Mom pointed out, "who'll have a chance to talk with Mark around?"

Even Bridget said, "That's funny, Mom. He does talk *a lot*."

From beyond the swinging door came her son's voice. "He's here, Mom! I see him coming. I'll go let him in."

Ciara's heart performed some gymnastics beyond her level of conditioning. She yanked open the refrigerator and let the chilled air wash over her as she struggled for calm. *I can do this.*

Only…it might have been better if she'd warned him.

CHAPTER THIRTEEN

WITHOUT REALLY THINKING through why he was doing it, Gabe shaved his beard off the day Ciara's family was expected.

Frowning at himself in the mirror once it was gone, he decided all he'd wanted was to look respectable. Not everyone admired beards. He didn't like the idea of her parents looking at him askance.

Now that it was too late to change his mind, he kept staring at himself, tilting his head this way and that, disconcerted by how unfamiliar this face seemed. Feeling uncomfortably exposed, he rubbed his hand over his chin, even the contours strange to his touch. Was this how he'd looked five years ago, when he first grew the beard?

Not exactly, he was loath to admit. Five years took a toll. Lines that didn't use to be there had formed on his face. Ones that were there had deepened. Damn, he was getting something like crow's feet beside his eyes.

And now his face and neck felt cold.

He should have done it a couple days ago, he thought uneasily, let Mark, at least, see him in advance of the big family occasion. Crap. Now his face wasn't the only part of him that was cold. His feet were, too.

Yeah, and what was he going to do? Not show? Right. He wouldn't do that to Ciara and Mark, even if a powerful curiosity wasn't driving him.

"Damn it," he growled at the mirror then flipped off the bathroom light.

He'd decided to walk. It was just plain silly to drive around now that days lasted long enough for him to make it home before dark. Hoodoo and Aurora seemed to enjoy the stroll, too. From experience, he knew they'd hang around at that end of the pasture, waiting to amble home with him, too.

Careful not to step in a pile of manure as he crossed the pasture—now, that'd be a social faux pas, stinking when he showed up—Gabe felt as nervous as a teenage boy heading out on his first date. He assumed he hadn't been expected to dress up, but her father was white collar, probably well-to-do, not a man who worked with his hands, so Gabe had changed from his usual T-shirt to a button-up sports shirt. Defiantly, he'd stuck with jeans. That's who he was. Work boots, too. He couldn't hide the calluses on his hands, either, and wouldn't want to try.

Didn't mean he looked forward to seeing disdain on the faces of Ciara's mother or father. Something told him they didn't know he was anything but a neighbor, though, who was spending some time with Mark and coming to dinner now and again, so maybe they wouldn't be judging him the way they would if they knew he wanted to marry their daughter.

God. His stomach was so tied up in knots, he didn't know if he'd be able to eat a bite. It had been a long time since he'd felt inadequate, and he didn't like it one bit. As down to earth as she was, Ciara had never made him feel this way, but he had the feeling her parents were from a whole different world.

One she'd run away from, he reminded himself.

No, he wouldn't be apologizing for who he was. They could like him, or not. If Ciara chose to take a look at him through their eyes…well, what would be, would be.

Man, he desperately wanted to have a do-over. Never get involved with the new neighbors. Go back to vaguely thinking the woman was pretty, but never even dreaming he'd kiss her, much less be willing to expose himself to this kind of apprehension.

Yeah, except he'd still be dead inside. He wouldn't have made passionate, searing love with her.

He cursed as he ducked through the fence at the top of the pasture, unaware he'd been spotted until the front door of her house opened, and Mark and Watson came out.

"Gabe!" The boy waved as if Gabe wouldn't see him. "Hi, Gabe!"

Mark hovered on the porch, but Watson raced to meet Gabe. The horses, heads hanging over the fence, didn't even bother to shy from the rambunctious dog.

Gabe had reached the foot of the porch steps before Mark's mouth fell open, his lips slack. It wasn't a good look for him.

"What happened to your beard?"

"Weather's warming up." A stupid thing to say. It was July. The weather had been warming up for some time now. "I decided to shave it off."

"You look different." It was an accusation.

"Still me," Gabe said shortly.

"But—"

He raised an eyebrow.

"Everyone's here," Mark said unnecessarily. Voices could be heard through the open door, and Gabe hadn't missed the shiny black SUV sitting out front beside Ciara's Dodge Caravan.

"Figured that."

"Oh. Well." He eyed Gabe as if he were a stranger. "Um, I think dinner's ready."

Mark had to turn back, whistling for his idiot dog. As Gabe entered, a man rose from an easy chair in the living room, setting aside a newspaper.

He was tall and thin, his dark brown hair receding. Gabe was relieved to see that his khaki pants were wrinkled and his sportshirt nothing special. He dropped a pair of reading glasses on top of the newspaper and held out a hand. "Ben Malloy. I'm Ciara's dad."

Gabe felt a small shock at the blue eyes so much like hers.

"Good to meet you." They shook. "Gabe Tennert."

"We talk to Mark at least once a week. We've been hearing nothing but Gabe, Gabe."

Relaxing in the face of obvious friendliness, Gabe smiled. "Nothing about Hoodoo and Aurora? Maybe a little about Watson?"

Her dad had a laugh that sounded like hers, too. "Could be. Sounds like he has some new friends, too."

"He does seem to be making friends."

Despite the smile, those eyes studied him keenly. "That's been a relief to hear." He cocked his head. "I think we're being called to dinner." He raised his voice. "Mark?"

Watson galloped in to greet Gabe anew, and then tried to brace his feet when Mark grabbed his collar and led him to the stairs.

"Has to be shut in when the family is eating," Gabe explained, seeing Ben's surprise.

"He begs?"

"I hear he steals food right off the plate."

Ciara's father laughed. "Okay. I'd as soon not see that."

In the dining room, a pretty, older woman was setting a salad on the table. Ah, Gabe thought, seeing copper-colored hair threaded with silver, worn in a long braid—hippie, he remembered with amusement. Her smile was like her daughter's. The lines that crinkled beside her eyes suggested she often smiled. Her husband made the introductions, and Janet Malloy, too, appeared relaxed and friendly before saying, "Sit down. We'll have dinner on the table any minute."

The knots in Gabe's stomach might have unwound, if he could forget Ciara's odd behavior this past week and her obvious constraint when talking about these people.

He hesitated, not sure where to sit. Usually, he had a place, but with six place settings...

The swinging door opened and Ciara appeared, carrying a casserole dish in mitted hands. "Gabe— Oh!" Like her son, she stared, although her mouth didn't hang open. "You shaved," she said finally.

Aware of her father's interest, he nodded, repeating, "Weather was warming up."

"Oh," she said again. She tore her gaze from his long enough to set the casserole dish down before staring some more. Then, slowly, a smile curved her mouth. "It's you."

He touched his jaw self-consciously. "I guess so."

Foolish thing to say, but she didn't seem to find it so. But the door opened behind her, and her smile vanished as if it had never been. He didn't like the fleeting expression of despair he'd have sworn he saw on her face before she said stiffly, "You met my mother?"

He agreed he had. But then he saw Ciara's mother returning with another woman, who looked...scared to death? She didn't want to meet his eyes, that was for sure.

He started to rise in automatic courtesy, before understanding slammed into him. Immediately he sat back down in an effort to make himself less imposing.

"Who is he?" the other woman asked in a high, agitated voice. "I don't know him."

"Remember?" Janet said gently. "Ciara told us she'd asked her neighbor to join us for dinner. This is Gabe. Gabe, Ciara's sister, Bridget."

"I'm glad to meet you," he said, by instinct keeping his voice equally gentle. "Bridget. That's a pretty name."

Bridget swung around as if to bolt back to the kitchen, but her father moved swiftly to urge her to a chair. "Look, Ciara made your favorite dinner, honey."

Gabe checked: macaroni and cheese that didn't smell much like the kind he cooked up out of a box. "It's one of my favorites, too," he said.

She plopped gracelessly into the chair, and he realized all her movements had been awkward. She looked a lot like Ciara, but the way she walked and held her shoulders made her seem heavier than he thought she really was.

Mark burst into the dining room, and she jerked, but he didn't seem to notice. "Gabe shaved his beard off," he announced. "Did you see, Mom?"

Ciara's gaze stole back to his face. "I saw. Did you wash your hands, Mark?"

"You already asked." He sounded offended.

"I'm sorry. Oh—the peas." She fled for the kitchen.

Eventually, they were all seated, food being passed around. Janet served Bridget, who clutched her fork as if she was going to stab someone with it but seemed to do okay getting food to her mouth. She didn't have a lot to say, and her sentences never seemed to be more than three or four words. His gaze wasn't the only one she avoided meeting, he realized; she didn't like looking directly at anybody, family or not. Her glances at their faces were quick and furtive.

She hadn't eaten more than half her dinner when she suddenly jumped to her feet. "I'm done. We can go home now."

"No, honey," her mother said, "but you don't have to stay at the table."

"Okay." She marched toward the living room. After a moment, they all heard the television come on. It sounded as if she was flicking through stations without stopping at any of them.

Janet Malloy looked across the table at Gabe. "I imagine Ciara told you Bridget is autistic," she said quietly, confirming his guess. "High functioning and quite verbal, but she finds new surroundings difficult."

"And meeting new people, I bet," he said.

"Yes."

"Is she younger than you, or older?" he asked Ciara.

She didn't want to meet his gaze, either. "Younger. Three years."

Pieces to the puzzle she'd presented were effortlessly dropping into place. And Mark—she was in deep denial about the echoes of her sister she couldn't help seeing in her son. Now he understood why she didn't want to accept the diagnosis that put Mark somewhere on the Asperger's spectrum.

Had she not wanted to tell him about her sister because she was afraid that would have him jumping to conclusions about Mark?

"Mark tells us you're a cabinetmaker," her mother said, smiling at him.

"That's right. One of the barns is my workshop. I specialize in solid wood cabinetry for historic renovations or custom-built homes."

"He makes gorgeous furniture, too," Ciara put

in. "You should see the dresser—" Now her mouth formed an O of alarm.

You should see the dresser in his bedroom. That's what she'd been about to say. Gabe would swear he saw a twinkle in her mother's eyes.

"I do," he agreed easily. "It's a sideline, though. I could sell more if I had time to make it." He shrugged.

"Mark has really enjoyed the lessons you've given him," her father put in.

"He has a knack," Gabe said. "He has great concentration and memory, and is careful with tools."

In obvious pride, Mark seemed to hold himself straighter. "It's fun. Gabe's good with math, too. He helps me when I don't understand something. And he's teaching me to ride. His horses are trained for cutting cows. I told you that, right? Someday *I'm* going to do that."

His grandmother chuckled, and his grandfather said, "I have no doubt, if you put your mind to it." His eyes smiled.

Gabe came to the surprising conclusion that he liked her parents. Maybe they were judging him, but if so, it wasn't overt.

"Does Bridget live with you?" he asked.

"Yes." Janet's expression remained placid. "We've looked into group-home situations, but until recently we hadn't found anything that seemed quite right. She does go to a day care with other autistic adults that's given her the opportunity to have friends, and outings that make her feel more independent."

"Until recently?" Ciara cut in, her surprise obvious.

"Yes, we've been talking to the parents of several of her friends and are considering going in together to create and staff a home for them," her father said. "Workers at the day care have come and gone, but a woman in her forties has been on staff for, oh, close to two years now. We really like her, and she's interested in initially, at least, taking charge in the home."

"We were planning to tell you what we have in mind when there was a quiet minute," her mother added, sounding apologetic. "You know we've never wanted you to feel as if someday…" She broke off with a glance at Gabe, as if she'd just remembered he was there.

"You've said you didn't expect me to take Bridget," Ciara said slowly. "That's why you want to be sure you have something set up."

Again her mother glanced somewhat uncomfortably at him. "That's right."

He wondered if he ought to be excusing himself, but Ciara bounced up from the table and said, "Ready for dessert? Cherry pie. Let me see if Bridget wants some."

Bridget did. She came back to the table and

wolfed her pie à la mode. Well, they all did. Ciara was a hell of a good cook, and an even better baker.

He drank his coffee faster than usual, and then suggested he ought to be getting going. As he pushed back from the table, he was surprised when Ciara did the same.

"I think I'll walk Gabe partway home. Mom, if you wouldn't mind clearing the table? I can load the dishwasher when I get back."

"What," her father complained good-naturedly, "you don't think I'm capable of carrying a dirty dish into the kitchen?"

She kissed his cheek. "Carry away."

A smile aimed at her parents didn't reach eyes darkened by some anxiety when she looked at him, Gabe saw. His stomach clenched on too much good food.

Predictably, Mark wanted to walk with them, but Janet had him helping clear the table instead as Gabe and Ciara let themselves out the front door.

"Good dinner," he said, as they started down the front steps.

Her "Thank you" was stilted.

He'd have reached for her hand if he hadn't seen the careful distance she maintained from him. Noticing that didn't help his roiling tension. He shoved his hands into his pockets instead.

She didn't say anything until they'd left the porch steps and were crossing the lawn that was turning brown and crunchy underfoot. The sun was still high in the sky, with the days so long right now.

"Now you've met my family," Ciara said suddenly, her tone sharp, even hostile.

"I have," he agreed after a moment.

"My sister has dominated my life." The sharpness was still there. Bitterness? "Bridget has always been my parents' focus. They're good with her." Her head turned. "You saw."

"They seem like nice people," he said mildly, guarding his expression when he didn't know what she was looking for on his face.

"Nicer than I am."

"Don't be ridiculous."

They stopped at the fence. The horses grazed not far away, the soft sound of their teeth grinding grass the only sound.

He might as well not have said a word, for all the attention she took.

"Do you know what it's like, having a sister who constantly throws screaming tantrums? Oh, and throws food, too? If we went to a restaurant and she didn't like what was brought to her, she'd heave it at the waitress. These awful, guttural bellows…" A shudder shook her. "Everywhere we went, people stared. Half the time, she had bruises, and then I could tell they were thinking awful things." Even in the darkness, the rigid way she held herself could be seen. "When I was little, my parents insisted on bringing her to see me if I was in a school play or getting an award. 'Because we're a family,' they'd said. So I quit doing plays and made sure I didn't get any awards." Defiance formed a glaze over murkier emotions. "I didn't want anyone to know she was my sister. I didn't invite friends home, because she was always there. My parents wouldn't—" She choked on what she didn't say.

Hide her. My parents wouldn't hide her. Make sure sometimes she wasn't there.

Gabe wondered if they'd had any idea what they were doing to their older daughter. But how could they not?

"Ciara…"

She ignored him. "Mostly, people don't even know I *have* a sister."

Another puzzle piece fell into place. "But your husband did. You pretty much had to introduce him to her, didn't you?"

"She came to my wedding. Of course she had to be at my wedding."

The way she said that could have been bitterness or simple matter-of-factness. Gabe couldn't decide.

"He was repulsed by her." More softly, "I didn't blame him."

Oh, Christ. His chest felt as if she was tearing it open. But when he reached for her, she backed away.

"That son of a bitch—" he began.

"No! Listen to me." Her intensity felt like a live wire. "This is who I am. I have spent a lifetime ashamed of my sister, who can't help herself. That's who I am," she said with self-loathing. "Not...not whoever you imagine I am."

And, before he could say a word, she bolted.

"Damn it, Ciara!" He was two steps too slow. She stumbled up the steps before he reached the foot of them. Gabe stood rooted where he was as she let herself inside and slammed the front door behind her.

He waited for...he didn't know what. One of her parents to come out? Raised voices from inside? But nothing happened. He suspected she'd torn upstairs and hidden in her bedroom to cry. He also guessed she wouldn't be fooling either of her parents when she reappeared after an interval with puffy eyes.

Or maybe he was wrong. They might genuinely be oblivious to Ciara's complicated feelings about her sister, and therefore about herself. They'd raised an autistic child and devoted a substantial share of their lives to her with admirable love, kindness and loyalty. Had that blinded them to Ciara's conflicts?

Both thoughtful and disturbed, he walked back toward the pasture. When he reached the fence, he gave one last, frowning glance back toward the house. He didn't like knowing he wouldn't be able to talk to her until tomorrow, at the soonest, about the destructive feelings she'd been harboring.

How could she believe herself to be a terrible person, when her feelings were likely commonplace for kids with a seriously disabled sibling? Or did she hate herself because as an adult she hadn't instantly sought a warm, close relationship with her sister?

Striding through the pasture, he found his footsteps slowing. *No, I'm missing the point,* he thought. Had to be. As an adult, Ciara wouldn't be embarrassed by her sister anymore. This evening, her interactions with Bridget had seemed comfortable, kind. Natural.

The poisonous witch's brew that had just bubbled forth, he knew suddenly, wasn't about Bridget at all. Or, at least, not directly about Bridget.

Mark had a whole lot to do with it.

WHEN THE DOORBELL rang the next morning, Ciara was in the living room with a dust rag in hand. Her heart squeezed tight. She hadn't heard a car engine. Unless this was one of the Ohler boys, it had to be Gabe.

"I've got it," she called, when she heard a thunder of footsteps upstairs.

Gulp. Open door.

Gabe stood on her coir mat, looming over her, even though he was a step lower. He looked…handsome, she thought weakly, contradicting that long-ago first impression. The blunt angles and planes of his face were strong and interesting. She wished suddenly he *hadn't* shaved off his beard. She hadn't adjusted to the change yet. This man felt too much like a stranger.

"Gabe."

He inclined his head. "I wanted to talk to you."

Mark came galloping down the stairs accompanied by Watson. "Gabe! Cool. I didn't know you were coming."

He stuck out a foot to foil the dog's dart for the opening to the outside and repeated, "I wanted to talk to your mom about something."

By this time, Bridget and Mom had appeared from the kitchen. Only Dad was missing. If she wasn't mistaken, the audience was making Gabe uneasy.

"Fine." Ciara dropped the dust cloth on a side table and said, "Let's go outside. Unless you'd like a cup of coffee?" The last was hopeful.

A twitch of one eyebrow suggested he knew she sought a reprieve. "No. Thank you."

Everyone was still staring, Mark with mouth agape, when she stepped out on the front porch and shut the door in their faces. Oh, God—what did he want to say? Would he tell her she'd been ridiculously melodramatic? Or that she'd shocked him? Or…what?

"Enjoying your company?" he asked politely,
"Yes, of course."

"Why don't we walk around back?" Gabe suggested.

She nodded. She had an awful feeling they were being watched from the house. The whole family would probably run from window to window and try to lip-read.

"I think you stunned Mark," she said, going for light. "You're supposed to be *his* friend."

Lines gathered on his forehead. "Do you think he's jealous? Is that part of the reason you didn't want him to know we were…seeing each other?" The pause was almost infinitesimal, but she heard it.

"No. I mean, I don't know how he'd feel about us being involved." Funny that she hadn't worried about it. Because she'd never expected them to get to a point where Mark *had* to know? "He…seems happy when we're all together," she said stiffly.

They rounded the back of the house. The day was hot and dry, the sky a pale blue arch.

They were still walking, still both looking ahead, when Gabe said, "Mark isn't Bridget. That's what's been eating at you, isn't it?"

Her feet stopped. *"What?"*

"You couldn't admit Mark had a problem at all, because if you did, you were afraid you knew what it would be."

Aghast, horrified, angry, she could only stare at him.

"When you looked at Bridget, and then you looked at Mark, you were afraid, so it was easier not to look at Bridget at all."

She backed away from him, stumbled, but took another scrambling step when he reached out for her. "You don't know what you're talking about," she said breathlessly.

"Maybe this is a mistake to say—" Gabe sounded weary "—but I think somebody has to. Ciara, I know you love Mark. He's a good kid because you're a good mother. *But he's not Bridget.*" Intensity vibrated in his voice. "You're acting as if he is. Like your parents do with your sister."

"That's not true." Her voice shook, as did all her certainties.

"He won't need you forever, the way she needs them." Every line in Gabe's face deepened, making him look older. "Not if you let him grow up. Take some knocks, learn to stagger to his own feet instead of you picking him up."

"You think I'm…I'm…"

"You're trying to protect him." There was that kindness, but this time it seemed mixed with pity and…something else. "To keep him safe, you've got him wrapped so tight he can't…" Gabe hesitated.

Ciara didn't let him finish. "You don't know

what it was like for him!" she yelled. Oh, God, she sounded vicious, hateful. "You don't know anything!"

"Breathe," he said quietly, although anger had sparked in his gray eyes, too. "He can't breathe. You're smothering him. Which is fine if what you really want is to devote the rest of your life to him—"

Feeling sick, she stumbled back a few more steps. A hot fire burned inside her. *I loved this man. I do love him. And this is what he thinks of me.* Then the irony struck. She'd been so afraid he would despise her, and here it turned out he did. Just not for the reason she'd thought.

"How can you say things like this?"

"Tell me, Ciara." His voice was hard now. "If I hadn't been around, would you have taken one single step since you arrived to give Mark a chance to meet other kids? To join an activity, play a sport, learn anything you didn't teach him?"

No. The answer hit her like a blow. *No.* But because she'd been afraid, not because she wanted to coddle Mark or…or keep him to herself. Give herself a reason for living. That's what he was suggesting, wasn't it?

"I don't mean this the way you're taking it." Compassion looked different with his face shaved clean. "This is why I keep my mouth shut most of the time. I've made it sound—"

"You said what you thought." She sounded almost calm, although her fingernails bit into her tightly crossed arms. "I suppose I should say thank you, because it's Mark you're worrying about."

He looked at her with resignation. "But you're not going to, are you?"

"I...have to think. Please leave now."

"Ciara." The way he said her name, a husky plea, shattered what was left of her composure, but she wasn't going to run away from him again, not the way she had last night. "What you said last night—"

"You've said your piece," she interrupted. She could not bear to hear what he thought about last night's admissions. "That's what you came for. Now I'm asking you to go."

Muscles flexed in his jaw. "All right. For now." After a last, long look, he walked away, disappearing around the corner of the house.

Ciara, unmoving, heard voices, both male. Mark? Or had her father come out to talk to him? She couldn't face either. She turned and hurried the other way, through the open woods. Not until she was close to the creek did she finally hear the murmur of it, so low now in midsummer that much of the rocky bed was dry. Sunlight refracted off the rippling ribbon, momentarily almost blinding her.

You're smothering him.

She thought of her terror when Mark disappeared, that first time, to ride his bike down to Gabe's. And all the terror since—when she knew he was using power tools, when he went in the pasture for the first time, first got on horseback. Left her side to hang out with the group of kids at the cutting-horse competition. Was invited to go trail riding.

You were afraid.

Of so much. A keening sound left her throat. So much.

Was what she'd done really so terrible? Weren't parents supposed to keep their children safe?

Of course they were. But they had another imperative: to teach those same children to fly, so that when the time came they could go confidently into the world. Even her parents were doing their best to find a way for Bridget to do that.

He won't need you forever, the way Bridget needs your parents.

That's not what she'd wanted. It wasn't.

She stood there dry-eyed, and tried to understand her most corrosive fears, the ones whose existence she'd never let herself admit.

And, like Gabe, she finished the experience not much liking herself.

CHAPTER FOURTEEN

"WOULD YOU LIKE me to make you a pillow?"

Bridget rarely wanted anything new, but she was showing unusual interest in the pictures of custom pillows that Ciara had hung on a giant corkboard on the wall as well as using on her website. Bridget had already fingered fabrics and said she thought the pillow Ciara had just finished was ugly.

Privately, Ciara agreed. Sentiment did not always equate with beauty, especially when that sentiment was felt by a customer who knew *exactly* what she wanted and wasn't interested in suggestions.

But business was business.

"I like this one." Bridget stared at the photo of an over-the-top mass of satin and frills and seed pearls created from a wedding dress with a few embellishments thrown in. The bride had loved her pair of pillows. Ciara hoped the groom didn't have to actually rest his head on either of them.

"I still have most of those fabrics," she said. She usually hung on to bits and pieces left over. Who knew when they would be perfect for another project? "The lace, too. Let's see." She opened a drawer that held some of her collection of lace.

Bridget grabbed. "There it is."

"Yep." Ciara hoped her sister didn't tear it. That was bound to result in a record-breaking tantrum.

Or maybe not. Bridget had done astonishingly well during this visit. Tolerance was still not her way; she hadn't liked a sandwich Ciara made for her yesterday, so she'd grabbed it, stomped out of the kitchen and thrown it on the floor in front of an astonished and delighted Watson, who gobbled it up.

"There!" Bridget had declared. Her eyes had narrowed when Ciara laughed, but even then, no tantrum.

And giving the sandwich to the dog beat having it smack her in the face, Ciara had decided.

"Tantrum? Oh, she still has them," Mom said later, when Ciara commented. "Just not as often. And she seems embarrassed afterward."

"Embarrassed?" Ciara refrained from snorting. Barely. *"Bridget?"*

Her mother chuckled. "I did qualify it with *seems*. But really, I think she's starting to measure her behavior against her friends'. Sometimes she'll definitely be disapproving when somebody disrupts an outing she'd looked forward to."

Bridget *had* changed. Not only recently, Ciara was disconcerted to realize, but over the years. She hadn't let herself see how much. As a girl her sister had been closer to a wild animal than human; inconsolable when she sobbed or flailed her entire body in rage, unreachable when she drew into herself. Language had been slow to come, slower to develop.

Maybe better verbal expression helped. Or Mom and Dad's never-ending patience. Physical maturity probably hadn't hurt. The teenage years had been awful.

On this visit, Ciara was increasingly disconcerted to discover that she could actually enjoy Bridget's company. She was reminded of times she had in the past. Bridget had definitely matured— *And maybe,* she thought, *I'm more patient.* She found she liked the idea of making something Bridget would keep with her, that would make her think of her sister.

A connection, when she'd spent so long wishing she could deny the relationship.

"Do you want me to make you a pillow like that one?" she asked.

"Yes!"

"Okay. I can work on it today," she promised recklessly. Not like she didn't have a backlog of orders, but she suspected those customers would handle waiting better than Bridget did. Besides... Bridget was here. She could watch the work in progress. That would reinforce the knowledge that this was something special from Ciara. She felt absurdly flattered at the covetous way Bridget still stared at the picture.

"Mom!" Bridget bellowed, making Ciara wince. Fortunately, before she had to repeat it, their mother appeared in the doorway.

"Oh, my," she said, closing in on the corkboard. "You have some new ones here I haven't seen on your website."

"You keep an eye on the website?"

Mom shot her a look. "Of course I do."

Of course. Who knew? she thought bemusedly. It seemed she'd misunderstood everyone, not only herself.

She located the various fabrics she'd used in the pair of pillows, suspecting she shouldn't deviate from what Bridget saw, at least not without asking permission. She hoped the customer wouldn't mind her wedding dress being used to make someone else happy.

In the next couple of hours, she worked steadily, measuring, cutting, sewing and pressing seams, starching the lace. She was grateful for something that required her focus, that didn't let her think.

If I hadn't been around, would you have taken one single step since you arrived to give Mark a chance to meet other kids?

Don't think, remember? Not now.

Bridget came and went, unable to settle, although

she liked to touch. Ciara had to warn her away a couple of times when the sewing-machine needle was flashing up and down.

Mom, too, watched for up to fifteen minutes at a time. Ciara hadn't even noticed she was there when, at one point, she said, sounding bemused herself, "I admire your power of concentration. And you always loved textiles of any kind."

Ciara let her foot lift from the sewing-machine pedal and turned in her chair to see her mother standing in the open doorway. "Really? I don't remember being that interested until I decided to make my own prom dress."

"Come on! You were already an expert seamstress. The only reason I sewed when you were younger was because you insisted I should. You'd march me into fabric stores and pick your own fabric. Remember that green dress with the velvet pinafore?"

Ciara did. She'd worn it her first day of kindergarten. She'd wanted something *special*. She remembered begging. Mostly now what she envisioned was the photo of her in the dress that was part of a collage at home, but she had a wisp of memory of twirling and loving the way the skirt of the dress and pinafore both belled. She'd felt so pretty.

Her mother laughed. "I think that was the one and only time you were entirely satisfied with my sewing efforts. By the time you were eight or ten, you'd decided you could do better."

"I didn't do that much sewing."

"Only because you'd also become a tomboy. And when you were a teenager, well, you wanted to wear the same brands everyone else did."

Ciara found herself smiling, too. "Oh, God. I so did. Thank heavens I have a boy! I can't imagine Mark ever caring what he wears."

"Nope."

"Bridget didn't used to, either."

"Sure she did. Only her tastes were eccentric. She'd throw a fit because I suggested the blue-and-brown-plaid leggings didn't look so hot with that petal-pink top with sequins."

Ciara suddenly remembered those battles. Maybe she'd blocked them out. Bridget always won, of course. No one could make her leave the house if she wasn't wearing what *she'd* chosen. One more cause of humiliation for her sister.

Ciara dipped her head so her mother, shoulder propped against the doorjamb, couldn't see her expression. She had been so shallow. Had she really believed she'd be shunned if people saw her with a sister who marched to a different drummer?

"I always knew it was hard for you," her mother said softly.

"Did you?" Ciara frowned, tilting her head on a

sudden, unrelated awareness. Automatic parental instinct. "Why's it so quiet?"

"Mark, your dad and Bridget went to Gabe's to pet horses."

"Really? Did they ask Gabe first?"

Her mother smiled. "Mark called."

"You didn't want to go?"

"A little peace and quiet sounded nice."

"I wonder how it's going."

"I don't know."

"We might be able to see from the front porch." Ciara bounced to her feet, her focus broken. Of course she hadn't been invited, not by Gabe. But… if someone had asked, would she have gone? No. She wasn't ready to face him. Didn't know if she ever would be.

Her mother raised her eyebrows, but followed her downstairs and out the front door. There, Mom gasped.

"Bridget is *on* a horse."

She was. "Aurora," Ciara said softly. Gabe led her, and she could just see her father's head on the other side of the quarter horse. He must be walking right at her side. Mark sat on the fence watching. Hoodoo was nowhere in sight, which probably meant Gabe had shut him into the barn.

"I never thought she'd do anything like that." Mom had lifted a hand to shade her eyes, but what astonished Ciara was that tears ran down her mother's face.

"Oh, Mom." She wrapped an arm around her mother.

"I think your Gabe must be an amazing man," she said shakily.

"I…think so, too," Ciara whispered, but it was grief that seized her, because he hadn't so much as called since she'd asked him to go, the day before yesterday. To say…what? That he loved her? If he did, how could he have looked with such laser clarity at behavior even she hadn't understood?

She had to accept that this family visit had done exactly what she'd been afraid it would—she'd convinced him she wasn't good enough for him.

THE TRIO WENT back down to Gabe's the next day for a second ride. Before they departed this time, Mark called up the stairs, "Mom, you want to come? I'm going to ride, too, and show Aunt Bridget how to canter."

"No," she called back. "I want to finish her pillow. She was proud of how much like usual she sounded. "Take Grandma."

"Grandma says she wants to stay home if you do. Bye," he added, and she heard the slam of the door.

A moment later, it was her mother who called up the stairs. "I just made some lemonade. Why don't we sit out on the porch and watch the lesson?"

Because I don't want to see Gabe, even across the distance of a large pasture? Not something she could admit to her mother.

And—she'd lied. She was done with the pillow, which was just as overblown as the one it was modeled after. And yes, she wanted to see Gabe, too.

She laughed…and then her laugh broke. She swiped angrily beneath each eye and then went downstairs.

She could tell from Mom's glance that she hadn't hidden a thing, but her mother didn't say anything. They went outside, to see that the distant figure of Ciara's son was saddling Aurora while Gabe led a prancing Hoodoo into the barn. Dad and Bridget waited on the other side of the fence.

"I hope it wasn't us you were trying to get away from when you moved so far away," her mother said out of the blue.

"Of course not!" She started thinking this was a lie, too, but knew suddenly it was the truth. She really had missed seeing her family. Maybe not Bridget…but, these past few days, she had realized she didn't feel the same discomfort she had in recent years. One more painful thing to admit— Gabe had been right about this, too. She'd clung to her self-centered, teenage misery long past it having any reality.

I looked at Bridget. Then I looked at Mark.

So much happening in subterranean depths,

unknown to her conscious mind, swimming on the surface.

"Then why?" her mother persisted, dragging her attention back to the here and now.

"You don't like it here," she accused.

Her mother's eyes met hers. "I didn't say that. I wouldn't want to live in a place this rural, but it's beautiful, and it looks to me like you and Mark are both thriving since the move."

"Mark is." *I was.* "It was because of him. To give him a new start. To put some distance between us and Jeff," she confessed.

"Well, *that* makes sense," her mother said practically. "I'm glad I don't have to see the jerk anymore. I don't think I could keep myself from smacking him."

Ciara gaped at her. "Mom!"

"Don't *you* want to?"

"I'd like to do more than that when I see Mark's face after he gets off the phone with his dad or comes back from a visit. I want to put on heavy-duty work boots and *stomp* on him. How could I ever have thought I loved him?"

"Well, I did wonder." Her mother laughed at the expression on her face. "I knew better than to say so. And…I'd hoped I was wrong."

"You weren't," Ciara said, voice stifled.

"No." Her mother's hand closed over hers and squeezed. "I'm sorry."

"I was stupid."

"Just young. And he's handsome and smart and ambitious. He just lacks…"

"Heart." The word came instantly. Jeff didn't deserve to walk on the same planet as a man like Gabe Tennert.

"I suppose that is it," Mom said.

Across the pasture, Mark had mounted Aurora, swinging himself onto her back as naturally as if he'd done it a thousand times. Gabe seemed to be leaning on the fence talking to Ciara's dad. Bridget…well, who knew? From this distance, Ciara couldn't make out expressions.

She sipped her lemonade, and her mother did the same.

"We hoped you'd invite us for a visit."

"Well, of course I planned to!" Not for anything would she admit how reluctant she'd been to issue that invitation, or why. *Oh, Gabe.* "I'd love it if you come any time. You don't have to wait for invitations."

"I know you thought we didn't understand how hard it was for you to grow up with a sister like Bridget, but we did."

Ciara turned slowly to face her mother, who seemed very determined to talk about a subject they had always avoided before. Old hurt rose to choke her. "Did you?" she said, a bite in her voice. "It never felt that way to me."

"I know. And I know that's our fault. My fault," she amended, more softly. "Your father used to argue that we shouldn't force your sister on you the way we did. I'm the one who was determined to give her the chance to be fully part of our family. I always thought you'd see—" Her voice shattered.

Nothing existed but the two of them, and memories. So many memories: an entire school assembly stopped, everyone in the auditorium staring, until a screaming Bridget could be carried out, or the open house where she'd started ripping student work from the walls, making Ciara's classmates cry and their parents stare in shock. All the times Ciara had tried to curl into herself and become invisible, praying no one knew that was *her* sister.

"Do you know how much I wished she didn't exist?" she heard herself say. "Not always. I mean, she was my sister. Sometimes we played together and…I loved her." The tightness in her throat eased. "I did. But I hated her, too."

Compassion altered the lines in her mother's face. "Do you think I haven't sometimes? That your father hasn't? When you're carrying a baby, you dream about everything he or she will become. It's not easy, when one day you realize she will forever be a difficult child in some respects, and too often unhappy. I saw her taking over all our lives, and I resented it. Oh, I resented it," she said with quiet force.

"I never knew."

"No." Mom's smile twisted. "Nobody except Ben did. I was such a model of serenity. And sometimes such a hypocrite."

"Mom." Ciara was so stunned, she couldn't think what to say.

"Your father was freer in some ways, because at least he left the house to work. But even he had his moments."

Had. Ciara noticed the past tense.

"Are you…excited about having her move out?"

"Yes." There was another laugh that wasn't quite a laugh. "And no. I know it's right for her, but I'll miss her terribly, too. Maybe you don't understand that—"

"Of course I do. She's been the center of your life."

"Too much so," her mother said sadly. "You suffered for that, but I didn't know what else to do. I couldn't send her to an institution. I just couldn't."

"No." That shocked Ciara. She hadn't known her parents had ever talked about anything like that. "I never would have wanted that." She was glad to realize that much, at least, was true.

Mom grabbed her hand again, her grip almost painful. "I wanted to say how sorry I am that her struggles impacted you so profoundly." Her eyes bored into Ciara's. "But I also need you to know that I believe I'm a better person because of Bridget. I think maybe we all are."

Ciara's lips parted, but no words came. She could see that it might be true for both her parents. She both loved and admired them. Her father's quiet sense of humor never seemed to fail him. Mom had achieved a serenity that awed Ciara.

But...me? At first sight, she rejected the idea. She'd been ashamed to introduce her sister to Gabe. Ashamed by the comparisons she'd drawn between Mark and Bridget. What kind of person did that make her?

She was shaking her head even as she thought, *But maybe I am a better mother because I knew Bridget. More...accepting. More willing to fight to protect Mark, to give him everything he needs.*

Like Mom had done for Bridget. *As long as I can also learn to open my hands and let him fly free.*

Now the lump in her throat reached gargantuan proportions. She quit shaking her head. "I'm... going to have to think about that."

"Good." Her mother's eyes shimmered with unshed tears. "That's all I can ask." She turned her head and said, "Oh, my. Look at her."

Ciara looked, and found herself smiling in astonishment. Bridget was on Aurora's back again, but this time she sat up straight, looking, from a distance, almost…queenly. And then she laughed, her head thrown back.

Oh, my said it all.

WHEN MARK HAD called earlier, it was Gabe who said, "Why don't you ask your mom to come along?"

"Mom?" Typical, unthinking kid, he sounded surprised. "Oh. Sure. I guess."

But only Mark, Ben and Bridget emerged from the Toyota ten minutes later. Gabe strode to meet them, hiding his dismay. What was going through Ciara's head? Did she hate him? Plan to move again, and not make the mistake of getting too friendly with a neighbor? Let him have access to Mark, but only in a controlled way? He wished he had a clue.

He wished even more that he could go back and recast the whole talk. What he should be wondering was what *he'd* been thinking. Had he really been stupid enough to imagine she'd gasp with excitement and say, *Oh, Gabe! Of course you're right!*

Hell, no. Trying to make himself understood, he'd trampled all over her feelings. He had said what he meant, but not the way he'd meant. He should have started by saying *You're a gentle, smart, amazing woman, and Mark's lucky to have you for his mother*. But him, he wasn't so good with the compliments. After Ginny and Abby died, he'd spent countless hours remembering everything he'd thought but not said. He'd too often kissed his wife but not said *You're beautiful*. He hadn't told her anywhere near often enough that he loved her. Or said to his small daughter *You're the sunshine of my life*.

And look at how little he'd learned! His idea of a high compliment was *He's a good kid*.

Even so, he'd come to realize that his wife and daughter both had *felt* loved. He could close his eyes and see Ginny's smile when he walked in the door, or the way his little girl had run to him with complete faith that his arms would open. They'd known.

So how could *Ciara* not know how he felt about her, how much he admired her strength and fierce defense of her boy?

But he knew the answer. He'd always been aware she was protecting not only Mark, but some deep wound. And then, in opening his damn mouth, he'd done the same thing her SOB of an ex had: he'd dumped a load of blame on her.

I have to fix this, he thought desperately, but didn't know when or how he could. He couldn't even blame her for avoiding him.

He tried to ignore the niggling little voice in his head suggesting that she had invited him that first evening to meet her parents only because she knew they'd been curious after hearing Mark talk about him. Didn't mean she'd admitted to them that he and she had a relationship beyond neighborly. He couldn't possibly be the kind of man she'd proudly bring home to Mom and Dad.

And yeah, he knew it was his own insecurities talking. It was hard to get past the fact that he'd spent his whole life in this rural corner of the state. He still didn't read very well. He'd barely graduated from high school. His computer skills were limited, which left him unable to speak the same language as most of his contemporaries. He was a craftsman, not a professional like her father and her ex-husband.

He'd been good to her boy, though, and she was grateful to him for that. They'd had sex half a dozen times. Maybe it hadn't meant that much to her.

A groan vibrated in his chest, but he suppressed it, going to greet Ciara's family.

Damn it, he thought, *she's not like that. I know she isn't.*

He had to quit being such an idiot. Find the right words to say and then corner her.

"Your mom didn't come?" he said to Mark, aware of Ben's interested expression.

"Uh-uh. She's sewing something for Bridget. She wanted to finish it."

He nodded and smiled at Bridget. "Are you ready for another ride?"

Her expression was tense as she shot glances around his yard. "Yes."

He slapped Mark on the back. "You tack up Aurora while I put Hoodoo in his stall."

"Sure," Mark said nonchalantly. There was a swagger to his stride that would have amused Gabe if he weren't so tangled up inside about the boy's mother.

Today it didn't take nearly as much coaxing to get Bridget up in the saddle, and after clutching the horn in terror for the first five minutes, she noticeably relaxed and even began to look proud of herself.

"I'm riding," she told them all.

"Smile," her father said, holding up his cell phone. "We've got to have a picture."

She opened up with a big, wide grin. "This is fun!" she yelled. "I *like* horses."

Gabe tightened his grip on the reins just beneath the bit, but Aurora's only reaction to her exuberant rider was to swivel her ears. She continued her placid stride even as her passenger threw an arm out, flung back her head and laughed. It was as if she understood. This was one horse who had depths he'd never appreciated. He stroked her sleek neck, and she turned her head to look at him with a liquid, dark eye.

"Good girl," he murmured, and she tossed her head the slightest bit.

After Bridget had dismounted and while Mark was unsaddling Aurora, Ben approached Gabe.

"Mark is growing up," he said quietly, making sure neither of the others could hear them.

Gabe glanced at Mark. "That's natural. He's thirteen this week."

Something else that stung; he hadn't been invited to any birthday celebration.

"That could be it." Ben Malloy sounded doubtful. "He's not as clumsy. He also seems…a little more sensitive to other people's feelings."

Gabe had noticed both, too. "I think the horseback riding is helping his balance and ability to center himself. I was going to suggest you think about looking into a riding program for Bridget. She seems to enjoy it, and she was a lot more confident today."

"She was, and I think that's a great idea." He smiled. "I also think you're responsible for a lot of the change in Mark. Thank you."

Thrown for a loss, Gabe said only, as he had to Ciara, "He's a good kid."

Nope—still couldn't spit out words like *likeable, fun, smart.*

When they left a minute later, he felt lonelier than he had in years.

HE'D HAVE BEEN more pleased by the eventual invitation to Mark's birthday party if Ciara's voice hadn't been so constrained when she called to issue it. Gabe had a really bad feeling he was being asked at Mark's behest, not because she wanted him there, too.

Not that long ago, before he blew it so bad, he'd have taken for granted that he'd be part of anything important in their lives.

He didn't say any of what he was thinking, though. He thanked her politely, verified the time he was expected and hung up the phone.

Turned out Mark had also invited Jennifer Weeks as well as both the Ohler boys. Gabe arrived as Ciara was still talking to Sabine on the doorstep.

"You really didn't have to send a gift."

Sabine laughed. "So you said, but my boys decided that wasn't right. And we do own a sporting-goods store."

Ciara laughed, too. Behind her, Mark was clutching a perfectly round, wrapped present. From the size, it had to be a soccer ball versus a larger basketball. "Jennifer brought one, too."

Both women greeted him, Ciara looking shy. Sabine raised her eyebrows and said, "*He* brought a present, too."

"I give up," Ciara said with another laugh, not admitting that she not only knew he'd bought something for Mark's birthday, she'd also been with him when he did.

She accepted the box from him, said, "Thank

you for coming," and led the way in before stopping. "Oh, dear."

Her sister had backed into a corner of the living room and clapped her hands over her ears. "They're so loud. I don't like it. Mo-om! They're loud."

Ciara thrust the box back in his hands and went to her sister. "Come on, Bridget." Her voice was very soft. "Let's go into the kitchen. It'll be quieter there."

She was careful not to touch her sister, he saw, but she stayed between her and the admittedly rowdy group of kids. Jennifer appeared to be demonstrating a cheerleading routine, which had him shaking his head. Good God, was the rough and tough rider going to morph into a girly-girl in the next couple of years? Hard to imagine.

Mark caught sight of him just as his mom and aunt disappeared through that swinging door into the kitchen. "Gabe!" His eyes locked greedily onto the present. "Is that for me?"

"None other."

The desire to start ripping open the paper was in his eyes, but he carried the gifts from the Ohlers and Gabe into the dining room and set them with a heap of others on the buffet at the end. A couple of leaves had been added to the table to extend it, and it was already set for nine. Gabe wondered how Bridget would handle sitting down with so many.

Not well, as it turned out. She liked the hot dogs and baked beans, but gobbled her food quickly so she could say, "I'm done," and leap up and rush out. When they got around to Janet carrying in the cake with candles lit, Bridget hovered in the doorway, joining in the singing although her voice was discordant. Nobody minded, though; the youngest set of guests displayed no interest in her at all, and Mark was obviously used to her.

Ciara seemed constantly on edge, jumping to her feet to anticipate everyone's wishes before they were expressed. Either excitement and all that nervous energy or the discomfiture that kept her from so much as meeting his eyes had also brought spots of color to her cheeks. A couple of times, her mother laid a gentle hand on her arm and spoke to her in a low voice, as if trying to soothe her, but Gabe couldn't see her efforts making any difference.

It didn't help that Mark was hyper, jumping up half a dozen times himself, knocking over his glass of milk once, interrupting people who were speaking. Being the center of so much attention was something like sticking his finger in an electric socket, as far as Gabe could tell.

When they finally got to the main event, opening presents, his mother fixed a look on him that had him pausing after inspecting each gift to thank the giver. Fortunately, he seemed genuinely enthusiastic about all of them. Gabe kind of doubted he'd have had the social skill to pretend to be pleased if he wasn't.

Jennifer had given him a book about cutting horses. He started trying to head the soccer ball until Ben deftly relieved him of it. About three-quarters of his presents consisted of computer software and games. Ciara had to dissuade him from rushing to try them out. Gabe's was one of the last to be opened.

When he lifted the black felt Resistol Western hat out of the box, his face was a study in awe and happiness. "This is so cool!" he exclaimed. "It's *perfect*."

It was the one time Ciara's eyes met Gabe's in a moment of shared pleasure.

"Try it on," she urged.

The fit was just right. Giggling, Jennifer showed him how to tip it low when he wanted to look brooding. The Ohler boys appeared jealous, although Gabe felt sure they, like pretty much every other local kid, had similar hats of their own.

Gabe made his excuses shortly thereafter. His hopes rose when Ciara stood to walk him to the door.

But that was as far as she went.

Her "Thank you for coming" was polite. Aware of too many people within earshot behind her, all he did was thank her for having him.

Turning to leave, everything he wanted to say, unsaid—that was hard.

CHAPTER FIFTEEN

WAS THERE ANY going back? Ciara couldn't even imagine. *I'm sorry* wasn't relevant. She'd been honest with Gabe, and he'd been honest with her. The clear result was a distance between them as deep and wide as the Columbia River Gorge.

So, okay, she'd reacted badly to his gee-I-thought-you-should-know revelations. But he was the one who'd retreated. The one who'd never said *That stuff about how you're a lousy person? You know it's crap, don't you?*

He had tried to say something about her tirade, honesty made her admit. But it had been an afterthought, and when she shut him down, he hadn't bothered to pick up the phone and finish it.

He'd apparently invited Bridget and Mark to come down to his place, and he'd showed up at the birthday party for Mark's sake. But her? She'd said *I am a lousy human being,* and it appeared he agreed.

No longer being able to call him and talk at night, not seeing in his eyes how much he wanted to kiss her, was more devastating than her divorce had been. Her relationship with Jeff had been so damaged by then, she'd been so enraged by his treatment of Mark, she wanted the divorce and was only sorry she couldn't cut him off entirely. She didn't like feeling as if she'd failed, or the sickening knowledge he disdained his own child and her because *her* genes were at fault. She'd hated the deep, gut-clenching sense of shame she hadn't a hundred percent understood, but now realized had to do with the implication that on a DNA level she was like Bridget, which meant…that every complicated thing she'd ever felt for her sister, she should have been feeling for herself, too.

And, oh God, maybe she had been. Maybe that always had been the real trouble. Where was the line between them? Maybe she wasn't normal, either. *Jeff* didn't think she was.

And maybe, maybe, she'd been so fixated on the times she'd wanted to pretend Bridget didn't exist, when she'd been embarrassed about her, that she'd forgotten she mostly accepted her exactly as she was.

Standing on the porch, she watched Gabe striding through his pasture, his horses trailing him like friendly dogs, and wished desperately that he would look back. The fact that he didn't, not once, felt like a stiletto to the heart.

Since the door stood open behind her, she wasn't

aware she had company until an arm came around her. Her father gave her a gentle hug.

"I like him," he said.

"Gabe?" She managed surprise, if a poor facsimile. Oh, who was she kidding? She swallowed. "I do, too." It came out not much above a whisper. Because she felt small?

"Is something wrong?" he asked.

Her laugh was closer to a sob. "Everything."

He brushed her hair back from her face. "Wanna tell me?"

"I—" She looked over her shoulder.

He did the same then reached out and closed the door. "No one will miss us."

After a minute, she nodded.

"We can walk if you want, or sit here on the porch."

They sat on the steps, her father looking entirely comfortable. He had a talent for that, she realized. How had she ever picked a creep like Jeff to marry, when she'd had as a role model a man as confident and kind as her father?

"I hadn't told Gabe anything about Bridget."

He looked interested but not judgmental, and only waited.

"I never told you what Jeff said." She did, watching the rare sight of her dad getting mad. Really mad. "The thing is," she said miserably, "it's true."

"What's true? Mark isn't autistic."

"No, but I think he's on the Asperger's spectrum. The school psychologist said he was, and I blew up."

"As you should have," he said stoutly. "I don't much like labels. Some people are good socially. Some aren't. Some are generous, some selfish, some athletic, some not. *Everyone* is on a spectrum."

"Yes, but—"

"No *but*," he said firmly. He smiled. "Gabe said Mark's a good kid."

"I know. And he is." She told him what Gabe had said about normal, too, and how it had revolutionized her thinking.

"So if he takes Mark in stride, what is the issue?"

"I've fought really hard not to let Mark be labeled. Partly because it would hurt him for no reason. But also because I didn't want to believe he was anything like Bridget," she said miserably. "I've always felt so ashamed because I didn't want friends to come home with me or even know I *had* a sister like her. I guess I started out being ashamed of her, and ended up ashamed of myself."

His gaze suddenly stern, he said, "That's nonsense! You were a good sister. Always sensitive to her moods, and able to coax her to do something when neither your mother nor I could. You should have heard her during the drive. She was really excited about seeing Ciara."

Another broken sound. "And me, I've been dodging her. Visiting with you or Mom when it didn't mean me having to see Bridget, too."

"She's a challenge. We all know that."

"But...she's my sister."

"That's true," her father agreed, "but she's not your responsibility. She never has been. I think we made a mistake dragging her to things like school events or insisting she be part of your birthday parties—"

"Mom said she overruled you. That she was the one determined to make sure Bridget was part of everything."

"That's true," he said again, "and I still don't know who was right. I didn't want her hidden away, either, but I could also see what her presence did to you. It wasn't fair."

"But it was good for her," Ciara said slowly, as if she was looking through a viewfinder that allowed her a perspective she'd never had before. "I was thinking just a couple of days ago how far she's come. I mean, there was a time she'd never have been able to handle such a long drive or a stay in a strange house. All the racket today." This last was hard to say. "Getting on a horse being led by a strange man."

"That's all true, too." He smiled at her. "But Gabe, he has a way about him."

She bit her lip and nodded.

"You still haven't said what the problem with Gabe is. Or am I wrong that there's something going on between you?"

"No, you weren't wrong. It's me." She pulled her feet up so she could wrap her arms around her knees and curl into a tight ball. "I told him how I felt about Bridget. I think…um, I shocked him."

"Did you say, 'I love my sister, but sometimes her behavior was embarrassing because I was a child and then an adolescent who was hungry to fit in but couldn't always because other kids associated that weird girl with me?'"

She blinked. "You make it sound so natural."

Her father was smiling at her. "Because it *is* natural. I had no idea you were torturing yourself like this."

"But I've been an adult for a long time. Gabe said—" After a pause, she told him. *You looked at Bridget, and then you looked at Mark.*

"That makes sense," he said thoughtfully. "If you didn't see Bridget, it was easier to block your fears."

So simple. She sat thinking about it, separate from the devastation of everything *else* Gabe had said, and to her shock discovered tears were running down her cheeks. She put out her tongue to catch them, tasting the saltiness. She didn't even know why she was crying.

"Oh, sweetheart." Her dad scooted over to engulf

her in a hug. She laid her cheek against his chest and felt such astonishing *relief.*

"I love you," she mumbled, and he laughed.

"I know. And I love you."

"Sometimes I feel like such a mess compared to you and Mom!"

His chuckle was so comforting. "We both had our breakdowns, you know. We just hid them from you two. And maybe that was a mistake." He eased back enough to look gravely into her eyes. "We had each other, too. When one of us faltered, the other one was strong. You didn't have that. You've been too much on your own. I wish your mother and I could have done more."

"How could you, when you have Bridget?" For the first time in her life, she didn't feel even a pang of resentment. They had their hands full. She could take care of herself. And…they'd have given her more, if she'd asked for it.

"You're our daughter, too." He kissed the top of her head.

"I do love her."

"Of course you do," he said comfortably.

"Gabe says I can't give Mark everything, that he needs other people." She could say it, after all. "He thinks I've been wrapping him in cotton wool." *Smothering him.*

Her father remained silent.

Ciara closed her eyes. "I can see that he's right.

It…might be different if I loved being his teacher, but the truth is I feel inadequate. I think I *am* inadequate. It wouldn't be so bad if he loved history or literature, but no. It has to be math and sciences. I *hated* geometry, and I never even took chemistry or physics or…" She stopped. "I'm just so afraid if I send him to school here, it'll end up just like it did before."

"You know, I have the impression he wasn't as shattered as you thought he was. He's a pretty darn confident kid, considering."

"About some things."

"At twelve or thirteen years old, is *any*body confident about everything?"

She had to laugh. Of course they weren't. She'd once believed the popular kids brimmed with confidence, but now knew better. The very cruelty of the boys who'd attacked Mark might have its roots in some deep-rooted fear or sense of inadequacy. "Point made."

"You know we'll support you no matter what you decide."

Now she did. She slid her arm around his waist to hug him back. "Yep."

"Why don't you visit the school?" he suggested. "Talk to the principal, to teachers."

"They're out for the summer."

"I'm betting they're around. This is a pretty small town. Besides, I seem to remember that by

August they're back to work getting ready for the next school year."

Ciara made a face at him. "As always, you're right, o wise one."

Her daddy laughed, kissed her and said, "Good to know I'm appreciated."

"I suppose we should get back to the party."

"I suppose we should."

She heard a crash inside and winced. Soccer ball. Reluctantly, she stood. "Here goes."

"Give Gabe a chance," her father said, as he, too, rose to his feet and crossed the porch with her.

She had only a moment to nod before they went inside, where she immediately heard her son's voice raised as he tried to explain why the soccer ball hitting the lamp had just *happened*.

GABE HAD JUST stepped out his kitchen door in the morning, a second cup of coffee in his hand, when he saw a flurry of activity up at Ciara's that told him her family was departing. Ben was loading suitcases in the rear of the SUV as doors were opened, the three women talked and Mark and Watson circled around them all. There were hugs—even Mark submitted to one from his grandmother, and Ciara and Bridget…well, Gabe couldn't tell. They at least said their goodbyes.

As the SUV receded down the driveway then turned left on the road, Mark and his dog wandered around behind the house. Ciara stayed where she was. From this distance, he couldn't see her face, but there was something forlorn about that solitary figure, watching long past the point where she'd be able to see the Toyota.

Gabe ground his molars and forced himself into motion. The Malloy family had taken enough of his time. Today he was putting a finish on an entire set of cabinets, then this afternoon riding Hoodoo to the Beems' place on the other side of his property to give him a workout with some cattle. Gabe had neglected him lately. Mark would have enjoyed coming with him...but he needed a break from *all* the Malloys.

He ignored his phone when it rang midday, and he recognized the number. He left the phone behind when he went out to saddle Hoodoo, who was even more fractious than usual. He didn't do his best cutting that afternoon, either. Partly the horse's fault, partly Gabe's. He caught himself using legs and rein in ways that only confused the animal.

They tried and tried again, until things went a little better, and he decided to quit on a high note.

He'd been aware that Henry Beem had come out to drape himself on the fence and watch the past hour.

"Ran some weight off those steers, did you?" Henry remarked.

Gabe shook his head. "They did a little more

running than they should have. Hoodoo and I aren't at our sharpest."

"Haven't seen you here in a while."

"Been busy." He asked politely after Verna's health, learned that their son Gerry had been promoted to manager at Boeing and their granddaughter was expecting what would be their fourth great-grandchild. Gabe knew only one of their three children lived nearby, which meant they didn't see all that much of those great-grandchildren, but he guessed that was the way it was for most people. There wasn't all that much work to be had locally. He'd been lucky to be able to pursue his livelihood and stay in the family home both, he knew that. Henry was tactful enough not to regret aloud that Gabe didn't have a family, although the pity was there in his eyes. Henry believed wholeheartedly in family.

Gabe tipped his hat and rode home, clomping along the narrow shoulder of the road, his thoughts consuming enough that Hoodoo was halfway up his driveway before he saw Mark, wearing his new cowboy hat, waiting outside the barn.

Gabe's "Damn" was heartfelt. At his growled outburst, the sorrel's skin shivered as his ears swiveled like a pair of miniature radar.

"Where'd you go?" Mark asked as soon as he was within earshot.

"Worked some cows over at the Beems'." Gabe jerked his head to the north.

"Oh. I wish I could have watched."

Gabe said nothing, only riding past the boy and dismounting when he reached the fence where Aurora waited, nickering a greeting.

He loosened the girth and hauled the saddle off, slinging it over the fence.

"You want help?" Mark asked.

"Not today."

"Oh." He shifted. "Grandma and Grandad and Aunt Bridget left today."

"Did they?"

He took that as encouragement and started to chatter first about the visit, then how Mom said maybe tomorrow they could do something together, but today she had to work.

"But she said to ask if you could come to dinner tonight," he concluded.

"Tell her thanks, but no. I'm going to grab a quick sandwich and work this evening."

"No?" Mark seemed shocked. As well he might, since Gabe didn't recall that he'd ever before declined one of Ciara's invitations.

"I've taken enough time off today."

"Oh." Apparently, that was his fallback word. "Can I come over tomorrow?"

"No, I'm delivering some cabinets."

"Well, then, can I—?"

Gabe raised his eyebrows. "I thought you and your mom were going to do something."

"She'd probably be happy if she didn't have to." For once, the boy seemed teenage sullen.

"Don't expect me to buy that. Your mother lives to make you happy."

He gave a sulky shrug.

Gabe set aside the rubber curry comb he'd been using on Hoodoo's sleek coat and reached for the stiff brush.

Mark backed away. "I guess I'll go home, then."

Regretting the effect his crappy mood was having on the boy, Gabe said, "Let's plan on a session day after tomorrow. That work for you?"

"Sure! Maybe you can come to dinner that night."

"We'll see," Gabe said noncommittally. Damn, he was going to look like a real son of a bitch if he kept saying no, but he couldn't imagine right now how he'd sit across the table from Ciara and pretend nothing was wrong when everything was.

A hoof shot forward, almost catching Gabe in the knee. He dodged it, smacked Hoodoo on the rump but also said, "Sorry, boy. I wasn't paying attention to what I was doing, was I?" He'd been plying the brush with unnecessary vigor on the horse's sensitive belly.

He used more care as he finished grooming Hoodoo, checked his hooves and turned him out, to be greeted by Aurora.

Gabe hadn't lied; he'd half intended to go back to work, but if anything, his mood was worse than it had been when he saddled Hoodoo. Instead, he went into the house, poured himself a rare whiskey and soda and carried it to the living room, where he planted himself in his chair and sat looking at the row of photographs on the mantel. The ones he had begun thinking he might be ready to put away.

And he made a discovery that wasn't entirely welcome: however savage the pain he felt now, he couldn't take refuge in grief too muted by the years to provide the shield he needed. That time was past.

"YOUR PARENTS AND sister get home okay?" Gabe asked as Ciara handed him a basket holding rolls.

His tone was killingly polite, and he had very carefully avoided touching her when he accepted the basket. Her heart sank.

"Yes, Mom called to let me know they'd got there."

"Grandad says he'll look for someplace Aunt Bridget can ride," Mark contributed.

If Mark had been anyone else, Ciara might have thought he had noticed the level of discomfort between the two adults and was trying to help ease it.

"I hope he means it," Gabe said. "Bridget seemed to really enjoy getting up on Aurora."

"It was nice of you to offer," Ciara said, hating how gushy she sounded.

He flicked a glance at her. "I'm a nice man," he said flatly.

Mark laughed as if that was uproariously funny. Ciara's hand trembled so she had to set down her fork. Which hardly mattered; her appetite was non-existent.

"More?" She nudged the bowl of peas Gabe's way.

"Thank you."

At the end of the meal, Mark dragged Gabe to the computer to see how cool his game was. She served them pieces of pie at the desk. Neither seemed to remember she existed. Seeing how engrossed they were, she quietly cleared the table, put away the leftovers, loaded the dishwasher and started it, all the while listening to them talk.

Some was about the game.

"See what happens here? You've got to be really fast."

Gabe, amused: "I don't know. I never was a whiz with arcade games. I'm kind of methodical."

But there were pauses, pockets of conversation that took her aback. Gabe told Mark about a new client. He'd never worked with the contractor before, either, and was therefore wary.

"They claim to understand why it takes longer to get their cabinets, but I'm not so sure they really do."

"Do you ever let anyone come and look around your workshop? Or even watch you work?"

"God, no!"

"Well," her son said reasonably, "they might be impressed. Like I was."

"And they might decide I'm a hick, one-man operation, not up to their standards."

"But all they have to do is look at your cabinets." Mark sounded passionate.

Gabe slapped him lightly on the back. "You're right."

A few minutes later, Gabe suggested they ride tomorrow. Work on "reining"—whatever that was. High-speed stops and starts.

"You're getting there," he said, "but I want to be sure you can stick on Aurora's back before I let you work a herd."

"Okay!" Mark's delight was obvious to Ciara, even when her back was turned.

They exchanged opinions on some country-music stars. She hadn't realized Mark was listening to local stations. There was passing discussion about finding the volume of spheres. Apparently, Mark had been continuing in his geometry book on his own.

Gabe sat back in his chair and said, "Huh. Now, that one I might have to glance at the book for. It's been a while, you know."

"You sound like Mom," Mark said with dissatisfaction.

"Bring the book with you next time you come."

"Okay, if I can't figure it out."

Boom! Something on the screen blew up. She didn't even want to look to see how violent the game was. Surely Mom and Dad had paid attention to ratings.

"You weren't fast enough," Gabe observed, the undercurrent of amusement back in his voice. He didn't sound horrified, so it couldn't be too bad.

She stood across the kitchen, looking at the backs of their heads and felt…invisible.

Like a ghost, she drifted to the back door. Not even the sound of it opening brought either of those heads around. Only Daisy was interested. With a grunt, she struggled to her feet and accompanied her person outside.

Ciara hugged herself and walked a few steps toward the trees that sloped toward the creek. Daisy plodded beside her, squatting once, as well as her arthritic hips allowed, to pee.

Had both man and boy really forgotten she was there? she wondered, and doubted it. She couldn't believe Gabe really gave a damn about a shoot-'em-up computer game.

He was making Mark happy, and that was what counted.

Her vision blurred as she looked straight ahead. What a fool she'd been to start something she'd *known* wouldn't go anywhere! Gabe's signals were clear. She should be grateful he wasn't cutting Mark off, too. Maybe…maybe she'd go back to sending goodies along with Mark and quit inviting Gabe to dinner. It was too hard having him here. She didn't have to torture herself.

The back door opened behind her. She didn't bother turning around.

"I'm taking off," Gabe said. "Thank you for dinner."

"You're welcome."

There was a long silence. He had to still be standing there, or she'd have heard the screen door slap shut.

But he said nothing more. The door did finally close, leaving her out there alone.

She kept walking. Somebody, long ago, had laid a couple of boards to span the distance between two stumps, forming a bench that would, in Western Washington with the never-ending rainfall, have long since rotted. Here, the boards were dry and cracked. She was careful to sit close to one of the stump supports.

She watched as Daisy contentedly wandered, sniffing the ground and tree trunks.

Ciara hugged herself tight, but after a while the peace of the early evening began to sink in. And the quiet. She couldn't imagine ever living anywhere again with the constant noise of traffic.

The conversation she'd eavesdropped on ran again in her head.

You sound like Mom. Useless, was what he meant. He *might* not have said that if he'd remembered she was in earshot…but he might just as well have.

Except…she found herself thinking about some of the other things he'd said. Telling Gabe that anyone seeing him at work would be impressed. *Like I was.* That was what her son had said, so simply. Demonstrating that he understood what Gabe needed to hear. Which was—unprecedented.

No, she thought, frowning, it really wasn't. She'd been surprised more than once lately when he read cues he once wouldn't have known existed. Tonight, the whole conversation had sounded so… normal.

She winced at using a word Gabe had dismissed. And of course he'd been right, but it was also true that Mark had made huge strides lately toward… okay, not seeming so overtly *different*.

Her arms loosened and she gazed, unseeing, at the rear of the house. This realization about Mark connected with the similar one she'd had about Bridget, and she thought, *What Mark's done is mature*.

And it also hit her, out of the blue, that he wasn't much like Bridget at all. And of course that was what she'd been telling herself and any school officials who dared to try to put a label on him…but she thought now her denial had been too vehement. Gabe was right. She had been burying her fear that he *was* like Bridget.

Mark, Ciara thought, was no more dependent on her than any other kid his age would have been. He was intellectually gifted enough; she couldn't possibly give him what he needed in the way of schooling. There wasn't a reason in the world Mark wouldn't go to college, be successful there, have a career, a girlfriend, probably a wife and possibly children.

She'd known all that in one way—but not in another.

In her fear and denial, she could have crippled him, she thought with stunning clarity. There were undoubtedly good reasons to homeschool, but hers hadn't been the right ones, nor did she love teaching for its own sake.

She sat there feeling so much, some of it contradictory, that she doubted she could have moved even if she'd heard Mark screaming. It was all knotted up in her. Ciara had a bad feeling it was going to take her a long time to untangle this muddle of joy and grief and sense of inadequacy and stupidity and, yes, relief.

One thing she did know—it was time she talked to Mark about what *he* wanted. She had a bad feeling she never really had. She'd yanked him out of school in the furious belief that, above all else, protecting him was the right thing to do.

It was probably another twenty minutes before she stood, imagining that her bones and joints creaked when she straightened, even though of course they didn't, and returned to the house. When she stepped into the kitchen, Mark, of course, was still utterly engrossed in his game.

It might have been the sound of the door closing, or the click of Daisy's claws, but he did turn. "Can I have another piece of pie?"

"You're *already* hungry?"

He didn't dignify that with an answer. He was always hungry.

"Why not? Bring it to the table, why don't you. I want to talk to you about something, if you can take a break from your game."

He already had the refrigerator open. "Do you want some?"

She almost shuddered. "No, thanks."

Daisy followed, settling with a heavy exhalation

under the table close enough to sigh and rest her chin on Ciara's foot. Ciara leaned down to scratch her head.

A minute later, Mark plopped down across from her. Watson had followed, of course, probably hoping for handouts. She saw that Mark had put a scoopful of vanilla ice cream on top of his pie. Well, if anyone could afford the calories, it was a boy his age, who seemed to be stretching out before her eyes. When Watson put his paws on Mark's lap and eased upward, Mark automatically fended him off with an elbow.

"What I wanted to talk to you about is school," she said. "I've been wondering how you'd feel about trying eighth grade at the middle school here."

His mouth fell open. "But you said—"

"I know what I said. But I want to know what *you* think."

He poked at his pie with his fork. "Well…doing the worksheets and stuff has been kind of boring."

"I think we can improve on that, if we decide to stick with the homeschooling. With the move and trying to take on more commissions with work, I took the easy way out, knowing we only had to get through two months to finish the year. But…" She hesitated. "I'm wondering if you don't need to be around other kids. If you were really into sports, we could sign you up for teams, but—"

He grimaced.

She smiled at that, even though she didn't really feel like it. "It might help that you've already met some of the local kids," she suggested tentatively. "I know Jacob and Will and even Jennifer are younger, but some of the kids you hung out with at the cutting-horse competition were your age, weren't they?"

"Yeah. Most of them don't go to Goodwater schools, though." He frowned. "I think Brandon does. And…some girl. I can't remember her name."

Ciara nodded. "Well, at least you wouldn't be a total stranger to everyone. Especially if, well, Gabe takes you to any more events like that this summer."

"He said he would." Mark hesitated. "The schools in Goodwater are, like, all together, you know. I mean, they all use the same playing fields and stuff. So I could take high school math classes. And biology, I bet." His voice was gaining experience.

She, too, had noticed the schools were clustered, logical when class sizes were so small.

"There might still be kids who are jerks," she reminded him.

He ducked his head. "You mean, because they think I'm weird or something."

"No, because they're jerks," she said, almost steadily.

He hunched his shoulders. "Yeah, well."

"Mark, this decision is going to be yours. I will do my absolute best as your teacher, if that's what you want to do. But if you'd prefer to enroll in school here, that's okay, too." She managed a smile. "I won't be insulted, I promise."

He stared at her. "Well…what do *you* think?"

Oh, he had to ask.

"I guess," she began slowly, thinking about things Gabe had said and knowing he was right, "I do think you should give it a try. You need friends. Teachers who have different styles, different ways of looking at things. You know?"

He nodded.

"It's…actually Gabe who has convinced me that part of growing up is learning to work with other people." She had to give him his due. "To make friends, to deal with people who don't like you or who you don't like. It may be harder for you than it is for some kids—" She held up a hand at his expression "—*not* because you're weird. Just because that isn't your strength. You were smarter than most of the kids in your classes, weren't you?"

After a minute, he nodded again.

"Some kids are athletic but lousy students. Some are good in one subject, not another."

"Like Gabe. 'Cuz he didn't read very well."

"Right. Some are shy, some outgoing. Hardly anybody is well-liked by everyone. But most jobs require you to work with other people. Gabe and I are exceptions, being self-employed *and* working alone. With your interests, you seem more likely to end up working in a lab, or even becoming a college professor. So…that's what I think. But I meant it when I said the decision is yours. And deciding to homeschool for another year doesn't mean you can't enroll as a freshman here in Goodwater. By then, you might really have made friends."

His face went through gyrations as he thought.

Ciara smiled. "And you don't have to make up your mind right this minute. We have the rest of the summer."

"No," he said. "I don't have to think. I want to try. Unless, I don't know, something happens this summer."

Like some boys who would be classmates giving him a hard time. She nodded her understanding.

"All right." She held up her right hand, and he gave it a high five.

"Cool! I can hardly wait to tell Gabe." He leaped up. "Maybe I'll go call him now. And Jennifer, too."

"You call anybody you want," she said with a laugh, hiding her pain, "*after* you load your plate in the dishwasher. You may note the kitchen is already clean."

His head turned. "Oh. Sure." With a few clatters and bangs, he complied. Before he could reach for the phone, she started upstairs.

CHAPTER SIXTEEN

GABE HUNG UP the phone, trying to decide what this meant. Ciara had been so adamant about shielding Mark from the bullies of the world. She'd been so defensive, he hadn't thought she'd easily change her mind. And he'd been afraid her sister's visit would, if anything, reinforce her fears.

So—what had happened?

Mom said it was you *who convinced her. You know, that I need friends, and that I have to learn to work with other people.*

Thanks to his ill-chosen words, she'd been pissed when he suggested as much. Although she'd also said she would think about it.

In his experience, angry people didn't usually mean that—but it appeared she had.

Damn, he thought. Would she listen now if he were to apologize? But thinking about her pleasant, noncommittal expression during dinner, her tendency not to meet his eyes, he had a bad feeling the answer was no.

The bad feeling got worse when, two days later,

Mark showed up to work on his second box with something in his hand.

"Cookies," he said, handing over the lidded plastic container. "White chocolate chip with pecans."

Gabe didn't move, only looked at the container. Ciara hadn't sent goodies this way since she started inviting him to dinner. She gave him cookies, homemade bread and leftovers in person now.

He closed his eyes momentarily. She hadn't had to write a note to send a crystal-clear message. Those dinner invitations were going to come as seldom as Mark would let her get away with.

"What's wrong?" Mark asked, sounding anxious.

Crap. Gabe thought a few other words, too, ones he wouldn't have said aloud in front of a kid.

"Nothing," he said. "Let's get to work." He set the cookies aside without so much as peeling off the top to inhale the sweetness.

CIARA WAS SCRUBBING out the refrigerator when Mark wandered into the kitchen. Carefully setting in place the glass shelf she'd just washed in the sink, she let her gaze linger on the sight of white athletic socks on skinny ankles. The two new pairs of jeans she'd bought that day at Costco weren't enough. With a sigh, she bumped the refrigerator door shut with one hip.

"You know," she said, "we have some serious shopping to do before school starts."

He looked horrified. "You can just buy me stuff, can't you?"

"You have to try some of it on. And maybe you should ask Jennifer what kids around here wear to school. I mean, do most of the boys wear Western-style jeans? What about shirts? Athletic shoes?"

"I bet they all wear their boots," he said eagerly.

"We have to find out."

His grimace was easy to read, but he also quit protesting. He'd have continued if he really didn't care. It would seem now he did; he just didn't want to go shopping.

"I'm bored," he said.

"Call and see if the Ohlers are home."

"Oh. I guess I could do that." But he kept hovering. "Do you think Grandma and Grandad will come back for your birthday?"

"Probably not, when it's so soon. Maybe we should go visit them." Then she thought of Watson and Daisy. "Oh, except what about the dogs?"

"We could take them," he said enthusiastically. "Or I bet Gabe would take care of them. Except... if we go then he can't be at your party."

She evaded her son's gaze. "But it would be nice to be with family."

"But it's Gabe," he said in puzzlement.

Oh, God. It was all she could do not to double forward in pain.

"Let's not worry about my birthday yet, okay?"

"But…"

"That's an order."

Expression discontented, he found the phone. From his side of the conversation, it was clear that Jacob wasn't home, but Will, the younger brother, was, and he'd like it if Mark could come over. Ciara took the phone briefly when Sabine asked to speak to her.

"Pretty, pretty please," she said. "Will's driving me crazy. If I hear one more whiny *I'm bored*, I may crack."

Ciara laughed. "You and me both. You know, you can send either of your boys over here anytime, too."

"Yes, but here they can ride."

"Sold."

When she hung up, though, Mark stayed.

"Can we ask Gabe to dinner tonight?"

"Not tonight." She injected a little steel in her tone.

"That's what you say *every* day."

"Maybe later this week."

Suddenly stubborn, he didn't move. "Do you not like him anymore?"

"Of course I like him." *I love him.* For a moment, aghast, she was afraid she'd said that out loud.

"Then *why*—?"

"I think that's between him and me," she said firmly.

He looked at her like she was crazy. "But it's not. He's my friend, too."

She hated to admit it, but he was right. If she'd thought she could ease back into something more like the early days with Gabe without Mark noticing, she'd been deluding herself.

"Did you ask Gabe?" she said finally.

He shook his head. "He won't come to dinner if you don't ask him."

"Maybe in a couple more days, okay?"

Her son shuffled his feet. "Did you guys, I don't know, have a fight or something?"

"Not a fight." She hesitated. "Not exactly."

"Well…I want to know!" he burst out. "Was it because of Aunt Bridget?"

"Why would you think that?" she asked, surprised.

"'Cuz that's when you two quit talking."

Startled anew that he'd noticed, she hesitated, studying him. He wasn't the same boy he'd been when they moved here, only a few months ago. Maybe he cared only because Gabe mattered so much to him, but she wasn't going to get away forever with not telling him *something*.

"I suppose you could say we had words." Words. There was an answer. "I—" She scrambled for the right way to say this. "There was a lot he didn't know about me. I think as he got to know me better, well, he cooled off. That's all."

She'd earned another are-you-crazy look from her son. "*He* cooled off? But— Gabe likes you!"

"You know, there's no rule that says he and I have to be best friends. He's good to you, Mark. Let's leave it at that, okay?"

"No!"

"Yes." Ciara made sure he could tell she meant it. "Now get. Will is waiting for you."

"But—"

She crossed her arms. "No."

Face sulky, he went.

Only when she heard the front door close behind him did she let herself sag. At least she'd avoided having to admit that Gabe had good reason for deciding he didn't like her all that well.

MARK WAS UNUSUALLY quiet the next time he showed up in Gabe's workshop. He handed over today's offering from Ciara—a loaf of pumpkin bread with raisins and walnuts—then got right to work.

They'd been practicing cutting dovetail joints, and today he was marking the wood he'd chosen for his next box and making the first cuts. With his need for perfection, Gabe had expected him to concentrate fiercely. This was different, though. Gabe kept sneaking glances at a face that was usually so open. Today he seemed to be brooding.

When they broke for lunch, he slouched behind Gabe across the yard into the kitchen.

"How about grilled cheese today?" Gabe asked.

"Yeah, okay." Mark watched him take a large frying pan from the drawer beneath the stove.

"You know where the bread is," Gabe said mildly, turning on the burner.

Now he looked sulky, but did take the bread from the drawer.

"I wish you came to dinner at our house the way you used to." He sounded sulky.

Gabe raised his eyebrows. "Your mom hasn't been inviting me."

"You could have us here!"

Gabe's mouth tightened. As the pan heated, he began to butter the bread.

"She says you don't like her anymore."

His hand stopped. He turned very slowly. "What?"

"Well, she didn't say that exactly," the boy mumbled. "She said…I don't remember."

"Try."

Mark flinched, making Gabe realize he'd injected the single word with something like menace.

"She said you didn't used to know her very well. And, I don't know, once you did, you cooled off."

His jaw jutted as he glared at Gabe. "But she's *nice*. Why wouldn't you like her anymore?"

Not like her? Stunned, he tried to wrap his mind around a completely different interpretation of what had gone wrong between them.

He flashed back on the evening she'd walked him out to tell him how much she despised herself for being ashamed of her sister.

He'd never managed to squash that idiocy. Him, he'd been tangled up in the later conversation, the one where he lost his temper and told her she was smothering Mark.

Could she possibly have imagined—?

He turned off the burner and yanked the pan off it.

"Why'd you do that?" her son cried. "I'm hungry!"

"I have to talk to your mother. Make yourself lunch. I don't care what you have. Just don't burn the house down."

The kid's mouth went slack before he pulled himself together. "But— I could come with you."

"You stay here until I come back. Got it?"

"After I eat, can I work on my—?"

"No. No tools when I'm not with you." Gabe left the kitchen at a near run. He took time only to close the barn doors and lock them before he jumped in his pickup, backed it in a sweeping turn and tore down his driveway.

DISSATISFIED WITH HER OPTIONS, Ciara frowned at the spool of thread she'd reluctantly decided was the best match to the crushed panne fabric she'd just cut out. There were moments like this when she wished she could dash out to a fabric store. As it was, she could use this or set the whole project aside and work on something else until—

The sound of a vehicle coming fast up her driveway had her dropping the fabric onto the ironing board and the spool of thread on top of it. Who on earth…?

It was Gabe's truck, she saw out the window, and she'd been right about the speed.

A clamp closed around her heart. Oh, God. Something had happened to Mark. Images of spurting blood had her descending the stairs recklessly. She flung open the front door to find Gabe with his fist raised to pound on it.

"Mark?"

He scowled at her. "You think *I've* cooled toward you?"

Bewildered and uncomprehending, Ciara said, "Mark's not hurt?"

The scowl didn't abate. "No, he's not hurt. God damn it, Ciara, he wanted to know why I don't like you anymore!"

She should have known her darling son would let his mouth run away with him. Why hadn't she stuck to her guns and refused to explain?

"It's true," she snapped. "So why the big act?"

"True?" He crowded her enough to get across the threshold. "That's bull, and you know it."

"I don't."

"*You're* the one who pulled back, not me. You told me to go away." He thrust his chin out, and clenched his jaws so hard he was in danger of cracking his molars.

"I told you I needed to think!" she yelled. "I didn't say you couldn't call or come back or—" Hot tears burned her eyes, and she backed away.

"Oh, damn." He moved faster than she could, pulling her up against him and wrapping his arms around her. Into her hair, he mumbled, "I thought—"

Digging deep for pride, she raised her head. "You thought?"

"You were telling me to get lost."

Seeing the torment on his craggy face, she gaped. "Why would you think that? I told you the worst thing about me because I thought you needed to know."

"Do you have any idea how chilly you've been since then?"

Her whole body stiffened. "You weren't exactly friendly yourself."

"You were mad when I said what I did about Mark."

She wrenched free, putting several feet between

them. "You told me what a crummy mother I was, and you didn't think I'd be mad?"

Gabe made a raw sound of frustration. "I didn't say anything like that. I said you're a good mother, that I know you love him and are only trying to protect him."

"You did not!" Except…maybe he had said something like that, she thought grudgingly. Only, somehow it hadn't been very convincing when it was followed up with the accusation that she was smothering her son in the name of protecting him. Trying to deny him friends, opportunities, anything *she* couldn't provide. "You made me sound like psycho parent."

"Don't be ridiculous," he growled.

"And where's Mark anyway?" She peered past him, toward the open door.

"I left him at home. I told him to feed himself and stay put until I got back."

"But what if he…?" Oh, Lord. There she went with the overprotective thing. "I don't understand why you're here."

"Because I love you!" he roared.

HER MOUTH DROPPED OPEN. She looked so stunned, Gabe didn't know what to think. God. Maybe Ginny and Abby *hadn't* known how much he loved them. Maybe he shouldn't have let himself off the hook.

And maybe Ciara looked stunned because she hadn't guessed, either, and was now grappling with how to deal with this new, unwelcome knowledge.

"I know you probably don't feel the same," he said woodenly.

"But…"

His eyes narrowed. "But what?"

"I thought…" she stuttered.

"That I didn't like you?" he asked roughly. "You really believed that?"

Her head bobbed.

"How could you?"

"I told you!" Her eyes had a suspicious shimmer again, but she also sounded mad. "I've spent years despising how I felt about Bridget. I decide you need to know, and what do you do? Attack me!" Her voice dropped. "At least…that's what it felt like."

"I was trying to help." He'd known he had been inept, but…this was worse than that. "I thought if you understood that your feelings about your sister had tangled with your fears about Mark, you could ease up on yourself."

"It did help."

Gabe shook his head, sure he'd heard wrong. "What?"

She swallowed. "I did think, and you were right. That's why I decided to encourage Mark to enroll in school here this fall."

"All right." At this exact moment, he didn't give a damn where Mark went to school. He didn't even know why they were talking about Mark. "Ciara…"

"Did you mean it?" she asked abruptly, those vividly blue eyes fixed on him as if she was trying to penetrate beneath the surface.

"That I was trying to help?"

She shook her head. "That you love me."

"Yeah." His voice came out so rough, he cleared his throat. "I don't want to make you uncomfortable—"

"But… Don't you want children of your own?"

"You're saying you don't?" He was getting more baffled by the minute.

"No, it's not—" She chewed on her lip. "It's just…I don't know if you're that serious about me, but—"

God. This was like stepping out on a high wire, and him scared shitless of heights. "I want you to marry me."

She stared and then whispered, "Oh."

A laugh that held no humor whatsoever huffed out of him. "Guess I shocked you."

"It's just…you've *seen*." She wrapped her arms around herself, her eyes beseeching. "Jeff was right. If I have more kids, we'd be *lucky* if they were like Mark."

He felt like a cartoon character with a lightbulb popping into sight above his head. The asshole had convinced her she was flawed down to the DNA level.

"Yeah." He smiled at her and took her upper arms in his hands, squeezing gently. "We would be. He's a great kid. I wouldn't mind having another one like him."

Her lips parted, closed, parted again. "But…but what if we have one like Bridget?"

"Then we'll love her, just as your parents love your sister." He shook his head. "Is this what's been the problem, Ciara? Or can't you love me?"

Tears brimmed in her eyes at the same time as she laughed. "Of course I love you! I'd be crazy not to."

He lifted a hand to wipe away tears. "I'm not that good a deal."

"You are the most amazing man I've ever met." Ciara sniffed. "Sexy, too."

He had no doubt his grin looked as foolishly hopeful as he felt. "Yeah, I've spent my life fighting women off."

"You did try."

"Yeah." His smile died. "I swore I'd never go here again. Staying to myself was easy until you and Mark showed up."

Her gaze searched his again. She seemed unconscious of her wet cheeks. "You're already more of a father to Mark than his own ever has been. You really won't mind that?"

"I'd be proud to claim him as my son." That required another throat-clearing. "You're sure, Ciara?"

She flung her arms around him, rising on tiptoe to press her mouth clumsily to his. Gabe took control of the kiss immediately, wrapping her tight in his arms and swinging her in a slow circle as he tasted and claimed, his tongue met by hers.

He was painfully aroused when he wrenched his mouth from hers. "Do you think he'll really stay put?"

The beautiful woman in his arms gave an impish smile. "If not—there's a lock on my bedroom door."

Gabe laughed, swept her off her feet and started up the stairs. "I can ignore him on the other side of the door if you can."

CIARA ENDED UP sprawled atop him, her head resting in the hollow below his shoulder, her hand over his heart, hammering as hard as her own. He let out a slow groan that had her laughing.

He lifted his head enough to give her a wicked smile, one side of his mouth higher than the other. "Can we get married soon?"

"So we can do this *every* day?"

His head dropped back to the pillow, although she could see the groove in his cheek that told her he was still smiling. "Maybe twice. Or three times.

You know, with us both working from home, we can coordinate our breaks."

Ciara giggled. "Especially once Mark is in school."

"Yeah." There was a moment of silence. "You think he's going to be okay with us? Or, I guess I should say, with me?"

"He worships the ground you walk on."

"He might be jealous."

"He's going to be thrilled," she said with sudden certainty.

His hand stroked down her back, the roughness of his fingertips astonishingly sensuous. "Much as I'd like to make love with you again, I keep wondering what he's gotten up to."

"He wouldn't be using your saws without you, would he?" Buoyant with happiness, she couldn't feel the alarm she probably should.

"Nope. Locked the workshop."

"Maybe he's decided to saddle up Hoodoo."

He sat up, effortlessly setting her beside him. The skin beside his eyes crinkled in a smile that didn't reach his lips. "Now you've scared me. I'll retrieve him."

Suddenly worried, she sat up, too, by instinct grabbing a pillow to clutch in front of her. "We'll almost have to live in your house, won't we?"

His eyebrows rose. Getting out of bed, he stretched, giving her a lovely view of his powerful body. "Yeah. You don't have a barn adequate for my workshop. Does the idea bother you?"

"I was more worried about whether it would bother *you*. I mean, I don't want you to feel as if you're replacing your wife and daughter."

Gabe stood looking down at her, his boxers and jeans hanging from his hand. "I think they'd be happy for me. If Ginny could have seen me these past few years, she was probably shaking her head in disgust. No, it's time I do some work on the old place. Make it our home." His mouth quirked. "Starting with new kitchen cabinets."

"Well, now, there's a concept," she teased. "We could go to The Home Depot in Spokane—"

He gave her a dark look as he stepped into his pants and zipped them up. "If you're real nice, I might let you have some say in what they look like."

"Thank you, sir." She hugged the pillow harder, older fears not quite gone. "You're sure…?"

"Yeah." That deep voice was impossibly tender as he flattened a hand on the bed and bent to kiss her. "We'll tear out some walls, modernize—"

"Get rid of the wallpaper in the living room."

"Meant to do that years ago." He momentarily disappeared as he retrieved his shirt from the floor, coming up with her bra and shirt, too. His face was suddenly expressionless. "Your parents going to be disappointed?"

"Oh, for Pete's sake! They loved you! They'll be thrilled."

"Okay." He didn't look entirely convinced, but sat down to pull on his socks and boots. Then he gave her another amused, sexy smile. "I'm off to get your kid. You might want to be dressed when we get back."

She stuck out her tongue.

He laughed and left.

GABE FOUND MARK sitting on the fence, chewing on a strand of hay and running his fingers through Aurora's forelock. She appeared half-asleep, her eyelids heavy. She stayed dozing when Mark clambered down.

"What were you *doing*?" he demanded. "Your computer is really slow. I was thinking of saddling Aurora and riding."

Gabe smiled. "That would have been okay."

The boy's face brightened. "Really?"

"Really."

"Well, then…can I? I mean, *now*?"

"No, your mom's expecting you." He hesitated. "Why don't I throw your bike in the back and drive you home?"

"Okay." He waited until both were in the cab. "Did you and Mom talk?"

"Yes. Thanks to you." Should he wait until they

were all together to tell him? Gabe's instinct said this was the time. "I asked your mother to marry me."

"Marry you?" Mark said it as though the concept was utterly foreign to him. "You mean, like, we'd all live together?" he said finally, awkwardly.

"Yeah. It'll mean moving again for you. Because of my workshop, you and your mother will have to move into my house." Gabe wondered if Mark had noticed the positive verb tenses.

"We'd live *here*?" He turned his head, as if he'd never seen Gabe's plain farmhouse or the two big barns and other outbuildings.

"Yes."

"Like…like you were my father?"

It caught at Gabe's throat, how off-handed Mark was trying to sound. As if he could shrug off a hurtful answer.

"I will be your stepfather."

He sat for a minute, taking it in. "Did Mom say yes?"

"She did."

"And…and Watson and Daisy can live here, too?"

"Yep." Gabe reached out and squeezed Mark's shoulder. "They'll be our dogs. Just like Aurora and Hoodoo will be our horses."

The boy's screamed *"Ye-es!"* came close to splitting Gabe's eardrums.

But they were both grinning when he put the truck in gear.

And everything in Gabe settled when they reached Ciara's house, and he saw her come out on the porch. Mark threw himself out of the truck and tore up the steps to grip her in a rare hug.

"We can have dinner together *every* night!" he exclaimed.

Gabe had forgotten what real happiness felt like. He hadn't expected a second chance. Had resisted the idea.

He was the luckiest guy on earth.

A dog trying to trip him all the way up the stairs, he couldn't take his gaze off the woman and boy he loved.

"Tell you what," he told her. "I'll even let you pick the color next time I paint the house."

He didn't think he'd mention how long it had taken Ephraim's heir to sell *this* house. What the hell. Maybe they'd do better this time around.

A smile snuck up on him. Hey, maybe having new neighbors wasn't such a bad thing.

* * * * *

LARGER-PRINT BOOKS!

GET 2 FREE LARGER-PRINT NOVELS PLUS
2 FREE GIFTS!

❖ HARLEQUIN®

Romance

From the Heart, For the Heart

YES! Please send me 2 FREE LARGER-PRINT Harlequin® Romance novels and my 2 FREE gifts (gifts are worth about $10). After receiving them, if I don't wish to receive any more books, I can return the shipping statement marked "cancel." If I don't cancel, I will receive 4 brand-new novels every month and be billed just $4.84 per book in the U.S. or $5.24 per book in Canada. That's a savings of at least 19% off the cover price! It's quite a bargain! Shipping and handling is just 50¢ per book in the U.S. and 75¢ per book in Canada.* I understand that accepting the 2 free books and gifts places me under no obligation to buy anything. I can always return a shipment and cancel at any time. Even if I never buy another book, the two free books and gifts are mine to keep forever.

119/319 HDN F43Y

Name _____ (PLEASE PRINT) _____

Address _____ Apt. # _____

City _____ State/Prov. _____ Zip/Postal Code _____

Signature (if under 18, a parent or guardian must sign) _____

Mail to the **Harlequin® Reader Service:**
IN U.S.A.: P.O. Box 1867, Buffalo, NY 14240-1867
IN CANADA: P.O. Box 609, Fort Erie, Ontario L2A 5X3
Want to try two free books from another line?
Call 1-800-873-8635 or visit www.ReaderService.com.

* Terms and prices subject to change without notice. Prices do not include applicable taxes. Sales tax applicable in N.Y. Canadian residents will be charged applicable taxes. Offer not valid in Quebec. This offer is limited to one order per household. Not valid for current subscribers to Harlequin Romance Larger-Print books. All orders subject to credit approval. Credit or debit balances in a customer's account(s) may be offset by any other outstanding balance owed by or to the customer. Please allow 4 to 6 weeks for delivery. Offer available while quantities last.

Your Privacy—The Harlequin® Reader Service is committed to protecting your privacy. Our Privacy Policy is available online at www.ReaderService.com or upon request from the Harlequin Reader Service.

We make a portion of our mailing list available to reputable third parties that offer products we believe may interest you. If you prefer that we not exchange your name with third parties, or if you wish to clarify or modify your communication preferences, please visit us at www.ReaderService.com/consumerschoice or write to us at Harlequin Reader Service Preference Service, P.O. Box 9062, Buffalo, NY 14269. Include your complete name and address.

HRLP13R

LARGER-PRINT BOOKS!

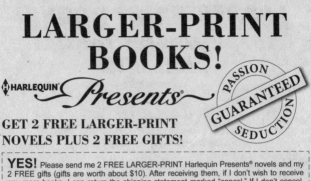

HARLEQUIN *Presents*

PASSION
GUARANTEED
SEDUCTION

GET 2 FREE LARGER-PRINT NOVELS PLUS 2 FREE GIFTS!